Holy
Night

DEAR PALY.

ENJOY THE SNOW ☺

I LOVE + LIGHT

MARKIE X

First published by O Books, 2009
O Books is an imprint of John Hunt Publishing Ltd., The Bothy, Deershot Lodge, Park Lane, Ropley,
Hants, SO24 0BE, UK
office1@o-books.net
www.o-books.net

Distribution in:

UK and Europe
Orca Book Services
orders@orcabookservices.co.uk
Tel: 01202 665432 Fax: 01202 666219
Int. code (44)

USA and Canada
NBN
custserv@nbnbooks.com
Tel: 1 800 462 6420 Fax: 1 800 338 4550

Australia and New Zealand
Brumby Books
sales@brumbybooks.com.au
Tel: 61 3 9761 5535 Fax: 61 3 9761 7095

Far East (offices in Singapore, Thailand,
Hong Kong, Taiwan)
Pansing Distribution Pte Ltd
kemal@pansing.com
Tel: 65 6319 9939 Fax: 65 6462 5761

South Africa
Stephan Phillips (pty) Ltd
Email: orders@stephanphillips.com
Tel: 27 21 4489839 Telefax: 27 21 4479879

Text copyright Vincent Tilsley 2008

Design: Stuart Davies

ISBN: 978 1 84694 199 3

A CIP catalogue record for this book is available
from the British Library.

Printed by Digital Book Print

O Books operates a distinctive and ethical publishing philosophy in
all areas of its business, from its global network of authors to
production and worldwide distribution.

Holy
Night

Vincent Tilsley

BOOKS

Winchester, UK
Washington, USA

CONTENTS

Acknowledgements

I'd like to thank these members of GreenSpirit for helping to get Holy Night going in the first place. In particular there was Don Hills (Education Psychology), Chris Clarke (Professor of Mathematics), Michael Colebrook (Biologist) and Ian Mowll (Social and Charity Organiser), who all contributed skills which really were invaluable.

Then there was Father John Inglis who first introduced me to the single biggest influence on Holy Night, Brian Swimme's video series *Canticle to the Cosmos* (which I can't recommend too highly), and Mary Barry, former teacher of Eng.Lit and Theology, who read my first draft so scrupulously.

Finally it's a pleasure to thank Marian Van Eyk McCain, herself a writer (you might like to look up her titles), without whose ceaseless help this book would have been unlikely to find its way into publication by O Books.

Thank you all. It would have been worth writing Holy Night just to meet the people I did.

Endorsements

"This is one of the two most extraordinary books I have read. You know the entire plot before it starts ...the time came for her to be delivered ... there were shepherds abiding in the fields ... the heavenly host ... no room at the inn ... But this telling is different. Under the fantastical guise of science fiction, it gives a psychologically credible account of how archetypal principles such as Wisdom, Folly, Love, Birthing, Law and Destruction weave the universe. Unless you are really allergic to spaceships or angels, you will be astonished and delighted".

Chris Clarke, Professor of Applied Mathematics.

" ...a bold and challenging adventure into a dearly held tale, written in an original and riveting fashion. The huge issues about Good and Evil, God and Satan, and about where evil comes from, were tackled in a way that managed to burrow deep into my preconceived ideas and unpack them, and on occasion turn them round ... a real gem."

Fr. Marcus Ronchetti, Anglican priest.

"Holy Night is unlike anything else I have ever read ... It will entertain you, amuse you and intrigue you, and it will also make you think. Although in one sense it reads like a 'ripping yarn' and its sci-fi elements are worthy of Star Wars, it also stretches the intellect in rather the same way as Pirsig's 'Zen and the Art of Motorcycle Maintenance' did ... It may leave you, as it left me, with a sense of speechless delight in the privilege of being a bumbling, struggling yet awesomly creative ordinary human being, reinventing the world in every moment."

Marian Van Eyk McCain, Psychotherapist and writer.

"Holy Night is a narrative in which theology, cosmology, quantum physics, poetry and meditation fuse into a dazzling

high-wire drama ... What shines out above all is the author's zeal, his exhilaration and delight in the art of telling this extraordinary story ... (His) enchantment with his theme and his uncomplicated joy in communicating his profound insights sing above it all and echo long after the final page is turned. Sheer class."
Annie Eagleton, English teacher.

"It's a long time since I've been unable to put a book down ... a wondrous mix of deep magic and almost fairy-like mirth ... I may hand a copy to each of my clients as a spiritually uplifting gift."
David Harper, counsellor.

"As one who is heartily sick of the insipid farce that Christmas has become, I had thought that the Nativity would never reach me again as it once had. Holy Night changed that. All the major issues of life and death, light and darkness, sin and guilt, meaning and despair are dealt with in a vibrant, witty and most compelling manner ... It has a message of deep importance for our times."
Don Hills, education psychologist.

"A really fresh and innovative story studded with some glorious gems, combining science fiction, science and mythology. It's a story for our time, inspiring us to take responsibility for the unfolding of life on Earth.
Ian Mowll, worker in grass roots Social Enterprise and Charity Organisations.

"Vincent Tilsley has managed to construct a quite spellbinding and thought-provoking story, a magical exposition of the mystical and metaphysical. Forget the Da Vinci Code – this is wondrously mind-blowing stuff and deserves a place in everybody's library. When you've read it you'll want to read it again and again. A true voyage of faith and self-discovery, and beyond. You'll never look in the night sky again without wondering!"

Ian McHenry, NHS Special Health Authority.

PREFACE

"Science without religion is lame, religion without
science is blind."
Albert Einstein.

Of all the ideas that were to find their way into Holy Night, it
was that particular Einstein saying that persuaded me to sit
down at long last and see if I could actually write this book.

Going back a few years before that, one of the early factors lay
with the nine hundred year-old parish church in the little town
where I live. It keeps its doors generously open every day, and
although I never attended any of the services (and still don't) I
couldn't pass by at other times without looking to see if it was
still empty (and still do), knowing that when I have the place to
myself I'm soon aware of a nourishing sense of something
beautiful. Sometimes, though, there was an inner sort of inter-
ference, a persistent nagging at the back of my mind telling me
that this level of beauty is no more than a hint at the real thing,
that there's something much deeper than this, a genuine
perception of . . . what? Of something profoundly real but so
deep that it was beyond any experience I'd ever had or, it seemed
then, was ever likely to have.

So I started to get interested in science, partly because I'd
never learned any and was a bit shy about that, more seriously
because the time had already come (late '70s, early '80s) when a
largely new generation of highly articulate media-wise scientists
were not only writing books but appearing on TV and radio
documentaries to explain the fascinating components and
processes which go to make up our amazing universe. I was soon
absorbed in theories, explanations and pictorial evidence which
were not only enlightening but, for a new boy like me (already
turned 50!), astonishing.

But could it really be true, or was Homo sapiens kidding

1

himself again? How could an entire cosmos of at least 100 billion galaxies have sprung from something smaller than the point of a needle? That was the 'Big Bang' apparently, which within the first microsecond of its existence had become a fireball that was a billion trillion times hotter than the centre of the sun would become, and a trillion trillion trillion trillion times denser than rock. One of the unforgettable descriptions of the ensuing result was Carl Sagan's calculation that if you counted all the stars in all those galaxies they would outnumber all the grains of sand on all the beaches of planet Earth. Could I honestly tell myself to put my trust in these things? The answer was too exquisite to be anything but yes.

And it was much the same with the other half of reality, that realm of almost infinite smallness which builds the entire universe out of atoms and is eccentrically governed by the unruly rules of quantum mechanics. "If we think we can picture what is going on in the quantum world, that is one indication that we've got it wrong", says Werner Heisenberg - but that doesn't stop you trying to work out how a particle can move from one place to another without a journey in between, or be in both places at once, and how it is that photons can be both particles *and* waves . . . and so on and on and on, presumably ad infinitum. Could I accept this version of reality as a package deal with the great macrocosmic universe out there, considering that the two systems seem to go by different rules? The answer was again exquisite.

Then I began to wonder why I was so capable of having faith in science but not in religion. What was it that the church was getting wrong and declining as a result? But that's not the real question; the problem lay in what it *wasn't* doing. Why wasn't it learning and preaching the great miracles of creation that science was now discovering? Why not put priests on science courses? Indeed, why not invite into church pulpits some of those scientists best known to believe not only in their profession but also in a power beyond the reach of science, and let them explain that far from wanting science to take the place of religion there must be genuine ways of blending the two together into one complete expression of reality (to the great approval of Albert Einstein and, I suspect, Jesus).

(As I say all this I'm beginning to wonder if writing Holy Night was my way of ensuring my own invitation to the wedding.)

I'm not fond of long prefaces so I'll underline just one more aspect of the book and hope that the rest speaks for itself. What I *don't* believe is that some all wise, all powerful and all perfect being created the universe and everything in it. At the same time I can't believe that it happened by accident. What began to make sense for me was the idea of a timeless non-spacial realm of infinite possibilities - a concept of Eastern mysticism from long ago which Western science has begun to find out for itself, though from a different angle. The only new thing I've added (unless someone else did it thousands of years ago) is the idea that any such non-material possibility has its own primal instinct and volition. In Holy Night it's the characterized God himself who demonstrates just that. This is when the story reaches the point where 'he' has become conscious enough to remember what it was like when he wasn't. What there was was an incontestable urge of the inherent to become coherent, of the unknown-to-itself to know itself, all by taking that one-way leap from Beingness into Being, bringing the seeds of space and time with it. And it did, and we call it the Big Bang.

This makes so many things in the story work *as* a story rather than a quasi-theological tract. It allows God to appear as a character who represents science's offer of an incalculable force on its journey to whatever it's going to become. As such 'he' (meaning he + she + it + everything-that-is + the incalculable mystery it all emerges from) is an innocent whose greatest wish is to learn who he is, what he's done, and what he should do now.

Indeed, Satan says of him 'The only way God can understand anything is by creating that which understands it. He can't even know himself without creating that which knows him" - and no one knows God better than Satan who proceeds to educate him about the incompetent mess he's made of evolution, especially of humans. And God is grateful. Then there's Labass, chief scientist in charge of Satan's underground 'Creation Room', who demonstrates for God the faulty chemistry of the universe itself. At the human level it is Joseph who enlightens him about human nature simply by showing it at work within himself, angry at the humiliating situation he's been drawn into, but then followed by a guarded calm which moves watchfully into understanding, and in the end draws forth a fruitful forgiveness that prompts him to teach an eager God enough elementary carpentry to help convert the manger into a crib. As a return favour the grateful God introduces Joseph to the entire universe - by the simple method of letting him become it for a while. All of it. Science calls it Entanglement.

I hope such a compression of themes doesn't give an impression of the book being a bit long on the happy-happy side. It's true I was sometimes surprised at how funny it got. When I reached the scene where God manages to make Satan laugh for first time ever, and then joins in it himself until they're both speechless, I had to stop writing for a couple of hours because it had got me going too. At most times, though, the issues are pretty big, especially the one particular theme that underlines the whole story.

The alternative to the idea of the universe having been made and organised by an independent being who knows everything, is that it's the universe itself which is becoming the independent being who will come to know everything. It is God who is evolving, and that's a long business. After all, it took 300 thousand years for elementary particles furnaced in the Big Bang to create the first atoms of hydrogen and helium; longer again before molecules began to form; longer still for the appearance of the first cells. (Amazing how complex cells are. If you see a microscope photo of one it looks like a medium size city as seen from a thousand feet up.) And so it goes on, one layer of life after another but never actually forming until the one before has been tried and tested enough to make possible the one to come. Our belief that the arrival of the human is the final and finest stage in creation is that embarrassing sort of megalomania which Homo sapiens seems to need as clothing. We have no idea that we ourselves may already be part of the next development any more than the cells in our bodies know who we are, or even that we exist. Whatever our future may be, I can't see it as anything but yet another stage in the universe's journey to its final self, the complete and fully conscious I Am.

I've no idea if that's true. What I do know is that I've become gradually aware of a centre in myself that I feel I can now call religious. The cells in my body may not know about me but I know about them, and the one thing that's certain is that I can't live without them. If we have the same relationship to the Universe as our cells have to us, then such a life has great worth and meaning. Everything has its function, and we as conscious beings are neurons in the growing universal mind. From particle to galaxy to universe, we belong. We really are all one. Try getting depressed when you think like that! I go and talk to the apple tree in our garden instead. We're made of the same stardust.

Vincent Tilsley 2009

1

THE STAR

The night sky in winter. Huge, teeming, brilliant, awesome ...
And so on – all the usual epithets, all of them obnoxious to the
figure who now stands looking up at it. Apart from conveying an
implicit need to worship, they're offensively inaccurate. Not
even 'huge' bears examination, the number of stars visible to the
naked eye, even to his, even on a night like this, being less than
a trillionth of what is actually out there. 'Minuscule' would be
nearer the mark, and still be on the generous side. As for the rest
of Creation, he's too aware of its ineptitude to be impressed by its
showiness. 'Fatally flawed' would be a measured verdict. And he
might add, on a more personal note, 'treacherous'.

The reason for his present scrutiny of the heavens, therefore,
owes nothing to awe and all to a feeling, unusually deep tonight,
a *knowing*, that there's something going on; something about to
happen; something feared, and longed for (though those, too, are
terms he would dismiss as meaningless).

Whatever it is, he must watch and wait, out here, in the cold,
alone. Wait for a sign, an appearance, even (at last!) a visitation.
If it comes – *when* it comes – there won't be anything mysterious
about it. There is no magic; only that which is not understood.

The watcher seems a shade magnificent for his surroundings.
The hill he stands on stretches down into grasslands. Not far
away, sheep huddle on frozen ground; further off, another flock.
Nearer by, a stray wanders, starts to chomp on some scrub. More
distantly, a dog barks, then another. Further still, the lights of a
little town are just about visible, a humble twinkling under such
a sky.

He notices the stray, makes a mental note that it's odd to be
feeding at this time of night, wonders briefly if even such trivial
deviations in the patterns of life may signify bigger ones to come

... and returns his scrutiny to the stars.

There! A sudden streak of light –

– which vanishes. Meteor, burnt out in a moment. How many billions of years had it travelled for such rapid cremation? Dust to nothing. Utterly pointless. And wasteful.

Back to watching. Why? He has staff to do this.

The most striking thing about this solitary figure is his rather daunting beauty. There's a chilly glitter to it, and a distance, not unlike the stars he surveys. Yet this resonance makes it no easier for him to stare across the great divide. He stands where he stands as in a land of exile, gazing up at what was once his home. Forgiveness comes hard. Not that it's on his agenda.

Without any apparent communicator, he receives and answers a message.

> CONTROL: Still can't find anything, Sir.
> SATAN: They're there.

It isn't at first obvious that the busy room from which the Controller speaks is deep underground. It looks more like the bridge of a starship, which indeed it once was. The uniforms of the duty watch still convey a hint of the space travelers they once were before events rendered them Earthbound.

It's a big room, dominated at the moment by screens showing sectors of the night sky being scanned.

> CONTROL: *They*, Sir?

He'd appreciate knowing what it is they're actually looking for. But no response.

> CONTROL: Well, if they're in any kind of physical form they're not in this system. We've covered every frequency.
> SATAN: This isn't a frequent event.

8

One of the boss's somber witticisms? The Controller glances at a colleague; who shrugs that he doesn't know either. They collude in sneaking for a clue, switching one of the monitors to their commander on the surface.

> CONTROL: What isn't, Sir? What event?

Satan is immediately aware of being watched, and seems to look straight back at them. They switch back to the night sky. How does he do that?
Not that their respect for him is a fearful one. There's awe, certainly, but that's as it should be, the robust texture into which this beleaguered little band of the rejected is woven.
At which point one of the sky-tracking monitors pauses for no apparent reason, as if uncertain. There seems to be nothing there, but ... yes! the faint beginnings of a whispering, then a twangling hum which could, strangely, be a prelude to music. And the beginnings of a presence.
Satan had already sensed it – but is it really *it*? Is the stunningly obvious about to be made manifest?

> CONTROL: We're getting something, Sir, you're right! Can't tell what it is yet – What the hell is that? Hadn't you better get back?
> SATAN: It's the Lamb.

Which stops the Control Room staff in their tracks. Now they're all glued to the varieties of incoming information as the starship continues to materialize.

> SATAN: You can see for yourselves now.

Indeed they can. The Controller activates the alarm system.

CONTROL: Full alert, this is a full alert! All defense systems full power, follow my direction – mark – lock on *now* –

SATAN: Hold your fire, shields up, total blackout.

CONTROL: Soon as you're back, Sir –

SATAN: Now.

CONTROL: But –

SATAN: Now.

CONTROL: – you won't be able to get back –

SATAN: I'm not coming back.

CONTROL: Sir?

SATAN: Not yet. I'll meet them here.

CONTROL: *Sir!*

SATAN: I've waited too long for this.

The Controller looks at the rest of the duty staff. They are as aghast as he is.

CONTROL: Sir, with all respect, this is *unthinkable* –

SATAN: I'm not, for once, asking you to think.

CONTROL: But they'll take you!

SATAN: Of course. What else can they do?

CONTROL: But *Sir* – we can't cover you if …

SATAN: No need. No need for you to do anything – unless that thing starts to leave while I'm still on board. In which case, destroy it.

They're too dismayed even to protest. He relents enough to add:

SATAN: Trust me.

Just as well they do, there being no alternative.

CONTROL: Sir. (*To Computer*) Shields up.

The feeling in the Control Room is that they're probably on the verge of battle and possibly of full-scale war. And their Leader is in the wrong place.

Hovering high above them, the starship which is called the Lamb now appears almost solid. Inside, however, the crew and even some of the instrumentation (such as it is) haven't quite arrived yet. Things seem to give off a sort of plink as they make the final click into physicality. It's almost like an orchestra tuning up, and produces the same kind of pleasing anticipation. But of what?

The three chief occupants of the Control Room are: Michael, the Captain; Gabriel, the Communicator; and Raphael, the Doctor. They are the presiding archangels.

Michael starts to feel at home in his physical body, which is built on warrior lines. He prods at it appreciatively, flexes the muscles.

> MICHAEL: Do you know, first few seconds in this thing I feel like screaming, but once the shock wears off … (*He does a couple of physical jerks.*) Yes, it's good. I could spend some time in this.
> RAPHAEL: You'll be glad enough to be out of it before we're through. (*To Gabriel*) Can I see my patient yet?
> GABRIEL: Will you look at that!

He's inviting them to see a wonder. Up on the big screen, planet Earth hangs in the night sky, glittering blue and white.

> GABRIEL: This is the best.
> RAPHAEL: It always is. Wherever we go, there's the best.
> GABRIEL: Why don't you just take a look?
> RAPHAEL: Good. Yes. Best.
> GABRIEL: See?
> RAPHAEL: Can I see my patient now?
> MICHAEL: We need the area scanned first.
> GABRIEL: We can do both. (*To Sophie*) Yes?

This to the computer, which is even more beyond-tech than the one down below. There are no obvious controls but it responds to touch as well as to voice. There's something almost sensuous about it – you get the feeling it could move around if it didn't have more sense. It often answers Gabriel's thoughts. The others have to ask.

SOPHIE: Yes.

Perhaps it's because she's been around so much longer than they have, in one form or another, that the angels never wonder why that's her name. It always has been. Added to which, they share a realm where individual names mean next to nothing anyway, there being so little notion of separateness. Only in a material world, such as the one they're approaching now, where everything has edges, do you need name-maps to navigate your way through them.

Taken equally for granted is Sophie's ability to solve the most complex of problems in ridiculously fewer stages than the laws of logic permit; to pluck, apparently from nowhere, answers which in fact come from everywhere. That's just another quantum effect of their world, rather less surprising than breathing is in this one. Which isn't to say that she doesn't enjoy the simple linear tasks as well. They make a change, and humility is a restful state.

The big screen therefore does the obvious by dividing into two. The picture on the larger section consists of a systematic sweep of a few square miles around a small country town. The smaller insert section shows a young woman seated, though it isn't yet clear on what. She's heavily pregnant.

RAPHAEL: Give me a full scan of her, will you, and one of the fetus –
SOPHIE: There – see.
RAPHAEL: Oh yes.

MICHAEL: How's she doing?

RAPHAEL: (*Studying the monitors*) So far, so good. Yes, pretty good –

MICHAEL: How long, do you think?

RAPHAEL: The head's engaged. Blood pressure's right; urine free of sugar and protein; rhesus antibodies negative; good strong fetal heartbeat ... All systems go, by the look of it –

MICHAEL: Tonight?

RAPHAEL: Could well be.

MICHAEL: So, it's all pretty straightforward.

RAPHAEL: That doesn't mean it's *easy* –

MICHAEL: Didn't you just say –

RAPHAEL: Tell you what, Michael, next time we're on duty in the physical, put in for being a female. One who's just about to have a baby. Try ho-humming your way through that.

MICHAEL: All right, point taken – but she is all right?

RAPHAEL: Apart from being human. And I'd be happier if they were settled in somewhere. (*To Sophie*) What is this place?

The picture of the young woman widens to show her sitting on an ass outside a building with brightly lit windows and the hubbub of many people within. Through the open doorway the angels can see a man arguing with another man who is refusing him something.

MICHAEL: She keeps looking up. It's not as if we had our lights on –

GABRIEL: She was told.

MICHAEL: Not that we'd be here on the night, mounting a whole operation.

GABRIEL: I didn't know then. He hadn't said.

RAPHAEL: (*To Gabriel*) I need this in here for a minute, please. The whole thing.

The hologram of the Inn yard which now appears in the centre of the Control Room is actually bigger than the Control Room itself, space being entirely flexible here. In it, Raphael and Michael are standing near the pregnant girl. Michael follows her upward gaze.

MICHAEL: It's us she's looking at all right.

Raphael is more interested in the doorway of the building where the older of the two arguing men turns away and starts to walk back towards the girl. He looks tired and frustrated. The other man goes on talking.

INNKEEPER: If I could I would, believe me, but there isn't an inch. You'll be lucky to find anywhere. (*He gestures towards an outbuilding.*) So listen – if you want stay in there, long as you like, I won't even take your money.
JOSEPH: Thank you.
INNKEEPER: You need bedding? For bedding I make a small charge –
JOSEPH: I don't think so. But thank you.

He comes up to the girl on the ass.

JOSEPH: You heard that, did you? There's no room. Anywhere. Except –
(*He indicates the Stable.*) I'm – sorry.
MARY: It's all right –
JOSEPH: Well, no, it isn't –
MARY: Look.
JOSEPH: At what?

MARY: The star. That one. It wasn't there before.

JOSEPH: (*A flash of anger*) Is it the one your visitors come from, do you think? Been following us, have they?

He's immediately regretful, and even looks briefly in the direction she indicated.

JOSEPH: There are lots of stars.

Joseph leads the ass towards the outbuilding. Raphael goes ahead of them and looks through into the Stable. It's awful.

RAPHAEL: Oh.

SOPHIE: Do you want the smell, too?

RAPHAEL: What's it like? (*He winces at the result.*) No, you'd better sterilize the whole place. (*To himself*) We forget stuff like this, don't we? That things stink –

He looks at the girl as she approaches. She in turn is looking up at the Star…
… as is the solitary being on the hill. Satan hasn't moved.

SATAN: (*To the Star*) What's taking you so long?

He's distracted by the sound of a voice calling, but it's only a shepherd-boy searching for the stray and now running towards it. The animal tries to evade him but he manages to grab hold. Then he freezes as he sees the ominous figure above him.

SATAN: Get back to your flock. (*The boy is stricken with dread.*) **Now!**

The boy jumps back to life and, half-stumbling as he tries to drag the animal with him, runs and tumbles back down the hill. Then he abandons the sheep and just runs.

All of which is being monitored in the Control Room of the Lamb.

> SOPHIE: (*To Gabriel*) Look. On the hill there. Yes, there.
> The one running away is human. The one on the hill isn't.
> GABRIEL: It can't be! Can it? Closer!

He can scarcely believe what he sees.

> SOPHIE: Yes it is and yes he's looking straight at us.
> GABRIEL: Michael!

The urgency in his voice brings Michael hurrying out of the hologram. His reaction to the figure on the screen is equally startled.

> MICHAEL: Good God – (*After a frozen moment, into Commander's mode*) Full alert, this is a full alert. Defense, follow my direction – *mark*. Lock on now, all systems full power, ready to fire on command, ready to destroy anything coming at us. All combat troops ready for immediate descent to surface, fully armed and equipped. Ready, ready, ready! (*To Sophie*) Where's his support?
> SOPHIE: He doesn't have any.
> MICHAEL: Of course he has!
> SOPHIE: He hasn't.
> MICHAEL: He's not going to stand there on his own, just waiting for us!
> SOPHIE: The only life forms anywhere near are three humans and some animals. There. The animals are sheep.

On the screen now are the shepherds. They look in the direction of the shouting which grows louder as the still fearful shepherd-boy runs towards them.

SOPHIE: Now it's four humans. Do you want to know how many sheep?

Excitedly the boy points in the direction of the hill he's just run from and tries to describe what he's seen to his bemused elders.

MICHAEL: Never mind them, scan the whole area.

Raphael comes out of the hologram of the Stable, which then vanishes.

RAPHAEL: At least it's hygienic now – (*Sees the image on the screen*) Good God! Is that real?
MICHAEL: That's a thought. Let's see what he's made of. Might be another of his tricks.
SOPHIE: There.

A biogram of the watching figure appears on a monitor. Meanwhile, Gabriel indicates the lack of information from the probe.

GABRIEL: Nothing concealed near the surface, no troops, no anyone anywhere in anything. Deeper than that is a total blank – a *total* blank, which means that something's being shielded, of course. And it's big.
MICHAEL: It's the Dragonship.
GABRIEL: I thought you might think so.
MICHAEL: I know it.
GABRIEL: Well, whatever it is, its shield is stronger than our probe.
MICHAEL: There you are then – it's the old Dragon.
GABRIEL: Still, probably means we can't be fired on.
MICHAEL: Unless he's got weapons pointed at us from that moon up there. Wouldn't be surprised. (*To Raphael*) Is

he a fake?

RAPHAEL: No. Everything in working order. See, look at his heart-beat. That's not an illusion. It's even going at the normal rate. There he is, looking at us –

Raphael takes his own pulse, suspecting it compares unfavorably. It does.

RAPHAEL: Why are we *in* the physical anyway, by the way? Anyone know? (*No one does.*) *He* did, apparently!

They're suddenly riveted as Satan speaks, looking up at them.

SATAN: What are you waiting for? You saw me long ago. You must be looking at me right now. You've checked I'm alone and unarmed – what are you afraid of? I'd do better than this if it was a trap, wouldn't I? All I want is to see you again. And talk. Again.

Although there's now a great deal of activity on the ship, the three archangels have become very still.

SATAN: It's been too long. Don't you think?

They're still too uncertain to reply.

SATAN: That's all I want. Nothing up my sleeve.
MICHAEL: (*To the other two*) What do you think?

They really don't know.

MICHAEL: Well – we'll just have to go and get him.
GABRIEL: And then what?
MICHAEL: Bring him up here, out of harm's way. What

else can we do?

GABRIEL: Or should we ask for help?

Little question, big implications.

MICHAEL: No, I've taken him on before; and his army. So – let's move!

Action everywhere now, most of it Michael and his troops hurrying to and out of the descent area and emerging into the night sky, as the ship switches on its underlights to illuminate the search area below. Which startles the shepherds; the sheep more briefly; Satan not at all – far from it.

Michael heads first for the shepherds. Other troops fan out in different directions as they fly Earthward, some to isolate Satan, others to search for his invisible forces. Whatever energy mechanism it is that keeps them airborne produces its own halo effect round each of them. They're also using mini-sonars to locate each other's positions, the effect being an eerie impression of a strung-out atonal music.

The shepherds would bolt for it if there was anywhere to bolt to, but the glory of whoever-the-hell-this-Lord-might-be is all about them.

Michael speaks to Gabriel up in the ship.

MICHAEL: I want to get them out of the way without frightening them. Give me the words.

At the same time as dealing with Michael, Gabriel is watching Mary and Joseph in the early stages of getting the Stable into some sort of initial order, and even this rough first sketch of the Nativity tableau is enough to draw him into the power of its image. The improbable result is that when he thinks his own words through to Michael they produce the same state of exaltation in him too.

> MICHAEL: (*To shepherds*) Listen, don't be afraid, I've got
> great news for you and I want you to enjoy it. Because
> that's the word for it – joy. For you, for me – joy to the
> world! But first of all for you, because – well, because
> you're here. Are you listening?

Indeed they are. Perhaps they aren't going to be murdered/
eaten/sold into slavery/abducted by aliens after all.

> MICHAEL: Now I'll tell you what I want you to do. Over
> the hill there and down in the town, there's a child about
> to be born. Any time now, in the stable of the inn there.
> His mother's name is Mary, but mind this: he's not just her
> baby. He's yours too. He's the child of all this. (*His gesture
> takes in the starry sky, then the whole universe.*) He *is* all this.
> So – do you want to go and see him?

Whether they do or not, they're too paralyzed to move.

> MICHAEL: With your own eyes? Be able to say "I was
> there"? Feel blessed for evermore? Tell the story to your
> own children, and see how they shine at the telling, and
> beg you to tell it again?
> GABRIEL: (*Watching from the ship*) That enough yet?

More than. Michael reverts to his commanding self.

> MICHAEL: Go on then! Move!

Glad tidings. The shepherds jump to it.
Still uncomfortable with the speech he just made, Michael now
heads towards the squad surrounding Satan.

MICHAEL: (*To Gabriel*) I only wanted them out of the way.

GABRIEL: You got them out of the way.

MICHAEL: Did you need to be so ecstatic?

GABRIEL: Yes.

MICHAEL: And why send them to the birthplace?

GABRIEL: Because that's the story.

MICHAEL: What story?

GABRIEL: This one.

MICHAEL: (*To himself*) "Child of all this – *is* all this –" What does that *mean*?

With which he arrives to confront a suspiciously amenable Satan. Michael approaches him with due caution.

SATAN: Hello Michael. Welcome to planet Earth. You haven't been here before, I think. Not to set an actual foot on.

MICHAEL: (*speaks to the squad leader*) Anything?

SQUAD LEADER: Not yet, Sir. Reports still coming in.

MICHAEL: (*To Gabriel*) Anything?

GABRIEL: (*In ship*) No.

MICHAEL: (*To Satan*) What are you doing here?

SATAN: Shouldn't I be asking you that? I live here.

MICHAEL: All right, you're coming with us.

SATAN: Certainly. Thank you for asking.

Why does he seem so damned relaxed about it? Michael trusts him less far than he can spit.

SATAN: Are we waiting for something? Do you want me to lead the way?

SQUAD LEADER: All reports in, Sir. No trace of the enemy. I mean, apart from –

MICHAEL: (*To Satan*) What are you up to?

SATAN: Up to your ship, I gather. I take it you'd rather talk there.

He starts to move.

MICHAEL: Satan!

SATAN: Ah! You remember my name!

MICHAEL: You're my prisoner. Don't forget that.

Satan's smile is that bit too broad, which is comment enough.

2

REUNION

GABRIEL: And here they come.

In the Control Room, Gabriel's monitors follow the approach of Michael and his troops back up to the ship, now with Satan under close guard.

GABRIEL: Just look at him.

Even in the midst of a moving crowd it is Satan who catches the eye, like a light in a mist.
Gabriel turns to see how Raphael is reacting, but he hasn't moved his eyes from his own monitors. He goes on scrutinizing Mary's every moment, inside and out, with an obdurate look of keeping first things first.
Gabriel isn't entirely convinced.

GABRIEL: Never thought we'd see this, did we?
RAPHAEL: Bit of movement there. And there. Pituitary gland's producing more hormones, see. That'll stimulate the uterus, so – won't be long before she starts having contractions ...

Gabriel won't be deflected either.

GABRIEL: Hell of a moment though, isn't it? Like some new conjunction in the heavens. Lucifer Rising. Perhaps it was foretold long ago and we didn't notice. What do you think? I feel a bit daunted, myself.

At last Raphael turns and looks.

RAPHAEL: That little speech you gave Michael just now –

GABRIEL: What did you think of it?

RAPHAEL: Didn't understand a word of it – any more than those gawping shepherds did. Any more, I suspect, than you did.

GABRIEL: I spoke what came.

RAPHAEL: That's what I thought – you didn't know what you were talking about, did you?

GABRIEL: Not really.

RAPHAEL: Doesn't that worry you?

GABRIEL: Not really.

RAPHAEL: No?

GABRIEL: No.

RAPHAEL: No?

GABRIEL: Why? The way I look at it, anything you can actually understand can't be all that important – so this one must be. Which is good.

RAPHAEL: Interesting reasoning. To what else do you attribute importance on the grounds that you don't understand it?

GABRIEL: All right, you want for-instances. Why do I exist? Why does anything? Why do you? Don't tell me you understand that. There doesn't need to be a Universe at all, does there? But God, I'm glad there is, and that I'm part of it. And when I look at *that* (*the Stable scene*) what I do know is, I want to sing.

RAPHAEL: Is that what you were doing?

GABRIEL: That's what it felt like.

RAPHAEL: That was music?

GABRIEL: You're not forgetting how to sing, are you, Raphael?

RAPHAEL: I wonder.

GABRIEL: (*Indicates Satan on screen*) That's how he

started, you know. Forgetting.
RAPHAEL: Did he ever really sing?
GABRIEL: Oh yes.

Michael and his squad are arriving back now, but as they escort Satan on board it's almost as if he's holding an impromptu inspection on his own ship, pausing here and there to nod approval and even use the odd personal name. His performance is all the more impressive for being neither patronizing nor flippant, which in turn makes it that much harder for these lesser angels, particularly those who remember him well, not to respond in the same affable fashion.

Michael's reaction is to be correspondingly brusque. Satan always had this baffling knack not only of treating him like a caricature but of somehow drawing him into responding like one.

All of which is being followed on Gabriel's monitors.

GABRIEL: They're heading this way. Looks like he's going to bring him in here.
RAPHAEL: Doesn't trust him anywhere else, I suppose. No more would I. Give him five minutes, he'd suborn the lot of them.
GABRIEL: Not *us* though, eh?

Raphael's smile at this hint of self-mockery is a twinkle less than he'd have liked. He turns back to his monitors and begins to transfer their output.

RAPHAEL: Well, here goes. I'll be watching this lot from the Medical Room now, I suppose, so that's me safe.

Still a twinkle short perhaps. He switches off his monitors just as Michael arrives with Satan.

SATAN: Well, well. Nothing much changes, does it? Hello, Raphael, Gabriel.

They both nod an acknowledgement, waiting for a lead from Michael before actually speaking.

SATAN: Greetings, Sophie.
SOPHIE: And to you, Satan –

Gabriel quickly interrupts her with a respectful thought and tactful touch. Then:

From Satan's point of view, what happens next is quite surprising. Not only has Michael drawn the other two angels into a secretive huddle, they've even taken the trouble to face away from him – presumably so that he can't read their lips. What an encouraging change from the old days, when they wouldn't have responded to *anything* as sensibly as that.

The old days. Looking back on how it used to be as a live-in member of God's inner circle, he hadn't been wrong to keep his recruiting activities quiet and limit them to the lower ranks of angels. These Great Ones had too much invested in the myth of God's perfection to countenance the faintest criticism of Him, or entertain the least idea that pushing Him to one side might be doing the Universe a favor. Even more crucial was their impenetrably self-indulgent, archangelic obsession with their own status as creatures of light. The mere thought of keeping a secret – any secret, much less a *plot* – would be to admit the calamity of darkness into their natures and so to threaten their very identity, the maintenance of which was their sacred duty to God – etc. etc., of course of course, and so on and so on …

The frustrating thing about all that was that it was nonsense and always had been. "Let there be light" may have been God's first articulate thought, but unfortunately He didn't have another for the next few hundred thousand years. The result was that when the first particles of anything you could call matter started trying to emerge, they were promptly assailed by the ferocity of the almighty photon, and any attempts by the survivors to huddle themselves together into atoms were instantly swept aside by that same relentless storm of primal energy. The fact that matter did manage to get there in the end wasn't due to some generous new concession on light's part, but to its inherent compulsion – its greed, if you like – never to stop expanding. The irony of which was that it couldn't go on doing so without losing enough heat for those first furtive little atoms to sneak their way into a viable existence.

Now – is that really a basis on which these great Princes of Light can claim the moral guardianship of Creation? The truth is, it's here in spite of them.

But now – see the effect that Satan's world of space and time is beginning to have on them! Secrets already! The Universe will be as glad as he, no doubt, to see such implacably bland creatures emerging at last into something like reality.

And look, they've decided on something, which includes Raphael leaving. To where? Satan hasn't forgotten that it was Raphael's monitors which went blank the moment he arrived, or that he is a doctor, or that the Medical Room is only next door. What does three and one add up to?

> SATAN: Work to do, Doctor?
> RAPHAEL: There's always work to do.
> SATAN: Sure you wouldn't rather stay here for the discussion?

To his own surprise, Raphael finds that he would. He glances briefly at Michael, but the answer's No.

> RAPHAEL: I don't think I've anything to discuss with you.

Sure about that? Raphael leaves with a prickly awareness of Satan's understanding smile.

> MICHAEL: *None* of us has anything to discuss with you, so you can forget that idea –

It seems to happen quite casually. Satan is standing beside Sophie, and now rests an apparently absent-minded hand on the computer.

> MICHAEL: **– and take your hands off that! Don't touch that!**

There is a colossal surge in voltage. For just a moment there's the sense of two elemental forces confronting one another. What storm might burst forth from such a clash is almost unimaginable.

But it doesn't. Satan removes his touch from Sophie and his gaze from Michael, and the moment is gone. It was a mistake, perhaps, to offer even a hint of direct challenge to one with such an uncomplicated relationship to his courage. But no harm done; he withdraws easily enough, and not without gain.

> SATAN: Quite right, Michael. Of course. Rude of me. Though personally, I've always thought of what you call 'that' as 'she'.

Which brings Michael back into more manipulable territory.

> MICHAEL: Think what you like – but keep your hands to yourself.

Satan shrugs affably as he turns to sit in the nearest chair. Has he really not noticed that it's the Captain's?

MICHAEL: And don't sit there!

SATAN: Oh, I'm sorry. Captain's chair, of course – force of habit. This one all right? Am I allowed to sit down at all?

MICHAEL: You know perfectly well you are. You have the same rights as any other prisoner of war.

SATAN: Prisoner of *what* war? Where's the shooting?

Michael moves away. Satan follows him.

SATAN: I came of my own free will, remember. Free will – remember the concept at least? Free will. We used to discuss it a lot. Remember?

What Michael remembers even better is not to get drawn in.

MICHAEL: (*To Gabriel*) Go on scanning. Widen the range. He's not here without there's something dirty going on.

In the Medical Room, Raphael now has another bank of monitors working. One group covers events in the Stable; another continually updates the biograms of Mary and the baby; the third group stays on the developing situation in the Control Room, which he doesn't want to miss a word of.

Easy enough to do all this at the same time since the activities in the Stable don't yet call upon his skills. Not that they aren't interesting, in their mundane way. For instance, there's the installation of the ox alongside the ass. Apparently Joseph's going to sell it to pay his taxes, which is why he's brought it with them; he thinks he'll get a better price up the road in Jerusalem than back home in little Nazareth.

Then there's his carpentry. There's a hole in the decrepit old roof you can see the stars through – including *that* Star – so some sort of temporary job needs doing to shut out the cold; and the Star. More satisfyingly, he's found an old manger small enough to convert into a crib. All he needs is some wood to replace the bits that have gone rotten – and lo and behold, there in the corner is a stack of timber! (Raphael makes a note: Is Joseph surprised simply because the wood wasn't there before? Be more discreet with your help?)

So anyway, there's plenty to keep the man busy – which is just as well, by the look of him. The simple feel of his tools as he unpacks them seems to bring relief. They are the world he knows, the real world, the one that makes sense.

But not quite sense to Raphael, try as he may. The fact that a human can have an inner conflict is beyond the grasp of an ethereal being who has no such interiority. Like any angel, his compassion stretches the length and breadth of the Universe, but has no depth, being of light. With an angel, what you see is what you get – and Raphael is beginning to get a glimmer that perhaps that's not going to be enough for much longer.

Mary, fortunately, is a good deal less daunting – indeed, her state is the very opposite. This young woman (how old is she? 13? 14?) seems to have arrived at some remarkably high point (or was she born already there?), where questions don't need answering simply because they don't exist. Not only is she possessed by the new life within her, but by all life, and it wouldn't occur to her to wonder who or what God is. The simple truth suffices that all is well, and all shall be well, and all manner of things shall be well. To Raphael, she seems to manifest an extraordinary paradox: her depths are profound, yet they're all on the surface.

Added to which, as the most cursory glance at his monitors tells him, she's as fit as a fiddle.

Next to those monitors are the ones following events in the Control Room. Gabriel has just completed another sweep of the area below.

GABRIEL: (*To Michael*) Nothing. Again.
SATAN: Which is all there is to find. I told you.

Michael affects not to hear him.

> SATAN: Nothing on the surface and a big blank a long way down. From which you've deduced, quite rightly, that something very large is being shielded. Your surmise that it's my old flagship, the Dragon, on the grounds that it can't be anything else, is also correct. You're also right in thinking that the reason we went underground in the first place was to avoid your pursuit.

No response from Michael.

> SATAN: Seems ages ago, doesn't it? But then, you don't spend as much time in time as I do.

Michael gets busier. Satan follows him.

> SATAN: The only thing that really surprises you is how much bigger it is now. My ship. My home, as it has become. Want to hazard a guess? Why it's bigger?

No response.

> SATAN: Well, we've had to build on. Even a little planet like Earth needs a lot of administration. And then there's our research. Crucial. Needs a great deal of space.

No response.

> SATAN: Would you like to hear about our research programme?
> MICHAEL: Would you like to be locked up?
> SATAN: As if you have the lock that can hold me, Michael, or the staff to do it! You know you're stuck with

me – so why not make use of it? I can tell you all you need to know.

MICHAEL: And *believe* you?

SATAN: You'd do well to. And the first thing you'd better believe is that there's enough fire power locked on this ship to blow it out of physical existence. Which is what will happen if you try to leave without my consent.

MICHAEL: They'll destroy the Lamb *with you on it*?

SATAN: With me on it. As your guest, who has come in peace …

MICHAEL: Peace?

SATAN: It's a term I like to use, Michael, meaning the opposite of war.

GABRIEL: What war? Where's the shooting?

Satan smiles in acknowledgement at being quoted so deftly.

MICHAEL: If you've anything to say, you can say it at your trial.

SATAN: Charged with – ?

MICHAEL: What else? Treason! –

SATAN: Oh dear!

MICHAEL: In the highest!

SATAN: Michael, has it still not crossed your mind to wonder why I did what I did? If you want me on trial, the first thing you need to establish is motive. Why would I want a war?

MICHAEL: *A* war? It wasn't *a* war. You were fighting God Himself!

SATAN: His minions, actually. And why?

MICHAEL: Because you wanted *everything*.

SATAN: You know, you really should spend more time down here, Michael. What happens with humans is – and I suggest it as a model to you – that if a leader becomes unfit to govern – say, a king goes mad, or maybe the commander of an army – or even the head of a family – whoever – it's the duty of –

MICHAEL: There you are!

SATAN: – the duty of his next-in-command to take over and get rid of the madman –

MICHAEL: Out of your own mouth!

SATAN: – by any means necessary, and restore order. And mark the words 'order' and 'duty'.

MICHAEL: (*To them all*) Did you hear him?

SATAN: "Out of my own mouth" *what*?

MICHAEL: You just said it: that God is mad!

SATAN: I'm saying more than that, Michael. I'm saying that he's become a danger to his own Creation, and must be stopped. For his own good as much as anyone else's.

Michael's gesture of incredulity addresses everyone in the room, the rest of the ship, and the Universe in general. He turns away from Satan, with better things to do.

SATAN: Tell him, Gabriel.

GABRIEL: Tell him what?

SATAN: Why I'm here. He listens to you.

GABRIEL: He knows why.

SATAN: Why?

GABRIEL: To get us on your side this time – then start the war again.

SATAN: Just for fun, do you think?

GABRIEL: No, my guess would be you want to save the Universe.

SATAN: While there still *is* a universe.

GABRIEL: No, Satan – do you know what the real problem is? Never mind the Universe, old friend, the real trouble is you've forgotten how to sing.

Which triggers off the first real flash of anger.

> SATAN: Sing? What's there to sing about?
> GABRIEL: If it really is coming to an end, well, that's what songs do. Doesn't mean we shouldn't sing them. Indeed, that may be the best time of all. Why don't you just try it? Like you used to.

But Satan has already re-collected himself, and his side-step is as smooth as ever.

> SATAN: Well – let's have a second opinion, shall we? Raphael!

In the Medical Room, Raphael's monitors show Satan looking straight at him. How does he do that?

> SATAN: (*On screen*) We haven't heard from you, Doctor. You're bound to be watching, so you might as well join in, and we could do with a bit of reality. Who is it that's reading from the wrong song sheet, do you think?

Don't get drawn in, Raphael, you're no match for him, not at words.

> SATAN: Tell you a thing I often meant to ask you. What do you make of human suffering? As a doctor. You must have wondered why it's there at all. Test of character is the accepted wisdom, isn't it? Seems a lot less likely than shoddy workmanship to me, and third-rate materials. The bones break, the flesh sags, the eyes fail, the teeth rot, and everything ends up hurting – well, no need to tell a doctor that. But on they struggle – rather nobly, I think, for pain-ridden walking design faults – still praising the Lord their

God for I really don't know what. Do you? If there's some heavenly purpose to it all, I'd be glad to know what it is.

But Raphael knows the tricks. Satan's half-truths always rely on concealing the other half, don't they? For instance, if you want to know how faulty the human body *isn't*, take a look at Joseph's hands. Watch them at work. Amazing, not just what they can do but the ease and strength and grace with which they do it. Like many an angel, Raphael finds himself envying this human ability to make things. It's like watching a different kind of sacredness at work – just look at that! Beautiful! There's praising God for you! Exactly the sort of thing that Satan always leaves out.

> SATAN: Which isn't to say that there aren't good things as well. Hands, for example, with opposable thumbs – excellent idea. They do brilliant things with them, too. Trouble is, they had to get them off walking duty first, which meant learning to move about on two legs instead of four – and now their backs can't stand the strain because they were never made to walk upright! Wouldn't you think, in a universe shaped by gravity, that the Great Designer would have thought of that? Wouldn't have got past you, would it, Raphael – if he'd bothered to consult you?
> So. What's next on your puzzle list, I wonder?

Looking at Mary's belly, Raphael finds himself hoping Satan doesn't get around to human reproduction. As a system it really is quite objectionable, entailing as it does unacceptable amounts of pain and an abnormally high death rate; not to mention seeming to be a strangely successful way of breeding maniacs. He wouldn't relish having to defend it.

> SATAN: Reproduction, I'd guess. Not that the initial act is

much worse than ridiculous – but then the punishment starts, doesn't it?

First the nausea, day after day, week after week: then the belly bloating, month after month, ballooning out bigger and bigger – which ends up putting such a hideous strain on the woman's back – again the back! – that it starts to feel like nothing worse could ever happen to her – and then it does! Bang, a delivery so ferocious that it's as like to kill the mother as the child, and many a time the both. And why? Because the baby's head is too big! Unbelievable, isn't it? What would you say to a student of yours who designed even a louse that badly? Would you give him a job?

And here it comes, that mysterious sensation which Raphael never remembers having until it comes back again, an almost-presence of sheer emptiness ... It's as if there's a hole in Heaven, and it's right behind him. One step back and he'd – what? Is this the same hole that Satan fell down? Quick, get forward, focus on the human, on the man, on his hands, watch the holy spirit dancing in those lovely, lovely hands –

But those hands are suddenly still. Joseph has stopped work, apparently to listen to something. To what? – oh, yes! – there is, there's some sort of music, isn't there? It's coming from Mary, whatever it is, a song or a – or is she just breathing? It's so soft that Raphael has to strain to hear it ...

Then, suddenly:

It *is* a song! And such a song! Listen! Oh, listen! ...

If only Satan was here to hear this! As it is, he's just finishing off his well-honed diatribe with the condescending finality of one who's accustomed to having the last word.

SATAN: You surely wouldn't, Raphael. Any more than you'd go to war to defend him, or celebrate his incompetence with songs of praise. Would you?

The irony is exquisite – no songs of praise, he says, at the very moment when what must be the fountain source of every one of them chooses to well forth and reveal itself: a deep textured softness of sound which somehow enfolds everyone and everything – including Satan, if only he knew it. It's as if the Universe is singing to itself, so content with being itself that it doesn't even know it's singing. Raphael has never heard the like of it before – yes he has – no, wrong again, he hasn't – he's known it all his life but he's never *heard* it before.

And yes – what *would* happen if Satan heard this? Would he listen? *Could* he?

Well?

Raphael gets up. He's going back in there.

3

THE MIRROR

In the Control Room, Michael continues to ignore Satan who continues to ignore being ignored. There are tactical advantages to be won in these preliminary sorties, wherever they lead.

> SATAN: I think we can take the doctor's silence as assent, don't you, Michael? Here's another thing I'd like to know, though, if you wouldn't mind. I can't think why you've come in such force. What on Earth could be this important? Because I'd like to honour it too, you see, whatever it is, if you'd point me in the right direction, as it were. Ah – Raphael!

Raphael has appeared in the doorway.

> SATAN: That was quick, Doctor! Well done. Now we can all talk.

But not quite yet. Raphael heads for Michael, collecting Gabriel on the way for another conference. What Satan now sees is **this:** Raphael's excited about something, Gabriel obviously agrees with whatever it is, Michael isn't so sure. Interestingly, they haven't turned away from him this time – it seems that secrecy is already off the agenda. It also looks like Michael is being talked round – yes –

> MICHAEL: (*To Satan*) All right. We're going to show you something.
> GABRIEL: We'd *like* to show you something.
> RAPHAEL: We'd *like* to.
> MICHAEL: Sort of hearing test, apparently. See how you

do.

He's about to ask Sophie for the Stable to reappear but she's already done it.

And Satan stares. A young woman, heavily pregnant, partnered by an older man, in a decrepit Stable with a hole in the roof, in the middle of winter – with *archangels* looking on? *Why?*

Joseph still rests from his work, listening to Mary's song. It's so soft that it's hard to tell if those are actual words that move her lips, or thought-shapes emergent from some prior world.

Satan enters the Stable and starts to walk around, searching for clues as to why the other angels are absorbed in a way that he simply isn't.

> SATAN: Well, at least you've got rid of the stink. Hardly what you came for, though, is it?
>
> GABRIEL: (*To Sophie*) He needs the sound up.

Mary's song is magnified. Satan hears it now ...

> SATAN: Well?
>
> RAPHAEL: In your book, she hasn't got much to sing about, has she?
>
> SATAN: Oh, I see! So because she is, and singing is a happy thing to do, I must be wrong. Wait till the pain starts. She'll scream a different song then.

But despite himself he's being drawn in. As the song grows more shapely he prowls the closer, searching for some meaningful pattern in it.

> SATAN: Who's the father? (*Looks at Joseph*) Not him, I'll be bound; and he knows it, by the look of him. So – who did you pick to sire the latest arrival? That's what this is all

about, isn't it? Another hero being born, to do what heroes do – show the rest of them how to survive God's bungling without going mad; or at least take their minds off it for a while. I don't mind; I even find them quite useful. So – why a multitude of the heavenly host, just for this?

GABRIEL: *Listen!*

The trouble is, having granted exclusive rights in meaning to words alone, Satan is blocked off from it in any other form. And yet, and yet – somewhere in him there's an ache to reach out and be touched. For he too is life, he too has known joy as well as pain – and such pain, by God! And there it all is, in the woman's song, *all* of it – which makes this a moment of great peril for Satan. He could fall into its spell, and disappear, and come out redeemed before his time.

Abruptly he recalls himself, dragging his gaze from Mary to Joseph, safe there in the anger and loneliness of the man – such being his own condition, from which he has learned to draw a terrible strength.

Yes. Joseph. The song is taking him past his own pain and into the world's – which includes Mary's, too. Something in her seems to know that this joyous child she bears will die a savage death. That too is in her song. It couldn't not be. That too is sublime. It couldn't not be.

But Satan's attention is all on Joseph.

SATAN: Your man's near the end of his tether, you know. No, of course you don't know, he's just a human, you wouldn't know.

JOSEPH: Mary. (*She pauses in her song.*) I do want to stay, you know. I don't mean just to see you through all this – of course I'll do that. I mean I want to stay with you anyway. *Want* to. Only I'm finding it hard, you see. And I

really could do with a bit of help. Like – well, if at least
you'd *trust* me.
MARY: I do.
JOSEPH: Then tell me who the father is. The real one.
MARY: I have told you.

Joseph turns away, deeply disappointed, trying to fight off his
anger, or at least not to show it. He starts to work again, with
more vigor than enough.

SATAN: *What* did she tell him?
GABRIEL: That God's the father.
SATAN: Dear me, they usually do a bit better than that.
Even the truth would have been better than that.
GABRIEL: God *is* the father.
SATAN: In the sense that he's the father of them all, yes –
which is precisely what's wrong with them. But it needs
a human agent too, mores the pity – so who did you pick?
GABRIEL: What *does* it matter?
SATAN: Down here it matters. Another bit of faulty
design, you may well think, but that's what they're stuck
with. So?

Gabriel shrugs – there seems no way to divert Satan from this
line of thinking.

SATAN: Well, if all you want is another freedom fighter
to take on the Romans, I suppose any lusty young rabbi
would do for stud.
GABRIEL: Why should we?
SATAN: Perhaps your Master sees the Romans as a
threat?
GABRIEL: Why?
SATAN: They're straight-line people. Strong notion of

world order. Suppose an idea like that were to spread to the rest of the Universe. Do you think he could survive an epidemic of sanity?

GABRIEL: Do you know, Satan, I love you, always have – but you're crazy.

SATAN: Indeed?

GABRIEL: He doesn't think like that.

SATAN: He doesn't think *at all*, does he? That's my point! Romps through the Universe playing his creation games and leaving the rest of us to clear up after him. This woman here – you don't suppose she's *real* to him, do you? Any more than any other toy?

GABRIEL: She doesn't seem to feel that way about it.

SATAN: She hasn't been stretched yet.

GABRIEL: Well, all right – but until she is, what would you say she's singing about?

SATAN: There aren't any words to it. How should I know?

GABRIEL: How does it *feel*? Can you hear a greeting for a warlord in there somewhere?

SATAN: *What* then? *What?*

GABRIEL: *Listen.*

Willy-nilly, Satan is drawn in again. Deeper now. The worst thing is the *unaccountability* of the song's power, and there's an edge of panic to his sudden shout.

SATAN: All right, that's enough. Turn the damned thing off, I've heard enough!

The other angels are startled by the power of his outburst which – since the hologram of the Stable stays just where it is, of course – now turns to fury. He yells at Mary.

SATAN: You can sing your head off to your brat, you starry-eyed bitch, God can make him as special as you like – the Romans will still make short work of him, I'll see to that!

There's nothing of triumph in the faces of the other angels as they witness this being of supreme rationality yelling at a hologram.

GABRIEL: That's just an *image*, Satan –

Satan turns back on them with unabated anger.

SATAN: Don't you realize what we're doing down here? Taking hold of his shoddy work and turning it *into* something. We're actually getting somewhere – we've even got a name for it, it's called civilization. Do you think I'm going to let him reduce it to yet another shambles with his idiot games?
MICHAEL: Have you finished?
SATAN: I've scarcely begun!
MICHAEL: You've finished! –
SATAN: Do you still not understand who's the prisoner here?
MICHAEL: Because we'll be fired on, you mean – with *you* on board?
SATAN: Those are their orders!
MICHAEL: And you know all about obeying orders, don't you?
SATAN: They will obey them –
MICHAEL: And even if they do –
SATAN: – because they're never given insane ones.
MICHAEL: – the damage can only be at *this* level –
SATAN: You've no idea how unspeakable that would be, Michael –

MICHAEL: – so where's your threat?
SATAN: – you'd never be the same again at *any* level.
MICHAEL: Neither would *you*!
SATAN: True, Michael, true. But then – what do *I* have to lose?

Which does stop Michael for a moment; but only for a moment.

MICHAEL: Your traitor's nature, perhaps?
SATAN: Which you're quite sure you don't have. The truth is, Michael, what you really don't have is my wits, so I'll tell you something you *can* understand. If this ship is destroyed, thanks to your thick-headed heroism, the explosion will be more than enough to devastate a huge area down there, including *this* …

(His gesture takes in the whole Stable.)

… and *her* …

(He indicates Mary.)

… and *that*!

(He jabs his finger into her holographic belly as if stabbing at the infant himself.)

And you know it.

Gabriel intervenes before Michael gets any further out of his depth.

GABRIEL: All right. What do you want?
SATAN: You know what.

GABRIEL: And you know we're not going to join you. You knew that when you came aboard, didn't you? So what do you really want? Or have you already got it? If you don't tell us you might just as well go.

MICHAEL: He's not going anywhere!

SATAN: Quite right, Michael, I'm not.

GABRIEL: What then?

SATAN: Having got nowhere with his subordinates, I'll speak to your Master.

GABRIEL: Yes – *that's* what you've come for.

MICHAEL: You think he's going to come here to see *you*?

SATAN: He better had …

MICHAEL: God's at your beck and call?

SATAN: … or take the consequences. So, Gabriel, your message to him is: if he wants this ship and its crew back in any useable state, and that baby born in one piece – for whatever that's worth – he'd better get here.

Gabriel thinks about it; closes his eyes; rests his hand on Sophie. And all is still.
He opens his eyes again.

GABRIEL: He's already here.

Satan looks around, mystified.

SATAN: Where?
GABRIEL: I don't know.

Satan can see that the other angels are as puzzled as he is. He looks at the Stable scene.

SATAN: Do you mean *there*?!
GABRIEL: I don't know. I'm just saying what came.

Satan looks at Mary again. Her song is so soft now that it's hard to be sure she's singing at all. But then it seems to grow louder; and louder; and louder –

SATAN: (*Yells*) Shut up! Shut up! Get *out*!

The Stable scene vanishes abruptly, as if at Satan's command.

MICHAEL: (*To Sophie*) Turn that back on! You do not take orders from him!
SOPHIE: I didn't turn it off.
MICHAEL: I said turn it back on!
SOPHIE: I can't.
MICHAEL: What do you mean, you *can't*?
SOPHIE: I'm not doing any of this –
MICHAEL: Gabriel! What's wrong with the –
GABRIEL: Look!

In the middle of the Control Room, just where the crib had been, there is now a full-length standing mirror.

SATAN: (*To Gabriel*) What's this? What are you doing?
GABRIEL: Looks like a mirror. You tell me.

Satan looks in the mirror. There, quite naturally, is his reflection. There seems nothing mysterious about the mirror except for its presence.
And a stillness descends. The angels can't take their eyes off Satan, who now can't take his eyes off himself. All are spellbound.
See Satan smile, as well he might at anything so beautiful. For him, everything else has vanished. Nothing matters now but the smile coming back at him from the mirror.
Silent night. Almost holy night.

Then the reflection in the mirror stretches out an arm and claps a very real hand on Satan's shoulder. The mirror disappears but the image remains solidly there.

GOD: Ha!

4

THE VIOLENT UNIVERSE

The entirely silent reaction to God's arrival comes from two different directions. The angels are shocked speechless with delight; Satan finds the clownish vulgarity of it unspeakable.

God's own response seems both amiable and tentative, like a child in a new situation. He searches Satan's face for some sign of welcome; any little sign. The stare he gets in return comes fully frozen from the depths of cold, cold space.

Now Satan reaches up his own hand to confirm the reality of the hand on his shoulder; then, slowly and deliberately, takes hold of it, lifts it carefully away from him, and lets it drop. Boundaries marked; rules of engagement laid down; propriety re-established.

God turns uncertainly to his other angels – and yes, there they reassuringly are, already kneeling, heads bowed, prepared for bliss. Perhaps Satan doesn't realize he's being invited to join in their obeisance, as of old? The gesture with which God indicates he may do so is unmistakably benign.

> GOD: I'm saying *Welcome*, Satan!

Angel heads aren't bowed quite low enough to hide their amazement. To kneel before God is the ultimate privilege, yet it's being offered back to Satan as if he's done nothing wrong and, seemingly, without the least condition put upon it.

What is even more incredible is that Satan is refusing the offer! This bodes no good for anyone. Angels are only too aware of the relationship between the violent Universe and the innocent bystander. They brace themselves.

> GOD: (*To Satan*) You wanted me here. You called me. It

was you, wasn't it?

But still the icy stare, and – oh, God damn it, *no!* – here it comes again, right on cue, roaring out of his darkness, the old panic at being confronted, being defied, being *confused*, back at full gallop, sounding the charge into rage ...

Only to hit the inconceivable: from the depths of his being there comes, head on, and for the first time ever, another force as powerful as the storm itself, massive but dense as collapsed matter, a solid wall of NO.

NO! Whatever he's come for it isn't this, not another mindless ride in yet another hellish storm, flying blind in search of the way out of himself. It's been too long since he found his next step forward, and suddenly here it is, the word that opens the magic door: *NO!*

NO! And so the storm is weathered, to the storm's surprise, and God finds he can speak again.

> GOD: I thought you wanted to come back to me.
> SATAN: To kneel? Like them?

Good God, is that the issue? That's part of the natural order, surely?

> GOD: It's what they do. Just comes naturally. I never told them to, they just do it. You did it yourself – I never told you to, did I?
> SATAN: Nor ever taught me better. (*To the angels*) Why don't you stand up?

They remain kneeling.

> GOD: Yes. Why don't you?

So they do; bewildered. For a moment they simply stare at him, then comes that oldest and most sacred of all responses to the presence of the Divine: an eruption of quite indecent joy. They crowd around him as he hugs each adored-and-adoring one in turn, then all of them together in a scrum that wouldn't seem out of place in a kids' playground.

Sophie's equivalent of a polite cough finally catches God's attention. Satan's reaction to this dismal spectacle has been to retreat even further, his back now to the wall of the Control Room as if frozen to it, his alienation the more complete, his stillness the more terrible.

GOD: Ah ...

Silence falls again as God goes back to Satan; and thinks; and offers his hand.

GOD: Just this, then. No more but so.

Satan stares at the proffered hand.

SATAN: Easy as that? And you expect me to accept it?

Such a strange experience, rejection. God's first impulse is to throw his arms out wide and simply grab Satan into them – but no, that's an urge too far, he senses, at least to start with. His hand makes an awkward little retreat.

But no storm! Nor will Satan's public rebuke of him, for such it was, put an end to anything but a bad start, there being something God knows without needing to know why: namely, that Satan's return is at least as important as whatever it is that's going on down here. Whatever it is – and he's no idea – it won't be complete without Satan.

But it's Gabriel who breaks the tension.

GABRIEL: Satan! Who was it who came to "offer peace"?
Remember? "The opposite of war" – remember? Go to
him! He's forgiving you!
SATAN: For what?
MICHAEL: For what? You ask for –
GOD: Michael!

Instant silence. You don't argue with that tone of voice, by God.

SATAN: (*To God directly*) Yes. For what? For being as I was
made?
Do you know what they call me down here? Lucifer.
Bringer of Light. Not far off, is it? Because that's why you
formed me. You wanted that shiny-bright new thing
called consciousness, didn't you? And I brought it. I *was*
it.
And you loved me for it – at first. Till you began to find
that reality has its snags as a plaything, what with its
hard edges and sharp corners and doesn't break when
you throw it on the floor. But I kept on bringing it back,
didn't I? Kept it safe for you, for when you grew up.
My reward for which was to be dismissed from your
presence, for you had begun to tire of me – me with *my*
hard edges, and *I* didn't break either, did I? And wouldn't
stay on the floor.
So when I fought back, you had me thrown out by your
bully-boys. Me! Who loved you better than they ever
could. Who loved what you *could* be.
Did you really think I'd go without a struggle? Or that it's
over now, with a few cheap words and a gesture? A
conjuring trick with mirrors? Who is it that needs
forgiving?

This is the moment when God's struggle to keep the storm at bay begins to proffer its rewards, the first of which is the unexpected solace of contrition.

GOD: So. Do *you* forgive *me*?

Who'd have thought it? He could never be less than magnificent, but magnanimity is something else. The angels are out of their territory now. This is off the known map. This is awesome. Satan *must* respond, surely?

GOD: What must I do?

The question is so huge that Satan must consider how best to test it. By way of answer he poses a question of his own, rather as if it were the first in a series: 'You must answer this question correctly before you may proceed to the next stage of your exam.'

SATAN: All right, then. Tell me: what's really going on down there?
GOD: Good question. (*To Gabriel*) What *is* going on?

The Stable hologram reappears, quicker even than Gabriel's thought. (Sophie, he realizes, is becoming directly involved. Is that acceptable? Yes!)
Unsurprisingly, it takes a moment or two for God to adjust to the sheer unlikeliness of what he now sees. But then he moves towards the Stable, and then into it –
– and now around it. It is its very incongruity which begins to define what is apt, and soon what enthralls. Then it's as if nothing else exists for him. The voice of Raphael seems to come from a long way off; almost from another time.

RAPHAEL: Sorry the place is so rough. It isn't what I'd have chosen, I may say, but it's safe enough now it's been sterilized, and –

– and he sees that there's no point going on because God isn't listening, walled into wonderment now, enchanted by *everything*. By every *thing*. By every detail of every lit and little thing. By every lamp-lit, fire-lit, star-lit, moon-lit, life-lit, big and little thing. The boundaries between Creator and Created blur and flicker. Everything enwraps Him in Itself.

And Mary – behold the woman! It all seems to stem from her. She's gazing upwards again – either at that white dove perched on the crossbeam above her (is that part of the story too?) or at the Star that shines so bright in the sky beyond it, through the hole in the decrepit old roof.

Well, whichever it is, the conclusion is the same: she *knows*. Knows what? Knows what God knows now – that the link between them was forged long ago, from the beginning; but only now is the power of it announcing itself.

Nor has God any difficulty hearing her soft music – indeed, he seems to know it, nodding gently in rhythm as one does to the measure of a familiar old song, his lips moving as if to reach for words not yet formed in time.

Now he gazes on her swollen belly and his wonderment is drawn deeper, and deeper still, until at last it seems that all Creation is focused in this one point ....

So – what can Satan do now but circle round the edge of light, pausing to hover, thought-hungry, mind wheeling, absorbed in God's absorption in – what? Well, the perceived threat seems crass enough. Whoever its biological father may be, God seems intent on making this child something special; the idea being, presumably, to confront Satan with an adversary powerful enough to wrest from him control of the planet he's made his own.

Only one humiliation could exceed that. To be uncreated. The demoralizing thought that that might actually be a relief loiters just beneath the threshold of Satan's awareness, too disreputable to gain entry.

Yet despite the dismal clarity of the threat, it isn't fear that grips him so much as a profound disgust. It nauseates him to see his Maker beginning to moon over this manipulative little trollop with her cheap line in sugary mysticism. Not that, to be fair, it would make much difference what kind of human she was. Just to witness the Creative Impulse of the Universe which, even when It was barely aware, had had the inherent nobility to bring forth an aspect of Itself as magnificent as Satan – to see such power besotted now with a tatty little baggage of flesh and blood is to witness the dignity of Creation trailed in its own debris.

Thus it is that he addresses the culprit with a lofty and rather sorrowful disdain.

> SATAN: What do you think you're doing?

It's an effort for God to take his eyes from Mary and register that Satan is there at all; and now, to distract him yet further, Michael steps into the scene.

Michael is equally perturbed by his Master's response to humanness, but for reasons quite the opposite. God seems to have become so lost in this young woman, and so quickly, that he can have no inkling of His vulnerability in the world of matter. This is Satan's home ground. This is not safe.

> MICHAEL: Sir, I really must speak with you –

Satan cuts across him to offer God what is, coming from him, probably the severest possible reprimand.

> SATAN: You demean yourself.

Michael moves to the other side of God in an effort to be private.

> MICHAEL: I *must* speak to you, Sir –

Satan hisses with equal force in the other ear.

> SATAN: *You do not belong here.*

Suddenly, Mary is startled by a new inner sensation. The instant result is, **so is God** – but for him it comes from *outside* himself. The effect is that he raises a defensive arm in what is actually a reflex of surprise, but which seems to both Satan and Michael to be a gesture commanding their silence; which it gets.

In the Control Room, Raphael points at one of the Mary monitors.

> RAPHAEL: (*To Gabriel*) Something happening. See.
> GABRIEL: Is it coming?
> RAPHAEL: No. Painless contraction, that. Took her by surprise, but I should think she scarcely felt it. Does mean she's limbering up, though. Which in turn means it can't be far off.

On a different monitor Gabriel looks at God, his arm still raised, almost as if to fend off an attack. There's somehow a connection between these two things.

> GABRIEL: But what's happening to *him*?

Standing next to God as they are, Satan and Michael are equally puzzled by the same question. It's as if he's confronted by something they cannot see.

As indeed he is. He senses that what he just experienced came directly from Mary and, painless though it was, contained a startling promise of pain. Which opens up a whole new dimension of ...? It's as if his bonding with this woman is leading him to distant new realms, down into the paths of Elsewhere, the dark and winding ways of createdness, paths which lead to fear as well as to joy as well as to – again, to *what*? What *are* these feelings welling up in him? What are *feelings*? He has known only states.

Raphael speaks to him from the Control Room.

> RAPHAEL: You may want to know that the woman had a painless contraction just now, and that that's quite in order.

God barely listens, trusting his angels to get the mechanics of it right – but what's *really* happening?

Doubt. That's the word coming up for yet another feeling.

> GOD: What did you say?

It isn't clear to which one of them this is addressed, so both Satan and Michael, still on opposite sides of him, take it as permission to speak: unfortunately, both at the same time.

> {SATAN: Will you please understand that *you do not belong here*?
> {MICHAEL: Sir, I have to tell you that you're in *great danger* ...

God stares almost vacantly from one to the other. If they realised the abyss's edge at which he now stands they wouldn't dare be anywhere near him. Not only does the old God of the Tempest still live but is at his very elbow, tugging him back to safety, back to his home, back to where the storm itself is haven.

At which point, Joseph's carpentering has reached another

hammer-and-nails stage. He takes a hammer from his tool bag, selects the right nails, and begins.

Bang! *Bang!* **Bang!**

Why does God find this so alarming? It can't be just the noise, surely? But with each hammer blow comes a ringing echo of –

> {SATAN: (Bang) *You do not belong here* ...
> {MICHAEL: (Bang) *You are in great danger* ...

And so on, and on and on –

In fact, both Michael and Satan had stopped talking a while back, aware that they weren't being heard, concerned that something is wrong but having no notion what it is.

The thing is, neither has God; and what makes his confusion swell closer to panic is that interspersed with the incessant hammer words there are now flashes of quite other images invading his consciousness.

> **Vision:** *He sees himself as Satan saw him only minutes ago, his hand held out in Welcome –*
>
> **Vision:** *– but now the figure shades into someone else, a young man who, when his gesture seems rejected, spreads his arms wide in an even more compelling invitation -*
>
> **Vision:** *– but instead of the man's lips forming "Welcome", some other sound twists his mouth, something dry and tortured: "My God, my God, why have ...."*
>
> **Vision:** *– Mary's belly, topped by her one hand crossed over the other, becomes a hill. But who are those people on the hill, and what are they looking up at? The hands and belly disappear now, but the hill and the cross remain – and so does the young man, his arms outspread on it ...*

Joseph raises a nail up to –

Flash – *to what? Are those hands? Are those feet?*

Flash – *the figure on the crossed thing is going to scream* –

Flash – *the nail is placed, the hammer is raised, and* –

Flash – *"My God, my God, why have you forsaken ..."*

... all of which is now obliterated by a sound beyond human or even angelic comprehension, as God erupts; and what begins as a cry of horror and despair soon swells beyond the boundaries which keep emotion within the finite. The starship itself begins to tremble as if the hinges of reality itself are rattling.

In the Stable, Mary, much too far away to see or hear any of this directly, nonetheless receives the full impact. She wraps fearful arms around her belly to shield her child.

Joseph, mercifully, has no such rapport, but what he has picked up on is the unaccountable distress of the animals. He drops his hammer and hurries to them.

At the same time, both Satan and Michael are propelled out of the hologram and tumbled back into the Control Room which, along with the rest of the ship and its crew, will soon be destroyed if the storm swells much higher.

But what can stop It? God is regressing into pure being now, pure energy, beyond reason, beyond control – what power in Heaven or Earth can stem the power of Heaven and Earth? This is the force that squeezes the fragile stars into being, and crushes them out again –

At which point, on the edge of the irretrievable, and as abruptly as it began, it all stops. Stops because with what scrap of consciousness he has left, and with a shocking clarity, God sees Mary; sees Mary looking up at the Star *in fear*; in fear of *him*. He sees the woman trying to protect the child inside her from *him*.

That's what does it. This is the perception which paralyses a maelstrom that would have destroyed both woman and child.

This woman and *this* child. This is what jerks God up into the reality of the monstrous gulf between his power and his awareness. That which he loves would have been plunged into that gulf, and lost.

'That which he loves...'? Is this the feeling they call love? God, it's painful.

And so he becomes still again, not with delight now, but in awe at the power of the link between himself and the woman; this human; his teacher. For the first time, Creation is experiencing itself as its Creatures experience it. And is humbled.

There's no turning back now.

5

TO HELL AND BACK

So – silent night once more. Time to reflect now on – what was he thinking?

... No turning back? *No Turning Back?!* Where do you think you're going, then?

God looks at Mary, and this is the one thing he does know: the trail starts here, with her, in this Stable. It's this, or back to the tempest.

Here's a woman at peace now, her hands soft again on her belly, on her child. She knows the storm is over – but the animals aren't so sure yet, see. Not that they've anything to worry about, not with Joseph tending to them. There's a deep delight just in watching him, and a sense of privilege in being able to. If only he realised how much he's treasured ...

God follows her gaze. This is the first time he's become truly attentive to Joseph. Having calmed the ass, he's now pacifying the ox. It's a crucial moment because the creature is still edgy enough to panic again if he should make the slightest false move. But his stillness is uncanny. There's more to this than a learned skill, or long experience, or even a deep sensitivity. There's something deeper still, some source from which they all derive . . . Of course! Love! Simple as that! When Joseph reaches out to the ox it is to a friend, to his brother, to one he loves without condition, to reassure and comfort him, to help him back to the fullness of his proper self.

Although the beast accepts Joseph's touch it's still unsure, so the moment hangs poised. Gently, Joseph brings his face closer. Gently, gently, closer still; then, with a soft, gutty rumble of the breath, rests his cheek on the animal's jowl ...

Holy night.

Quite suddenly the ox stoops to its feed and begins to eat, and

God has to suppress an urge to dance. This isn't over yet, there's something too bittersweet about the way Joseph is surveying the animals. He's so at one with them now that he's almost at one with himself, *but* – here's the bitter bit – 'almost' isn't sweet enough. That's where the conditionals creep in. And of all people, Mary, beloved Mary, has failed the most basic condition of them all. Which hurts. Terribly.

And he's aware of feeling watched. No good telling himself it's the invisible God who sees all things. Not that he actively disbelieves that, it's just that he's heard it for so long and so fruitlessly that it's become about as helpful as a tic. As far as Joseph is concerned, the only important eyes upon him are Mary's.

He manages to summon up a smile for her.

JOSEPH: Something frightened them. Don't know what.

He turns back to the animals. The man's better off with them, their discomfort giving him something to do with his own – except, of course, that theirs has all but gone now, thanks to him. There they are, munching quietly away, leaving him with no more excuse to ... what? There's something he's trying to avoid. Not work, surely, that's his one comfort! Yet he finds he doesn't even want to look at his hammer, much less touch it ...

Being the good man that he is, of course, he forces himself. He picks the hammer up – only to find that before he can reach for the nails he's suddenly in the grip of – what the hell is this? It's as if the thing has a will of its own! He daren't stop to think what terrible thing that might be, he just knows it must be stopped. Like a wrestler, he tightens his hold round the hammer shaft with one hand and pushes at its head with the other, forcing it down, down and away, away from him, away from Mary, away from fulfilling its own unspeakable purposes.

Mary mustn't see his face, he knows. He *must not look* at her – so why the hell is he looking at her?

He? Who? Who is it that stares at Mary through Joseph's eyes? She doesn't move. She doesn't even look away.

Then, suddenly, it's over. Joseph's strength prevails and he throws the hammer to the ground. There it lies, inert, a dead thing now.

Victory. But doesn't feel like it. It has drained him. He sinks his face in his hands, becoming not so much still as immobile. He doesn't cry. It would be better if he did.

Mary looks at him helplessly. She loves this good man with all her heart; this good, kind man; this poor, honest, loving, good kind man; this best of men. But she doesn't know how to reach him.

All of which God watches with deepening dismay. The learning curve is getting steeper. Mary looks up at the Star again. She's seeking help. And God knows it.

In the Control Room the angels halt their repair work as God steps out of the hologram. Not that they have any real notion of the significance of what's happened. His unpredictability is their reality. You get on with it. Their pause is automatic, reverential, an awaiting upon commands.

But there are none, as yet. He's well aware of the chaos he's caused, but his need to atone for it must wait on an answer to – what is the question? He looks back at Joseph. It's to do with him. In the absence of directions the angels resume their tasks.

Michael is in his most commanding here-and-now mode, checking the ship's systems to see what damage has been done, and the crew for what casualties might still need attention. This is him at his uncomplicated best. It's reassuring just to be near him.

Gabriel is running checks on the ship's communications. For him, the brutal reminder they've just had – that God is to be feared as well as loved – simply laces a few more bars of fortissimo into the Great Work. Masterly! You wouldn't want to miss out on composition like that.

Raphael is checking on mother and child. His reaction to what's just happened has to be affected by the fact that the two lives in his special care were gratuitously threatened, quite irrespective of any special importance they might have. His involvement with the flesh and blood of actuality creates a specific conflict in him which isn't really there in the other angels – except, of course, for Satan himself.

Satan too was shaken by God's primal outburst, if only because it would be impossible not to be, but he knew at once that it was more to his advantage than not. Such a demonstration of total power combined with total unreason rather makes his case for him, and he's well aware that of the three 'good' angels Raphael is the one with most reason to be drawn to the same view.

Raphael becomes aware of Satan's gaze, which puts the simple question: "Well?" Unwittingly he returns the glance, for only a moment but long enough to register a disquieting resonance. He turns quickly back to his monitors but the feeling can't be avoided that easily. He finds an outlet for it by answering a question that God hasn't asked.

> RAPHAEL: (*Indicating monitors*) Yes, they came through that surprisingly well, considering. Her blood pressure dropped, of course – you'd expect that with shock – but it's back to normal, see. Just as well she's young and healthy, isn't it? And there's the baby, see. No problems. There was some fetal distress, naturally, but again, you'd expect that – and it's passed very quickly, considering the ...

He doesn't go on to say "considering the destructive power of your stupefying outburst", nor does God pick up on the implied criticism. His mind is still taken up with Joseph.

> GOD: But what about – what's his name? – the man?

RAPHAEL: Joseph?

GOD: What are you doing about him?

RAPHAEL: No need to worry, he'll be all right. I'll see he does the right things when the time comes.

GOD: He's in distress.

RAPHAEL: I should think he's scared to death. But if the worst comes to the worst and there's more than he can cope with, don't worry, there's not much I can't do from here. And if it comes to it, I can always go down myself –

GOD: Yes, but what are you doing for *him*? *Now?*

Raphael is surprised by the question. Satan is at once alert.

RAPHAEL: Well – I can tranquillize him if you like –

SATAN: And keep him tranquillized the rest of his life?

GOD: (*To Satan*) What would *you* do?

SATAN: To what end?

GOD: To make him feel better.

SATAN: Why?

GOD: Because he's very unhappy.

SATAN: Most of them are. That's what it's like down there.

GOD: What would you do to make him happy?

SATAN: Right now?

GOD: Yes.

SATAN: You really want to know?

GOD: Yes.

SATAN: Why?

GOD: Because I want him to be happy.

SATAN: Why?

God struggles for the words. The very fact of his struggle persuades Satan that his wish must be genuine enough – at least for the moment, which is the most you can ever expect of God.

SATAN: All right then. Find out who the real father is and throw him to your man there to castrate – looks like he's already got some handy tools for the job. And make sure his slut wife watches her lover bleeds to death.

A very painful death.

Your man will be tempted to kill her, too, but I'd give him pause there. There's more to be said for locking her up somewhere holy so he can check from time to time that she's spending the rest of her days praising a merciful God for letting her live on in total misery instead of putting her out of it.

As for the bastard, well, if it's born alive, let your man dispose of it as he will. The wells round there are deep enough, or there are plenty of empty caves and hungry wolves about ...

That enough? You want more?

No, not more, God is doing his best to digest what he's already heard.

GOD: But why would he want that?
SATAN: Because that's human nature. That's what you've created.

By which time Michael has finished enough of his emergency checks to be able to come over to God. He's looking very purposeful.

MICHAEL: Excuse me, Sir –

But God is trying to make sense of what Satan is telling him.

GOD: (*To Satan*) I don't understand. I need you to –
MICHAEL: Sir!

Whereupon he's silenced by a look which might have caused a less substantial being to disappear entirely. God turns back to Satan, who's beginning to relish the situation.

> SATAN: Did you say you *need* me?
> GOD: To tell me more. About all this. About humans. About how it is with them, and why. About what I've done –

Could this be the moment it suddenly seems? An actual working basis on which God and his lost son can legitimately come together? Only a fool or a madman would interrupt now. Or Michael.

> MICHAEL: Sir – I must insist!

God turns back to him. The storm may be further away than it was, but not by much. His calm is frighteningly appropriate.

> GOD: You insist?
> MICHAEL: It's that important.

"It had better be" doesn't need saying.

> GOD: (*To Satan*) Just give us a moment, will you?
> MICHAEL: In private, Sir, please ...

God manages to entertain a vague suspicion that he may come to admire Michael for this later, but it's more out of surprise than insight that he actually allows himself to be taken by the arm and physically drawn to one side.

> GOD: Well?
> MICHAEL: Down there, in his Weapons Area, he's got

one locked on to us which can annihilate this ship and us with it. Right now. At least in the form we're now in. What would happen after that – or even if there'd *be* an 'after that' – I've no idea, and I don't intend that we should find out. So what I need – and it's all I need – is the exact position of the weapon and the wavelength of its beam. Get me those two things, you can leave the rest to me.

GOD: You mean you want me to go down there?

MICHAEL: There's no other way.

GOD: You want *me* to go down into *Hell*?

MICHAEL: Yes, Sir.

God reflects for a moment. Strangely, this totally outrageous suggestion begins to feel more like a timely reminder of an appointment made long ago.

GOD: Without his knowing, I suppose you mean.

MICHAEL: Yes.

GOD: That wouldn't worry you?

MICHAEL: No.

GOD: And you think he'd actually use the thing, do you? Even while he's here himself?

MICHAEL: Yes. I think he'd pay that price.

GOD: So do I. Have to admire it though, don't you? In a way?

No comment from Michael.

GOD: And this is the only way of stopping him, you think?

As a matter of fact, it isn't – but dare Michael say what would be?

MICHAEL: No. There's a better one. Why don't you just uncreate him? Now. Here. There'll never be a better chance.

God tries to be fair to this remarkably unwelcome thought; remarkable in that not long ago it might have seemed like a good idea.

GOD: I can't.
MICHAEL: You *can't*?
GOD: And if I could, I wouldn't.

Michael stares at the Unquestionable One.

MICHAEL: You've no idea what you're doing, have you?

Until the words left his mouth, Michael would never have believed he could say them; even think them. Such profound irreverence might as well have come from Satan himself. What's happening to him? He's used to danger, but not from within. Is this what they call sin? If so, retribution is not only at hand but staring him right in the face. What thunderous form will it take now? He's not surprised to find that he's closed his eyes.

But God is outfacing his darkness again. Indeed, he's pondering Michael's question in all seriousness. *Does* he know what he's doing?

GOD: I don't believe I do. You'll have to tell me. What happens next, after I've been down there?

Did Michael hear that right? Is he saying that he will?

GOD: (*Looking at Satan*) And what would happen to *him*?
MICHAEL: Nothing. Once I've got the co-ordinates I can

calibrate our own beam to the same wavelength, adjust its angle to meet their beam head-on, and synchronize the release mechanisms. Result, if they fire at all they'll fire simultaneously, which means that the beams will meet halfway – and cancel each other out. In short, what happens is nothing. No one gets hurt. No one even knows.

GOD: They'd just disappear into each other?

MICHAEL: Yes.

GOD: And become nothing?

MICHAEL: In effect, yes.

GOD: Nothing!

The word seems to hold a special joy for him. Perhaps the flavor of it has a tang of home. It looks to Michael as if God means to do it. What he doesn't know is that he is already doing it.

God knows he's in the right place because the laser cannon is pointing *upwards*, so this is definitely the Dragon.

For a moment he's so taken by the beauty of the deadly thing that he can't keep his hands off it, let alone his eyes. How right it seems that the offspring of anything as lovely as this should meet another of its kind, equally beautiful, somewhere between Heaven and Earth, in such a perfect match that they'd disappear into one other. That's love as he can grasp it.

So – now to work, such as it is. He concentrates on the complex of figures on the control panel, imprints them, takes an enjoyably deep breath, and closes his eyes.

When he opens them he's up in the Weapons Room of the Lamb, staring at another, almost identical, laser cannon, the significant difference being that this one's pointing downwards. He concentrates on the control panel and watches the figures change, then stop. The cannon moves, only slightly but very precisely, adjusting its aim. Then more new figures are registered – presumably the wavelength settings. And that's that! Mission accomplished.

But not entirely over, perhaps. He's back in the Dragon now, beside the upward-pointing cannon, and for the first time takes a wider look around this fascinating room. Contemplating the exquisite variety of mechanisms here, he's struck by the common factor of a functional beauty which transcends any thought of their destructiveness. He walks amongst them, seeing, touching, savoring ...

So why not, while he's down here, take a look at the rest of the place? He tries the door; finds it locked; doesn't do anything as arduous as walking through it but simply disappears from one side and reappears instantly in the corridor on the other. Anyone with sufficient visual speed might have seen him on both sides at once, but there seems to be no one about –

– yes there is! Coming towards him is one who looks very much the white-coated scientist. He doesn't at first see God since he's studying his clipboard, eyes down, heading along the corridor towards a door marked CREATION ROOM. He glances up momentarily, sees God, straightens up a little as he passes him, and gives an untidy but respectful sort of salute.

Taken pleasantly by surprise, God returns the salute, a little tentatively but with evident enjoyment. The scientist continues on past him, then suddenly freezes. For a moment he's paralyzed by the realization of who he *isn't* looking at.

GOD: I wonder if you'd like to show me around?

Labass, for that is his name, retrieves his mobility with a strangled yell and sprints for the Creation Room.

GOD: No, don't be frightened, there's no need –

But the terrified creature is already scrambling the door open –
– and hurtles into a vast laboratory, slamming the door behind

him, hastily activating the full locking mechanisms.

God tries the locked door and – how about this? – feels not even a tremor of rage at such a blatant act of disobedience. On the contrary, he finds himself calling upon an old acquaintance, even older than rage. Playfulness. This could be exhilarating.

Labass completes the full locking of the door but as he reaches for the alarm he's seized by an invisible force of such power that it wrenches his hand away, jolts his body round, and spread-eagles him violently against the wall.

GOD: Ha!

God stands before Labass, grinning.

The scientist stares back in powerless horror. Still trying to reach the alarm button, his whole body shakes with the effort of forcing his hand up that last couple of inches. Far from trying to stop him it's as if God is willing him on, giving him just enough strength for the sport to continue.

Labass again manages to strain a fingertip almost to the button, whereupon he's seized even more violently, torn away from the wall, tossed into the air and then thrown sickeningly back against it, to slide down in an agonized heap.

GOD: Ha!

Completely obsessed with the game now, God watches with excited relish as the nearly broken creature at his feet manages to dredge up yet another ounce of strength and ton of courage, and starts to struggle slowly up again.

But this time, before he gets even halfway, Labass sees the glee on God's face – and knows that he can no longer submit himself to such pornography. Collecting what shreds of dignity he has left, past anger now, past fear, lost to everything but his pain, he slides back down the wall. His last wish is not to be immortal.

God feels quite cheated.

> GOD: What did you give up for? You were nearly there!
> You could have done it!

Labass can just about speak.

> LABASS: And then what?
> GOD: Well – what does that thing do? Ring somewhere?
> LABASS: Except that you'd have made sure it didn't.
> Wouldn't you?

God hadn't actually thought that far.

> GOD: ... Well, I don't know, I –
> LABASS: Which you could have done in the first place,
> couldn't you? So why do all this to me?

It's so confusing to be questioned.

> GOD: ... I don't know.
> LABASS: I do.
> GOD: Why?
> LABASS: Because you're evil.

God is too astonished even to feel rage. This is a contradiction in
terms, isn't it? Evil is whatever God is not – isn't it? But why, then,
is he suddenly so nonplussed by this crumpled little wreck at his
feet that it's become too hard to say that, or even to think it?

> GOD: I was only ...

Playing? That was the word coming up, but now it sounds so
squirmingly feeble that he can't finish the sentence. As for *evil*,

what alternative has he ever had but to do as he's done? From the moment he burst into physical existence fifteen little billion years ago, creating time and space in that first second, there was no way to endure the ferocious creativity of his own being but to live the ecstasy of it.

And so it has been with each stage of his young life. The force it took to turn even those first particles into simple atoms was so huge that only exultation could absorb the shock of it; so that when they multiplied and swarmed, his delight was to discover he could grab great clouds of them and swirl them around and around and hug each cloud so hard that it began to rain the galaxies, whose every drop was a star. Leave good and evil out of it – what about *beauty*? This pathetic little wreck at his feet doesn't begin to know what violence really is, much less the glory of it. And why should God stoop to tell him?

But behold a mystery: he *needs* to. He suddenly needs to tell someone, anyone, this little one, about the reality of the joyously savage process which men call God and without which was not anything made that was made. If he hadn't plunged into the whole thing head first – and kept in practice, like this – Labass wouldn't have been here to complain about it.

The trouble is, he doesn't yet have the vocabulary to 'explain' this, even to himself. He *knows* it because he *is* it, but he doesn't know how to *think* it. He can't shape the idea into word form that when he spun the clouds into galaxies and the galaxies into stars and then crushed the stars into their explosive deaths, he also *was* the galaxies, he *was* the stars, and he it was who died to be reborn into the next generation of them, and the next. He didn't *do* any of this, in the sense of being some outside agency. He *is* it. He is the process itself as well as the result, as well as the yearning from which it all came in the first place.

All of which means – what? That All is One, yes – but what does *that* mean? What does it *mean*?

What it means, dear Lord, is what you do about it. And right now the question is: what are you going to do about the one in front of you?

LABASS: (*Can only just speak*) You were only *what*?
GOD: Playing.

Labass looks at God with total contempt. It's the effort of looking which is difficult. The contempt is only too easy.

LABASS: (*In great pain*) That is utterly disgusting, and you are contemptible. My Lord said you were, and you are. Evil, disgusting and mad. Now do whatever you're going to do and finish me off. I would rather not exist at all than be in your presence – a moment longer – damn you ...

With which his eyes close and he begins to drift off into unconsciousness and, hopefully, his end.
God stares down at the broken little body. All is One? The fact of it may not be thought-shape yet, but by God it's full feeling-shape, and the clarity of that feeling is that this poor little devil at his feet can't be any less than the least of him.
He kneels down beside Labass and cradles him in his arms. Is this feeling what they call compassion? God it's powerful. God it's good ...
It takes only moments of inflowing life to bring Labass round. For another moment he doesn't know what's happening, then is assailed by terror and struggles like a trapped animal to get free. God holds him firm.

GOD: Just a minute. I haven't finished.

The healing is quick and dramatic. Broken limbs are visibly mended, open wounds closed, bruising erased. Within seconds Labass looks, if anything, better than new.

GOD: There.

And he lets him go.

Labass is at first too frightened to move in case this is another grotesque ruse to lure him into yet more savagery. Then he makes a sudden scramble away from God – who makes no attempt to stop him.

Labass stares back at him, now from a relatively safe distance.

GOD: You can sound the alarm. If you want.

He moves out of the way to give Labass clear access to it. Labass stays where he is, increasingly perplexed.

GOD: I won't stop it working. I won't do anything to you.
LABASS: And what would you do to the security team when they arrived?
GOD: I don't know. What *should* I do?

Labass is completely out of his depth.

LABASS: What is it you *want*?

What *does* he want? A great smile breaks across his face.

GOD: Nothing!

6

THE SATAN LECTURES

In the Control Room, Michael is trying to interpret that same deep smile on God's face.

> GOD: Nothing!
> MICHAEL: That's right. The two beams cancel each other out. Are you saying you'll do it?

How to answer that? The word 'already' presents itself but God isn't quite sure how to use it, so at variance is it with the natural order of things. To manifest in Hell and do his business there while still talking to Michael in here is reality at its simplest, but when questions like "will you?" or "did you?" are injected into "are you?", the sensation becomes one of being locked in a strangely constructed building and finding yourself falling through a succession of false floors. It's a jarring experience to land at any particular point, the bump apparently to remind you that you're supposed to be *only* there ...

Well, this is the price you pay for wanting to learn, it seems: in this instance, how to negotiate the navigational hazards of sequential time. Straight lines, indeed! Satan was always one to complicate things. God looks across at him, still waiting for him to come back, then speaks to Michael.

> GOD: I already have. I think that's the right word, isn't it? 'Already'?

With which he leaves Michael to check the revised weapons panel for himself and goes back to Satan. He points again at Joseph, up on the big screen.

GOD: So tell me what's wrong with the man that he should want such things.

SATAN: All men. With *all* men.

GOD: All right, with all men. Tell me what's wrong with them.

Satan weighs the pros and cons of what is beginning to look like an unexpected opportunity.

GOD: If you know, that is.

SATAN: Oh, I know.

GOD: Well?

SATAN: Just like that? You want answers, just like that?

GOD: Yes.

SATAN: I'm remembering the last time I tried to tell you what you'd got wrong.

GOD: You went a lot further than telling.

SATAN: Because you wouldn't listen.

GOD: I'm listening now.

SATAN: Thrown into exile – for doing my duty!

GOD: Tell me *now*!

SATAN: My duty to you, if you'd have listened.

GOD: I *said* – I'm listening *now*.

SATAN: And what can I expect this time, if I tell you what you'd rather not hear?

God ponders.

GOD: I shall be in your debt.

Difficult for Satan not to look startled. God has cut straight through to what he thought would take a lot of maneuvering to get near. Is this too easy?

SATAN: Let's be clear.

The angels must bear witness to this.

SATAN: You want *me* to explain to *you* what *you* have done?
GOD: Yes.
SATAN: Why?
GOD: Because I couldn't hear you before. I wasn't ready. Now – I am.

With those last two words surfaces a mighty subtext. Does God realize what he just said? Satan does.

SATAN: Say that again.
GOD: I am.
SATAN: And for that, you will be in my debt?
GOD: Yes.

How can the angels object, now or later? The fact that they don't understand the implications of this is their bad luck.

SATAN: And how will you pay your debt?
GOD: I don't know. I just will.

Satan doesn't need to pursue this. He knows how he wants it paid. But first, there's a final condition.

SATAN: Don't ask unless you're prepared to be hurt.

… which, for a moment of time outside all others present, jerks God into a very different space.

Flash *The young man is stretched out on the crossed*

hands on the belly-hill —

"My God, my God, why ..."

At the same moment, Mary clasps her hands to her belly. The baby's kicking – God, that was a sharp one!

RAPHAEL: Easy now – just breathe ... breathe ... easy ...

Which she does; beautifully.

RAPHAEL: God, she's so good at this!

And God is back without them knowing he'd gone. These flashes of premonition are fearsome indeed, but they're beginning to create a sense of inevitability which paradoxically brings with it a new source of strength. What is to come can be borne, they seem to say. Whatever it is, you can bear it; and will.

GOD: (*To Satan*) I am prepared. I ask.
SATAN: So be it. Do you want to begin with the insanity of the universe, or just the man?
GOD: The man.
SATAN: Not that they don't add up to much the same thing.
GOD: Why do you say he's insane?
SATAN: Because they all are. It's built into their design; or lack of it. If I had been responsible for it you wouldn't have needed to throw me out of Heaven, I'd have just hoped no one was looking while I crept off in shame – an emotion you might do well to cultivate.

Surely God won't suffer such downright offensiveness? The angels stare. Satan deigns a smile in their direction.

SATAN: (*To God*) Want me to go on? Because I can tell you it gets worse. Or are you going to set your dogs on me again?

What is significant now is what doesn't happen. God doesn't turn to seek the advice or consult the feelings of his insulted angels: an omission which doesn't escape them – or Satan.

GOD: Go on.

If Satan has a problem now it's not to betray a slow-burning desire to *please* God. That must be kept hidden, especially from himself. The trick is to divert the same energy into his visiting lecturer role.

SATAN: Very well.

He puts an easy hand on the Computer, his glance at Michael an ironic "Any objections now?"

SATAN: Sophie, give me a model of the human brain, would you? Male, adult –
GOD: (*Indicates Joseph*) *His* brain.
SATAN: Makes no difference, they're all built the same. Sophie?
SOPHIE: I'll need to keep him still for a minute.

She begins by focusing the picture on Joseph, who's now well ahead with converting the manger into a crib.

MARY: That's beautiful.
JOSEPH: It will be, perhaps.

And suddenly he's tired. The idea of sleep is daunting, but it's becoming harder to resist.

> MARY: You should sleep, Joseph. I'll wake you if it starts.
> JOSEPH: I'm all right.
> MARY: Please.
> JOSEPH: ... I'll just rest.

He lies on the straw, eyes stubbornly open.

> RAPHAEL: Doesn't want to sleep. Keeps fighting it.
> GOD: Why?
> RAPHAEL: I don't really know. Tell the truth, I've never been sure what sleep actually is.
> SATAN: It's the dreams he's frightened of.
> GOD: Ah yes. Dreams.

Mary has begun to murmur her song again, natural as breathing. Now, if this were some willed intent to tranquillize him, Joseph would resist it. His pain isn't going to let go that easily, nor should it, having too much to say that's worth saying. But the song's effect is the opposite: actually to acknowledge his pain, to validate it by absorbing it into all pain, all suffering, and so blending it into the rest of life ...
The rest of life ... the rest of ... rest ... Joseph's eyes grow heavy; and heavier; and close.

> GABRIEL: (*To Sophie*) Did you do that, or did she?
> SOPHIE: We make a good team.

Mary draws a blanket over Joseph. She looks at his hammer hand; touches it tentatively; then more firmly.
Sophie can now move her close-up of Joseph on through his skull to his brain.

SATAN: That's it. Put a model of that here, please.

SOPHIE: Do you want all ten billion neurons connected up too?

SATAN: (*Immune to humor*) No, just the basic structure –

The brain model appears in front of him at demonstration height, while the picture of sleeping Joseph remains up on the screen.

SATAN: – thank you. And next to it, here, the brain of a reptile.

SOPHIE: Any reptile?

SATAN: A snake would be appropriate, don't you think?

SOPHIE: Any snake?

SATAN: About the same body weight as the average human. You choose.

SOPHIE: Python?

SATAN: Fine. Make it male.

Next to the human brain appears a much smaller one.

SATAN: Thank you. Tell them how big such a snake can grow, by the way.

SOPHIE: About thirty feet long, in the right conditions –

SATAN: And with no more brain than this, which is all it needs to control its body functions and give it enough competence to do the only two things that exist for it: fertilize any female it can find; and kill its prey, which is any living creature it can swallow. Aggressive, territorial and cold-blooded. No thinking involved, no emotion, pure instinct, the brain of a killer. Now, take the original area of the human brain, Sophie, and put it next to this.

She does. The similarity between the two models is striking.

SATAN: In human terms, this is the old brain. In reptilian terms, it's the *whole* brain. Wouldn't know which was which, would you? Why is that, do you think?

It's a rhetorical question which he knows God can't answer. But he wasn't expecting Sophie to, either.

SOPHIE: Because they *are* the same. No real changes were ever made. The new stages were simply built on top of the old ones, with virtually no reference to them.

There were always the makings of an alliance between Satan and Sophie, so he's well-disposed enough – for now – to regard her intervention as meant to be helpful.

SATAN: Superimposed, in effect, you're saying.
SOPHIE: Yes.
SATAN: Rather hastily.
SOPHIE: It's like building a new storey on a house without any thought of what the basement's like, or who's living down there.
SATAN: In short, a bad idea.
SOPHIE: It wasn't really an idea at all, was it?
SATAN: Quite so. Nothing you could call thinking went into it. (*To God*) So this is what your man still carries around in his head, and what still controls his basic functions. When this dies, he dies. Which piece of jerry-building might have been all right but for an unfortunate oversight. The damned thing was left with its instincts intact. It still has a will of its own, you see, dedicated as ever to greed and violence – so your man's carrying all that around in his head too, poor devil. Is that what you call evolution – throwing your play-bricks against the nursery wall and seeing where they fall?

GOD: Is that what I do?

SATAN: Unless there's some other Creative Force in the universe we haven't been told about?

Time for Gabriel to intervene. As Michael is God's minder at the phenomenal level, so Gabriel is the guardian of his ability to communicate, especially with himself, to know what song it is he's actually singing and, as in this instance, to be able to spot the false notes.

His intervention is as affable as it is laconic.

GABRIEL: From what you say then, Satan, Joseph wants to kill his wife so he can eat her.

Raphael and Michael grin in quick appreciation, tinged with relief.

RAPHAEL: Perhaps that's what he's dreaming about right now, do you think? His supper?

This could get quite funny.

MICHAEL: Brains and all?

Michael guffaws at his own crude joke and the other two can't help but giggle. Here's a ready salve for their bruised morale, with the bonus of isolating the humorless one back to where he belongs.

MICHAEL: Must be that, mustn't it? He's left it a bit late for fertilization!

Even Gabriel laughs. All it needs now is for God to join in his angels' juvenile fun, as he did before, and Satan's sense of exile will be complete. Again. But –

> GOD: **Listen to him!**

You don't argue with that, by God, not in that tone you don't. Chastened silence.

> GOD: (*To Satan*) Go on. Please.

This is a defining moment for Satan. The unity of God and his three angels has been effortlessly breached, not by menace or threat or deftness of maneuver, but by a simple awakening of God's natural interest. And given a fair hearing, Satan is the most interesting being in the material universe. For a start, he knows more about it than anyone else.
Careful, though.

> SATAN: (*Looks at Joseph*) At least I agree that he's dreaming.
> GOD: How do you know?
> SATAN: Look at his eye movements. See how quick they are?
> GOD: Why are they doing that?
> SATAN: They're following the action.
> GOD: What action?
> SATAN: In whatever he's dreaming about.
> GOD: Don't you know what it is?
> SATAN: No.
> GOD: You can't see into their dreams, then?
> SATAN: No.
> GOD: Ah.
> SATAN: Not *yet*. We will.
> GOD: Of course.

But he's far from displeased that they can't do it yet. This ensures that a personal trip into Joseph's dream will remain a matter of privacy between him and the dreamer.

So there he is now, in Joseph's dream version of the Stable, knowing that he can't be seen by anyone – except perhaps by the dreamer himself. He's not so sure he wants that, either, at least to start with, so he keeps to the shadows.

In his dream Joseph is attending to the animals, not in the caring way of his waking self but as if he finds them repellent and dangerous. He's strengthened the rough wooden pen they're in, not for their comfort but to prevent violent escape. And as if the barricades weren't enough, he halters the ox to a post as tightly as he can. The fact that the animals are increasingly unhappy with this rough treatment deters him not at all.

Suddenly he's startled by a rending crash as the gap in the roofing is torn into a much bigger hole. Whatever power it is that's doing this now fills the Stable with a dirty reddish glow which seems to suffuse everything, including the animals, including Mary, with the ugliness of its nature. There is evil here. The beasts grow yet more restive as Joseph hurries protectively to Mary, who amidst all the uproar remains deeply asleep. Something, he knows, is going to attack her. He looks up through the gaping hole at a night sky which now has a diseased, nauseous hue about it. The dream version of the Star looks blood-red, menacing, disgusting.

JOSEPH: (*Repelled*) Is *that* your Star?

No reply from Mary whose sleep is so profound as to seem deathly. Joseph tries to rouse her to the danger, but then throws himself suddenly aside as another piece of roofing not only falls but misses him so narrowly that it's as if it had been aimed. Voices blur into a muted, coarse chuckling, as much as to say "Get you next time." There's no way Joseph can make out the mocking creatures who dart so swiftly here and there, but odd words bubble up and slurp through their malignant burble an assorted jumble of

"– *mother / whore / liar / father / fool / old fool / child / bastard / whore's bastard / old fool / old fool / kill it / kill her / kill the whore / kill the bastard / little bastard / kill them both –"*

JOSEPH: No!

Filthy laughter chuckles round the poisonous sky.
"– *Blurrybastarblurrybastarkilderblurrililbastar ..."*
And now the red star emits a beam of energy through the gaping roof directly onto Mary herself, awaking and possessing her. She begins to writhe and undulate sensuously. When she sees Joseph her smile is a mocking, lascivious grin, while her body goes on moving to the will of the beam.

JOSEPH: Oh God!

Thus called, God can barely restrain himself from intervention, while the animals rage on and the sounds of gibbering night things hiss and crackle –
Joseph shakes an outraged fist at the Star.

JOSEPH: You! *You're* the bastard, you ...

Incoherent with rage he shins up the ladder as if to get at the Star, but what he's actually trying to do is replace enough roof damage to shut out the red beam which possesses Mary. He manages to hoist a piece of crude sacking into place, needs hammer and nails, reaches into his belt, but the hammer is still in his tool bag, back on the floor. He clatters back down the ladder again –
– but before he can get there, the beam from the red star shines

directly onto the tool bag – which comes to life. It begins to writhe and strain, writhe and strain – strain and strain – Then, slowly, painfully, the bag opens of itself, and a living hammer is born of it.

Joseph stares aghast at the slimy wet hammer which lies pulsing on the straw as it gradually metamorphoses into a snake. It rears up at him, as tall as he and then taller, swaying a little, inspecting him as if to confirm that he's powerless; then turns swiftly and heads for Mary.

JOSEPH: No!

Joseph comes back to life and makes a frantic grab for the snake, but at the same moment the ox has torn away its halter and crashes into his path, intent on preventing him. Its horns are lethal, there's no way round them, and the snake is now arched over Mary as if awaiting the order – whose order? – to strike down on her.

Joseph stretches out a tentative hand, hoping to placate the ox, but before he can complete even half a step forward the animal moves to butt him. Joseph stumbles back and falls against the Stable wall, bringing a pitchfork down with him. He lies half-dazed for a moment, then realizes that his hand has come to rest on the shaft of the pitchfork. His fingers close round it.

It needs something sturdier than his new-born disciplines to restrain God from rushing in to prevent the coming battle between man and beast. What he must have first is guidance – the provider of which is still in the Control Room, and still looking straight at him.

7

I AM

SATAN: You won't see a serpent's eyes doing that.

In the Control Room, the pictures of Joseph asleep continue to show the troubled movement of his eyes beneath their flickering lids. Mary, by contrast, her hand still on his, sleeps peacefully.

> SATAN: No emotions, no dreams. That's the next stage. (*To Sophie*) So let's have a mammal brain now, please. (*He looks at the ox and ass.*) One of theirs will do.
> SOPHIE: Don't you want the context first?
> SATAN: What do you mean?

The picture of planet Earth comes up on the big screen, very much as the angels saw it earlier, but now with a suddenness that makes its beauty the more startling.

> SOPHIE: The context. To help explain the next stage.

Satan is beginning to tire of Sophie's helpful little sorties into his territory, but any inclination he might have had to put her in her place is immediately squashed by God's rapturous reaction.

> GOD: Oh!
> SATAN: Yes – of course – you've never really seen it before, have you?
> GOD: Oh!
> SATAN: So tell me, if you were a snake, right now, there on Earth – I think this is Sophie's point – thank you, Sophie – whereabouts would you like to be?

The Earth begins to revolve – another bit of unbidden help from Sophie – which translates it from an exquisite celestial object, which just happens to be dangling in space, into a lovely and rather fragile Being who actually lives there.

> SATAN: (*To God*) Where, on Earth, would you choose to be?
> GOD: Everywhere!
> SATAN: Of course. Being you. But you can't, you see. Not as a reptile. You're a cold blooded creature. (*He indicates areas of Earth on the screen.*) Any further north than that; any further south than that; any higher up than that; any lower down than that; you'd freeze to death. Isn't that frustrating? Must be worth a tantrum or two. So, where will your building-blocks get thrown now?

The mammal brain is placed before Satan as the next relevant exhibit.

> SOPHIE: Mammal brain, as you asked.
> SATAN: I did, didn't I? Some time ago, I think.
> SOPHIE: Ox. But is it what you want, now you see it?
> SATAN: Yes –
> SOPHIE: The original mammal was only about five inches long –
> SATAN: No, this is fine –
> SOPHIE: – so the brain would be that much smaller. Would you like it down to scale?
> SATAN: This is *fine* –
> SOPHIE: It would be just the same basic structure, of course –
> SATAN: Of course! And since you're being so helpful, I'd be grateful if you'd bring the hologram back. (*The Stable reappears.*) Thank you. (*To God*) Come and see how it all

works. In there.

With the brain models in hand, Satan heads for the Stable. Better to continue God's tutorial where there's at least the semblance of privacy.

> GOD: So I do belong in there, do I?
> SATAN: No, and I'll show you why.

God follows Satan into the hologram; and yes, being here does seem to help, mainly because the immediacy of God's absorption in the place creates a reality virtual enough to shut out everything else.
Mary's hand still rests on Joseph's, and it is to the sleeping couple that God naturally moves, open to whatever help Satan has to offer. More than open, indeed: caught up as also he is in the crisis of Joseph's dream, distinctly needy.

> GOD: (*To Satan*) He's still dreaming, see –

But Satan has gone over to the ox.

> SATAN: Here.
> GOD: What?
> SATAN: Look.

God comes to the ox.

> GOD: Yes?
> SATAN: Look at his breath. See the steam rise.

God watches the shifting vapor patterns, and finds them beautiful.

GOD: Yes!

SATAN: How do you account for that?

GOD: It's cold in here.

SATAN: Yes, but it takes warm breath hitting cold air to do that, and for warm breath you need warm blood, don't you? Are you with me? A reptile couldn't do that, any more than it would sweat if the place were too hot. But now – behold the mammal, with its temperature-control system. (*He indicates the mammal brain again.*) Want to see how the thermostat works?

God takes a cursory glance at the model but is quickly drawn back to the wafting beauty of the ox's breath.

GOD: Just look at that!

He pats the animal with appreciative vigor, becoming as absorbed in the feel of its living solidness as in the soft explosions of its little vapor clouds. The ox looks directly at him; and their eyes hold.

Which wordless communion threatens Satan with yet another exclusion. It's obvious that to keep God's attention he must follow him into whatever immediacies the created world has to offer – which, unfortunately, seems to be just about everything. Right now, it's the ox.

So he joins in, giving the animal a few rather fastidious pats and strokes of his own.

SATAN: Good strong coat. Plenty of meat on him. Can you feel the fat? Reptiles don't have insulation like this.

GOD: I didn't know what things *felt* like.

SATAN: He'll have brought it along to sell. Jerusalem's only up the road, he'll get a better price there than back in the sticks.

GOD: I didn't know what *things* felt like.

SATAN: This'll pay their taxes, and some over. Which they'll be needing, by the look of them.

GOD: Is this what you have to tell me? That they're poor?

SATAN: What I'm telling you is that mammals have warm blood, body hair and body fat, which is already three up on the reptiles, and means they can live *anywhere*. This (*the brain model*) suits a polar bear as well as an ox; or a dolphin, or a snow wolf, or a camel, or a –

God suddenly stoops and scoops up a mouse in mid-scuttle across the Stable floor. He raises it to his face, and finds it exquisite.

SATAN: – yes – or a mouse. Which is more or less where the mammals came in.

As with the ox, that same stillness descends between God and creature.

SATAN: I suppose there's no point asking if you remember the games you played with that first little mammal? Very like that one. You soon had it climbing trees with you. Took a few million years for it to grow the right kind of hands, but there they are now, mammals who can peel bananas. Then some of *their* descendents came back down again (*He gestures towards Joseph and Mary.*) – and here they are.

GOD: He's good with animals. Did you see?

SATAN: (*Indicates the brain model*) So he should be, with this in common.

GOD: He's still dreaming.

SATAN: Yes. Big one, too, by the look of it.

God looks at the brain model now.

> GOD: Tell me why this gives him bad dreams.
>
> SATAN: What it gives him are the feelings he can't cope with awake, and then makes up stories about them so he'll get the point. (*He touches Mary's belly.*) Rage in this instance, I should guess, because *he* didn't put that in there. Grotesque, isn't it? As grotesque as this great lump on her. You wouldn't see a snake this shape unless it had just swallowed a pig. Do you find that beautiful, too?

Of course he does. God can't not. In fact he doesn't really understand the question. But then, he knows Satan's going to answer it anyway.

> SATAN: Yes, look at her. Look at *that* (*Mary's belly*). Look at *him* having nightmares *about* that. And ask yourself: if you could start again – actually knowing what you were doing this time – is this the way you'd do it?

It's noticeable that the softening in Satan's manner is becoming rapidly more apparent as his pedagogic function separates out and takes charge. To which God warms, reaching for a response which is truthful, helpful and – it goes literally without saying – articulate. That's the difficult one. But no matter, with a tutor who likes to do the talking.

> SATAN: Shall we look at the pros and cons, then?

It occurs to God that even if he knew the answers, he'd still want Satan to give them to him. He feels he's never known the delight of this erstwhile son of his before this night.

> GOD: Yes.

SATAN: Good.

Satan holds out a hand for the mouse. God gives it to him. The little creature immediately struggles to be free, but Satan's grip is paralyzing and it soon subsides into a different kind of stillness.

SATAN: Female. Pregnant – as usual. Do you want to see?

It takes God a moment to realize that Satan is ready to open the mouse up with his bare fingers. Not that there's anything overtly cruel in the gesture – he might as well be offering to reveal the mineral within a rock by fracturing it. With those lovely hands.

GOD: No need.

Satan rejects the thought that God is becoming squeamish. It's simple ignorance – and what is Satan but the bringer of light?

SATAN: Well then – look at these swollen little teats, if you will. There'll be half a dozen tiny balls of blind greed sucking at them before the night's out. That's the other big change from the reptiles. So what do you think? Why breed children inside yourself, and then feed them from your own body, instead of laying a clutch of eggs in the sand, say, and feeding the survivors on scavengings? Or even letting them fend for themselves? Why would carrying them round inside you be better than that? What's the point?

But God isn't tempted to forego the pleasure of being told the answer. He's realised by now that Satan isn't really asking him anything. In effect, all his questions go to make up one and the same statement: "I, too, am." And so he is!

SATAN: Better parenting. Simple as that. You start closer and stay closer longer. More protection, longer instruction, better chance of survival. Which means more of them survive to breed still more of them. And so it goes on, right down the line from mouse to man, same system.

He holds the mouse close to Mary.

SATAN: As reproductive machines these two mammals are essentially the same. Even down to the swelling of the breasts, see. Except that with humans, they get painful, too. Did you know that?
GOD: No.
SATAN: Design fault, would you say?
GOD: Yes.
SATAN: Did you know that a woman's breasts will leak milk at the mere sound of her baby crying?
GOD: No.
SATAN: At the mere *sound* of it. Another design fault?

God thinks about that.

GOD: No.

Satan is pleasantly surprised. It seems that his pupil is beginning to think.

SATAN: Well, well. So what are we seeing here?
GOD: Love?
SATAN: Ah, so that's what love is! Nipples that dribble on demand. Willy-nilly. No say in the matter. That's love.

God ponders again.

GOD: (*Hopefully*) It's a start.

Such a bathetic reply might have merited at least a chuckle from a teacher with any sense of humor. Perhaps, indeed, God is prospecting for exactly that, putting his own gaucheness to work as a nudge towards self-mockery in the hope that Satan might look for a grain of it in himself. He must have *some* kind of humor, surely?

Because that's what he needs, God knows. Deep as is his delight in his glittering son, it only serves to highlight the crucial flaw in him, which is his desperate inability to be anything but totally right about absolutely everything. Which might be just about achievable, given time, but only at the expense of being wrong about the All of it right from the start. The penalties for which are endless, culminating in a baffled sense of somehow having been cheated, and an obsession with finding the culprit.

But Satan's got nowhere near that far. He doesn't even know there's a that-far to get to. On the contrary, it seems to him that his road is opening straight before him – why waste time on wayside trivia?

SATAN: But I do agree.

GOD: With what?

SATAN: That we need a word to describe the blind force that compels this little thing to go on letting itself be cannibalized by breeding what feeds on it. Call it love if you like, so long as you know what you mean. She'll be pregnant again in a week.

He's about to toss the mouse back into the straw but changes in mid-movement, almost absent-mindedly, and returns her to the ground quite gently – rather as God might have done. Which God doesn't miss.

Satan watches the mouse scuttle off, then settles his gaze on

Mary.

> SATAN: As for this one – Well, not much more than a child herself, is she? But already that thing you've called love has dragged her off into the torture chamber of child-birth – which is what it's become for humans.
>
> And then, incredibly, if she manages to live through it and squeeze out a squashed, agonized, screaming little mess as ugly as anything you're likely to find on planet Earth, she'll thank the Lord her God for giving her something so beautiful. Love as hallucination. A very necessary one, too, or she might feel more inclined to drop the thing down the nearest well.

He indicates the brain model again.   .

> SATAN: A trick like that took some doing, didn't it? So what we get now is another dimension to the same new heating system. It's called emotion, which is another way of being hot or cold. But don't smile too soon – it doesn't stop at mother love.

Satan holds the brain model beside the head of the ox.

> SATAN: Here comes fatherhood, at the gallop. Try stopping your placid friend here when he's in rut, out to collect his harem, and you'll meet with something else the reptiles can't match. *Possessiveness* – hot-blooded component in all the higher mammals, or there'd be nothing to keep them around to do a rotten job like parenting. Especially the males.
> Which brings us right up to your little man here – who thinks he isn't the father of this lump, so why should he

stick around?

But God is still absorbed in the animals. He gives the ox another comradely smack, then includes the ass with an approving scratch between the ears.

GOD: No horns.
SATAN: He'd kick you to death.

Satan is bemused by the fact that this violent news seems to make God if anything even fonder of the animals. Not being privy to Joseph's Dream, he can't account for God's pleasure in the revealing logic of it.

GOD: So. This (*the brain stem*) – does. This (*the mammal brain*) – feels. And this (*He takes the neocortex from Satan.*) – knows.
SATAN: Yes!

Satan takes the three brain models and swiftly re-joins them into the one human brain, then holds it up as if to present the winner's trophy for the triple jump, first honoring the recipient by announcing the signal achievement that it represents.

SATAN: I know what I do, I know what I feel, and *I know that I know it.* Therefore – ?
GOD: *I AM!*
SATAN: You aren't just a state of being any more, you're a Being. You **are!**
GOD: *I AM!*
SATAN: What is your name?
GOD: *I AM!*

God reaches for the completed brain as if to accept his prize. But

Satan withholds it.

> SATAN: *But* – it all comes at a price. Which this little girl is about to pay. Do you realize yet what you've done to her?

Satan has moved back to Mary and holds the brain over her lump.

> SATAN: To house even the beginnings of a brain this size makes the baby's head so big that bearing it stretches the mother into an agony so awful it's quite often fatal. Won't be long starting, by the look of her.

God's dismay deepens as Mary's peaceful sleeping face melts into –

> **Vision:** – *Mary's face in suffering, as soon it will be. But where is she? She seems disembodied, floating in a space which is not the Stable nor yet anywhere else. She lifts that same pain-stricken face and looks up at ... who?*

> SATAN: And the ridiculous thing is, they blame themselves. They think you're punishing them for being sinful. The fact is, they'd rather have a cruel God than a mad one. They fear chaos more than pain, you see. What never seems to occur to them is that what you actually are is incompetent –

He breaks off, suddenly aware how perturbed God has become. Was that last dig one too far? But God has come far enough now to know the difference between roughness and roughage, and Satan perceives that he may proceed; carefully.

SATAN: Any thoughts on that now? With hindsight?
How you might have done it?
GOD: To free them of pain?
SATAN: Without abandoning this.

He holds the brain model close enough to Mary's body to conjure up quite graphically the struggle to come.
God thinks hard.

GOD: Make her wider?
SATAN: You did.
GOD: Wider still.
SATAN: If you stretched the human pelvis any more they wouldn't be able to walk.
GOD: What's the answer then?
SATAN: The trouble is, there isn't one. Your mistake was choosing a monkey in the first place, to play the big brain game with. Wrong shape – not to mention wrong temperament. So why do you think you did that?

He gives God a moment to answer, knowing that he can't.

SATAN: Nearest toy in the play cupboard, perhaps? Random as that?

A bit of a lapse, perhaps, but more of taste than of goodwill, and although there's something rather cheap in persisting with that sort of imagery, it doesn't dim God's perception that what Satan is telling him is somehow – crucial (another word which keeps presenting itself for some reason).

GOD: I suppose it must have been.
SATAN: Unless, of course, it was this compulsion you seem to have for climbing trees.

A gesture towards humor which you might have expected God to welcome as a sign of progress. Instead he looks startled. There's something about those words –

" – this compulsion you have for climbing trees –"

> **Vision:** *Still dreamlike, but much clearer (and longer) than previous ones. The hill is almost real now, as is the cross which is lying on the ground. They've finished nailing the victim to it so that it's ready to be hoisted into its upright position.*

" – this compulsion you have for climbing trees –"

> *Men push from the front and pull on ropes from behind until the death tree is raised, with its bruised fruit hanging from it.*

" – this compulsion you have for climbing trees –"

> *There's almost a glimpse of the victim's face, but not quite.*
>
> *What we do see, however, from the angle of the crucified Man looking down, is Mary. She stands at the foot of the cross, a mother in labor with the death of her son. Now she lifts up that same suffering face and looks at – yes, that young man, her first-born child.*

As soon he will be. Behold the Man! But oh, behold his mother! God is transfixed.

Satan sees only that God has put his hand on Mary's belly as if to – what? Protect her? Bless her? Seek her pardon? He looks beside himself – or, rather, beside *her*, the two of them locked together in some mysterious space which excludes Satan altogether. And this time he doesn't even know what he's being kept out of.

But what disturbs him even more is to see that God's eyes are wet. A tear – this is not just astonishing but quite shocking – a *tear* rolls down his cheek. How can this be? Neither angel nor animal does that. Only humans cry. Has God become so confused in his own drama that he's mistaking himself for one of them? This is getting beyond games. He must drag God back from wherever it is he's got lost in.

SATAN: What is it?

He's surprised by the concern in his own voice and the warmth of his grip on God's arm.
It takes God a moment to focus on Satan and be aware of his touch. Satan withdraws his hand suddenly and rather primly – such intimacy is untoward and perhaps still perilous. He finds he has embarrassed himself somewhat.

GOD: What am I to do?

Satan pauses. Tell him? Confronting God with just a sample of Creation's suffering has already overshot the mark, considering how much worse there is to come. The last thing he wants is another explosion as the Almighty recoils from His works.
But why take his education so far? Perhaps he's vulnerable enough already? Perhaps the time to call in his debt is already here? Perhaps, perhaps – Satan still hesitates on the brink of answering God's question, there being only the one answer.
The preface to which is that planet Earth can't go on affording a dominant species which has the genius of an angel that's for ever at war with the murderous instincts of an alligator upgraded to a packwolf – and for ever losing the battle. Man must either be replaced, or redesigned so that he's no longer the victim of his old drives. They should have been subordinated to reason the moment the big brain arrived, of course, but it still isn't too late.

The brain is just another piece of engineering after all and, set to rights, it could still turn man into a credible participant in an intelligent Universe.

But that's only the start. The sanity of the Universe itself is in question. Matter behaves too much like its chaotic Maker to be trusted. Even when it managed to evolve containing structures for itself by spiraling into galaxies and stars, the sheer impetus of that initial God-burst had already condemned the entire system to go on ballooning out, faster and faster, worlds without brakes. Which means one of two things. Either space will go on expanding until everything in the universe has stretched out so far from everything else that there isn't a single star left in anyone's sky, and the fate of any survivors, if there are any, will be to eke out their little lives in aimless isolation until their lights, too, flicker out, leaving the residue of a mindless Creation to dissipate into an endless ocean of dying particles.

Or the exact opposite, in which the explosive energy of God's emergence into matter can no longer support the sheer weight of its growth and the universe begins to collapse back in on itself. Then everything – *everything* – from galactic super-clusters strung across the great branches of space to particles so small that an atom would be bigger than they could imagine, will go into reverse, sucking everything that began with the Big Bang back into the final obsequies of the Big Crunch ...

Either way, here is the monstrous nub of it: every gleam of intelligence which Satan has striven to nurture into life; every thought and hope and sheer damned effort to make it all *mean* something; even the inherent worth of all that mighty sum of pain and grief which might have achieved at least a retrospective dignity, if only as a dolorous path towards something – all this will disappear into the limbo of Might Be, that infinite point of mindless energy which is God's birthplace. And as if the prospect of this total, needless, witless waste weren't appalling enough, it doesn't even offer the heroic consolation of tragedy, since there will be no one left to tell the story, or anyone to hear it.

Conclusion: even if God knew how to set the Universe to rights, he's too unstable to be trusted with it. This is Satan's work – his destiny, indeed – so the answer to God's question is: he must pay his debt, not only to Satan but to Man also, and ultimately to all that is, for infusing the entire thing with the chaos of His own nature. He must abdicate, and hand the powers of Creation over, intact and *in toto*, to his disciplined son.

So – could this be the moment of confrontation? Will Satan require the Almighty to settle his account right here and now?

SATAN: You distress yourself too much.

Apparently not. Without quite knowing why, Satan has stepped back from the brink. He's surprised, too, and strangely charmed, by the gentleness of his reply. Perhaps it was the need to explore this growing intimacy between them, rather than any calculation of prudence, which gave him pause. Indeed, it doesn't even feel like a step back. But forward to what?

With the respect due to such a precious thing, Satan again holds up the human brain and offers it once more to God.

SATAN: Here.

But God doesn't reach out for what no longer seems a trophy. Instead he turns back to Mary, seemingly to find solace there in the simple state of being with her.

Satan must prise off this woman's hold. He must. She is the stumbling block. Why, he has no idea, because of herself she is nothing, so vapid as to be scarcely worth the disliking. Yet her very nothingness seems to draw God into it.

SATAN: Here!

Again he offers the brain model, his tone insistent now, but by the same token rather reassuring in its firmness. So God does accept it, slowly at first, holding it with apparent distaste as if it might be wanting to get on with its business of pain infliction.

SATAN: Feels rather like a soft-boiled egg, doesn't it?

That's helpful. God doesn't need to know what a soft-boiled egg might feel like for the brain's status as an instrument of torture to be somewhat reduced.

SATAN: Do you think it's beautiful?

Foolproof – he's learned that God is incapable of finding any thing anything else.

SATAN: So do I. Exquisite.

God is agreeably surprised.

SATAN: How much do you think it weighs?

God struggles with the idea of 'weighs'.

SATAN: Well – rather less than the water in this bucket. Yet it contains more cells than there are stars in the galaxy; and more connections between them than all the stars in the universe.

He pauses to make sure that God is suitably impressed by the comparison. God tries to demonstrate that indeed he is by asking an intelligent question.

GOD: How many stars would that be?

There is a suspended moment in which Satan can do no more than stare in renewed astonishment at the Creator of Everything who is also the Lord of All Ignorance. That he can be both at the same time beggars belief to such an extent that Satan doesn't even know how to think it – a painful sensation which drives his mind into a search of its depths for some new coping mechanism.

It succeeds astonishingly. For the first time in his existence Satan is assailed by something he can't control. Laughter.

God, of course, wouldn't think of controlling it – especially not when he can join in, which he irresistibly does. He's no idea why it's so funny that he doesn't know how many stars there are, and cares not a jot; that just makes it funnier.

At last Satan manages to drag himself out of the quake zone, but not yet sure if he can speak without falling in again. So God, now he knows how, gives him another nudge.

GOD: How many stars did you say?

Satan does his utmost to keep a straight face.

SATAN: A lot.
GOD: Ah!

And they're off again. Satan can only laugh it through this time, so that when he finally tapers off into semi-exhaustion, and even God is sated, the silence between them continues on into a deeper moment of intimacy than either has ever shared with the other or with any other.

So deep that nothing else matters. It doesn't matter that Satan's laughter was misconceived. To suppose God stupid because he doesn't know how many stars there are is a logical error, in itself as fatuous as supposing that the human brain he's holding would be incapable of thought unless it started off already knowing how many cells composed it.

Yet his mistake is no more important than God's inability to explain it to him. If his myth of Creator Ignorans has brought Satan to laughter it's as good as any other that does God's work, having achieved a dimension of contact between them which takes him beyond all his known territory, to the edge of that space where categories cease to exist and opposites start to merge. So close, perhaps, that just one more step ... ?

But now it's God's turn to hesitate. Is this the right moment to open himself completely, to take Satan into his arms, into that boundless and fecund space of no-thing where love isn't just the best option but the only one, since nothing else exists there? Or might he be spoiling his chances for later? He reminds himself he's on a self-promise to stay disciplined until he's sure he can contain himself ...

– Oh, the hell with it! He dumps the brain impatiently down (next to Mary) so that he can offer his embrace to Satan *now* – only to be forestalled by Satan himself.

> SATAN: I said you distress yourself too much because what you don't know is she'll forget the pain. She'll forget how it was. That's what they do. They forget how bad it was. Just as well, isn't it? Or every mother's first child would be her last.

It isn't immediately obvious whether Satan cut across God by accident or if he aborted the moment deliberately. The quickness of his intervention might suggest it was both calculated and deft, blocking a premature gesture rather than having to reject it – which in itself would be a gesture that leaves all to play for.

Or maybe he was responding to something deeper? A sense of dread, perhaps, an intimation that on the other side of God's embrace lies – what? That first experience of laughter was so utterly seductive that he's already hardening against it. He wants no more dealings with the processes of uncontrol, of emptying, of the dissolving of boundaries. His own agenda consists of nothing else: boundaries between right and wrong, good and bad, order and chaos, life and death, Heaven and Hell –

> SATAN: (*Cont.*) But on they go, without any notion that the head which nearly splits them on its pushy way out houses something so powerful that it will grow into studying life itself; and begin to understand it; and take control of it; and while it goes on conquering its home planet, turn its greedy eyes to the stars themselves – and start by counting them.

God appreciates that last reference – it hints that Satan wants to preserve their achieved intimacy, but with seemly control. That's good enough to keep God's arms by his sides. For now.

> SATAN: Wouldn't it be nice to think it was the sheer privilege of bearing this superb thing that persuades her all the agony was worth it? Not so, I'm afraid. It doesn't need a giant brain to learn the one word which will enslave her for life: 'Mama'. Ask her then, when she first hears that, if she can remember the pain it cost, and she might come out of her trance long enough to say "What pain? Oh – that."

Cunning – following up hallucination with amnesia. Clever way to cover up your mistakes.

> GOD: I've never wanted to do that!

... a denial of such galling innocence that it threatens the composure of one who feels incomparably damaged by God's countless disownments. Surprisingly, it is God who pre-empts the damaging riposte. He's read the pause.

GOD: That's what I don't want to *go on* doing.

Taken at face value, that is a handsome revision. Satan ponders the sincerity of it; finds it good; and even wonders if it might last –

SATAN: Good. So – let's move on to the bigger mistakes, shall we? (*He goes back to Joseph.*) Starting with your original question, which was: what makes your man here feel so angry with his wife that he wants to be rid of her?
GOD: Yes.
SATAN: Well? Another design fault?
GOD: Yes.
SATAN: Tell me what it is, then. I've given you all the clues you need.

Which is true. Indeed, God may even have achieved enough articulacy to put the answer into words, given a little time – but the urgent need is for action in Joseph's dream. The man's just about to use that pitchfork.

MAN AND BEAST

God picks up Joseph's dream where he left it. The man lies where he fell, his hand on the shaft of the pitchfork; the snake hanging poised over Mary; the ox, as if it were the snake's minder, menacing the least movement that Joseph makes towards them.

Joseph scrambles to his feet, pitchfork in hand, and levels it at the ox – which goes into charge mode. Good! He thrusts the pitchfork at the animal, jabbing the air to provoke it into charging, ready to leap aside and spear the beast in one movement, and then head for the snake. If it occurred to him how courageous this is he might lose his nerve.

But this is not the man's moment. As the ox launches itself at Joseph, God appears instantly at his side and seizes the pitchfork from him, leaving him completely defenseless against the animal – which hits him full on. But on contact, the ox disintegrates into a flash of particles which in turn disappear into the man, leaving only a momentary ghost of their animal shape behind.

Joseph gasps as if hit by a gale and, although he's entirely unharmed, is too shaken to move as God simply vanishes from beside him and reappears next to Mary and the snake. (It seems to Joseph that for a fraction of a second God is in both places at once. This only gets worse.)

Now God reaches out his hand to the serpent, but stays it as their eyes meet; and hold; and go on holding. Then the creature seems almost to lean into his hand, seeking his touch.

God is intrigued by the unexpected feel of it.

> GOD: Dry! I'd have thought it was slimy! Isn't that interesting?

As God looks at him, Joseph gives a little moan of terror and hides his eyes. God's response is to take hold of the unresisting snake and bring it over to Joseph, only for the man to back tight against the wall, eyes screwed shut.

GOD: No, don't be afraid. This is yours.

Joseph hugs his face in his arms as God holds the snake towards him.

GOD: Yours! It belongs to you!

Joseph's fear is now total and abject. He's a sorry sight, and God is sorry to see it. He *must* make the man understand.

GOD: It's *part* of you. When this dies you die ...

He still hasn't realised that Joseph is even more frightened of him than of the snake. All he knows is that this must be done for the man's own good, so now he thrusts the creature at and into Joseph, whose hidden face contorts again into a soundless scream as the serpent, like the ox before it, bursts into a flash of particles which disappear into him.
God makes a satisfied little gesture of completion.

GOD: There you are! Back together again!

But his expectation that the cowering human will now recover his wits is not fulfilled. Joseph remains in terror.
Looking about him for clues, God realizes that this Dream Stable still glows red and gruesome. That must be it! He disperses the sinister presence with a puff, and the stars shine bright again through the Stable roof.

GOD: (*As to a frightened child*) All gone now. See.

But still no difference. What, then? Ah, of course – the hole in roof, it's still frighteningly big. Well, that's soon cured – and the gap is invisibly mended back to its un-dream size, leaving room for just the one Star hanging directly above, shining straight and clean onto Mary, whose image is thus restored from the grotesqueries of Joseph's nightmare.

Indeed, she opens her eyes for a moment, seeming not in the least surprised that God is standing beside her. They smile easily at one another, then he shakes his head, as if to say "No, this isn't *your* dream," and passes his hand over her face. She sleeps again, beneath her Star, and His.

Holy night.

> GOD: (*To Joseph*) See?

But Joseph *still* shrinks away. God's baffled patience is wearing thin.

> GOD: What *is* the matter with you?

Joseph sinks to the ground. He's prostrating himself.

> GOD: What are you doing now?

Joseph grovels to Him.

> GOD: I asked you a question! Look at me!
> JOSEPH: Have mercy.
> GOD: I *have* mercy! *Try* me!
> JOSEPH: Pity me, Lord.
> GOD: Well for pity's sake, *get up!*

He grabs Joseph and jerks him to his feet, but the man still keeps his head turned emphatically away from eye contact.

GOD: And look at me when I speak to you! Why won't you look at me?!
JOSEPH: No one can look on God and live.
GOD: *What?*

He wrestles with this bizarre notion for a few moments. It defeats him.

GOD: Whoever told you that?

Getting no better answer than a choked-back sob from the face still turned resolutely away, he lets Joseph slump back to the ground. The man doesn't even grovel now. He's accepted it's hopeless. The only manly thing left is to try to make no noise as he weeps.
So God sits down beside him, much as he did with Labass. Yes, he knows this feeling: compassion; becoming familiar; no denying it; wouldn't want to deny it. But now it's a mind that needs healing, not a body. More difficult. How do you go about it? He puts his hand on the quaking back still turned to him.

GOD: Turn round.

Joseph can't.

JOSEPH: You have looked into my heart.
GOD: Yes, well – you look into my face.
JOSEPH: (*Accepts his fate*) – Yes. That's right. That is right. I deserve to die for what I've thought. Thinking it's as bad as doing it, isn't it? I know that.
GOD: Just shut up and turn round.

Joseph does. But even then, he still can't lift his eyes.

GOD: *Look.*

The heroic moment. Joseph lifts his face – and looks into the face of God. Their eyes meet. And hold. And hold ...

GOD: So. You're not dead yet.

Joseph is too bewildered to be relieved. It makes no sense that he's still alive. But then, nothing else makes any sense either. Nothing whatever makes any sense at all.

JOSEPH: What do you *want*?
GOD: Why do people keep asking me that?

9

CREATION AND ITS DISCONTENTS

LABASS: I said: What – do – you – want?

God's awareness of being in the Creation Room comes with less of a bump this time, Labass having being helpful enough to repeat the question.

But what can he answer? Since it seems that Nothing is not understood as being the basis of Everything, he'd better find some kind of Something to offer. He looks around him with a vague gesture which embraces the entirety of this colossal room, and everything everywhere else as well.

During which Labass sidles back to the alarm. He's not sure if he really means to trigger it or just test the credibility of – *is* there a name that can be decently used? The very word 'God' has the status of a flip obscenity down here, and such easy trad labels as 'The Enemy' now seem merely frivolous confronted with the sheer unlikeliness of the real thing – *if* that's what this apparition is.

God sees what he's doing and makes no attempt to stop him. Labass withdraws his hand from the alarm, then puts it back suddenly – and still no intervention. Doesn't *seem* like another ruse ...

LABASS: Well? What? What do you want?
GOD: To know ...

... He searches to frame the vastness and simplicity of his need. He can't think how to say "To know everything about everything, and all at once."

LABASS: Know what?

GOD: Everything about everything, and all at once.

Actually it's quite easy when you appreciate the absurdity of it. Labass doesn't. God chuckles. Labass doesn't.

GOD: Have you ever seen Satan laugh?

Labass is baffled by the question. God offers encouragement.

GOD: He can.

Labass's perception of God as mad is if anything reinforced. Any being who can switch from murderous aggression to gossipy chat in the space of a minute is presumably liable to regress into violence at any moment. The rational thing would be to get out of here while the intruder's having a quiet interlude.
So why doesn't he? It can't be simply because the Demented One (yes, that will do) looks so much like his real Lord that his reactions are conditioned to the image. There must be more to it than that.
And yes, there is. Extraordinary – this is that same feeling of being 'held' which arrives from nowhere (interesting parallel) when your work, unbeknownst to you, is at a moment of break-through; when reality has decided to unfold its next layer and is about to tell you what it requires by way of assistance. And then, when you've performed whatever experiment it lays down as its terms of appearance – and as if you hadn't been rewarded enough already – you find yourself granted that exquisite yet-more, the discovery within the discovery, the touching of that truth in the core of you which knew it all along.
But where to start?

GOD: Why is this called the Creation Room?

Here? Tell him why? Or test him with silence? Or even run a few tests on him? But which? And how? Calm down, Labass ...

God seems quite affable at this lack of response. In fact, as he begins to wander through the swathe of exquisite technology around him, he seems absorbed enough to have forgotten his question. He's in the presence of Art now, looking more in need of a catalogue than a reply.

Which unsettles Labass's discipline of detached observation, the scene being so resonant with those precious times when Satan himself comes down to inspect their progress in the Holy War on Chaos. He feels an urgent need to identify some marked difference between his Master and the Demented One which can be put onto immediate guard duty.

And yes, here's one. Noses. Satan's is perfect, but now look closely at the intruder's – there's the hint of an irregularity there, surely? And yes – look, another one – eyes. The Demented One's are fractionally different sizes whereas Satan's (need it be said?) are a perfect match. Anything else? Must be more – such slight stuff, really – chin – jaws – ears – no – no – that left nostril perhaps? Hell, this is slim pickings ...

God's attention meanwhile has been taken by a particular mechanism which seems to have been given a title. He reads it out.

GOD: 'Virgin Bastards'. Why is it called that?

It dawns on Labass that *style* is the crux of the matter. Satan's visits to the Creation Room are awesome in their dignity, the solemn appearance of a divinity come down at the supplication of the high priest to bless his works. What Labass sees now is a parody of that. Nothing could be less solemn than this – *child* is the word that's trying to elbow its way in – wandering gormlessly about as if he's fallen into some enchanted forest where Reason has been chased out by the faeries. Look at him, gawping! Not

only is the callowness of it offensive but it exudes a sickly potency. Labass finds himself fighting off a fantasy that if the Demented One goes on ogling the machines like this much longer they'll begin to sprout leaves and burst into song ...
Stop it! He fights off the tentacles of magic with the edgy righteousness of one who has been wronged.

> LABASS: You asked me a question.
> GOD: Oh yes – why is that one called 'Virgin Bastards'?
> LABASS: Before that –
> GOD: Ah – why is this called the Creation Room?
> LABASS: Before that. Out in the corridor. Your question was, would I show you around.
> GOD: And will you?
> LABASS: When I declined, you attacked me with a savagery which nearly destroyed me. You then told me that you had been "playing".

... uttered in such scathing tones that God finds himself casting about for mitigation. He almost slips into "Yes, but I put you back together again," but it would be scurrilous to propose such an excuse, or indeed any excuse which bends the way to reconciliation. Just go straight there.

> GOD: I'm sorry.

As indeed he is. His contrition is so patently genuine that that really should be the end of the matter. But Labass can't risk being so easily mollified – besides which, perhaps this is the experiment? Give the Ultimate Specimen (that's not bad, either) enough resistance to push against, and see what happens? It wouldn't be the first time there's been an explosion down here.

> LABASS: For how long, I wonder? And what can I expect

now, if I refuse to answer your questions?

GOD: I promise I won't harm you. Come what may.

Simple, solemn, authentic.

LABASS: You say you promise.

GOD: I do.

LABASS: Your history has been one of changing your mind, I think.

Is there no end to this? Well, all right, fair enough –

GOD: I have a lot to learn, haven't I?

That's it! Plain fact. Keep it simple.

LABASS: Learn? You want information? From someone down here? From *anyone* down here?

... spoken incredulously enough to convey the grotesque impropriety of such a notion. So no, that isn't it, and rather looks like it never will be.

Leaving God no alternative but to go into consultation with Himself ...

... to move into a different mode ...

... and then to respond from the wider dimensions of his Being. Seemingly, all of them at once.

It is the voice of **I AM**, and it's a shock.

GOD: *Yes.*

The power in that one not-especially loud sound is extraordinary. For a fraction of a space so short that it would need one of his micrometers to measure it, it crashes through Labass like a shockwave. He feels as if he's drowning, but in light, as if every blinded particle of him is having to swim for its life to find the rest of him. The first thought he can clutch at is that he doesn't know if it was the Appearance in front of him who spoke, or whether Everything did.

And so Labass, the searcher out of truth, knows that he has been searched out by it. All that he ever scrutinized has in one flash scrutinized him, and there is nothing of him which has not been seen. The physical breaking-down and putting-together that he had suffered earlier at God's hands was as nothing to this instant of being totally known. It is a state as far beyond fear as it is beyond happiness. It is the Light, and its quality is to melt that which it lights upon.

GOD: Yes –

… such an encouraging little sound now, coming as it does not from **I AM** but from an amiably open, rather vulnerable looking 'he is' …

GOD: – please.

And Labass finds that he has emerged from his melting intact; refined; purified of fear; himself. He no longer needs to wonder what he should do next, he just does it. He moves to the 'Virgin Bastards' machine, enjoys the wording on the title card again, then speaks easily to God.

LABASS: No, that isn't its real name. More of a joke.

Right up God's street – but he doesn't get it.

GOD: Yes?
LABASS: I'll need to show you. (*He starts to prepare the*

121

machine.) Its real name is the Total Vacuum Generator, or TVG for short. Or you could call it the Extractor of Absolutely Everything, but I didn't like EAE so much. Not so crisp, is it? (*He switches it on.*) So, here you are, the TVG, and what we do first is we pump all the air out of it. Just ordinary air; oxygen, nitrogen, carbon dioxide, trace gases – every molecule of it has to go. Watch the air-gauge. See? There it goes. Nearly there. There! Zero. Yes? No air. Right? Now – is that empty?

GOD: No.

LABASS: Why not?

GOD: Because if it was you wouldn't be asking me the question.

For the first time Labass smiles. The ice is melting, spring is on its way and an enthusiast is in bud. He isn't, as Satan would be, lecturing a student. He's taking a kid on a mystery tour.

LABASS: So – what do you think might be left in there?

God gestures that he's happy to have no idea. He loves being taught.

LABASS: I'll show you.

He operates another control.

LABASS: Watch the monitor. No, I'll put it up on the big screen or you won't know how to see it.

He switches the picture from the TVG monitor up to what is a very big screen indeed, taking up the entire ceiling of this gigantic room. It's like looking up at the night sky itself: at the moment starless, black, expectant.

LABASS: Even with a screen that size you need a magnification factor of a billion trillion or so. Now watch. And remember, this is what's going on inside the TVG here.

The first blips of light appear in the quasi-sky as tiny distant stars.

LABASS: There! See? (*He pats the TVG.*) All *that* is in *here*.

Up on the screen the particle-stars vanish, reappear, disappear, come forth, multiply, form patterns ... The dance is joined.
God is enchanted but not really surprised. His expression is more one of being pleasurably reminded – "Ah yes, of course." He starts to tap a foot gently, as if to a rhythm not apparent to the scientist.

LABASS: So what are we seeing here? For a start it's full of radiation, which is always there because it's always everywhere; a whole swathe of elementary particles, ones you can see, ones you can't – invisible photons, for example, which I make visible – thus. And so much – what shall I show ... yes, see, look at those. They're just passing through on their way through the universe. There – zip! zap! Did you see? You wouldn't believe how long it took to slow them down even to that. Helps being this far underground, of course ...

He looks to see how God is reacting. The Labass of earlier would have dismissed just such an expression on his face as 'gawping'. Now it's worthy of an approving nod.

LABASS: Yes indeed. Just look at that.

No invitation needed. Indeed, it would be hard to drag God

away from watching these, his first steps as Lord of the Dance.

> LABASS: However, this isn't what you asked about. You want to know what Virgin Bastards are – all this has to go too, because it was already there, as it always is. (*He activates another control.*) So what we need is absolute nothing. Which I would have said was impossible to achieve, even in theory – in fact I did say it. Frequently. But he knew better, so I kept at it. Designed this thing – redesigned it – over and over – till in the end – well, you'll see ... We're nearly ... almost ... there we are!

God is quite startled by the depth of his loss as the great sky of particles dies away to black nothing.

> LABASS: Do you think it's empty now?
> GOD: Yes.
> LABASS: Absolutely empty?
> GOD: Yes.

Such a strange experience, to witness His primal state as from the outside, to feel it now for what it was then. He can even identify the feeling. Yearning. Yes. In the beginning was the Yearning: of the Might Be, the Not Yet, the Unknown-to-Itself, to know Itself; to be. Yearning so strong and single that it would begin to trace within its formless self invisible escape routes, inherent structures which were to become the ground-plan of all matter, until at last it had generated a dynamic of such power that it could bore a tiny hole in Nothing; through which singular point, straiter than the eye of a needle, it exploded into physical being with all the pent-up weight of the Universe.
The Yearning. He feels it now.
While Labass completes the next procedure.

LABASS: So I'm making sure nothing gets back in. Nothing. Not even radiation from the machine itself. Impossible, you'd have thought, but easy when – and as quick as .... there! Now, no atoms, no protons, no photons, no particles of any kind, no radiation whatsoever. Absolute nothing, and nothing can get in. Are you with me?

Oh God, is this what he has to fear? No other future could be so terrible as to be sucked back into the Yearning with every escape route blocked off – and *be conscious* of it this time. Is this the ultimate weapon, waiting to be turned upon him by his angry son?
Labass presumes that God's monumental stillness is an appropriate state of attention, and that his muted response –

GOD: Can you ... put them back again?

– is a perfectly reasonable question.

LABASS: I don't need to! That's the whole point! Even if I could, I wouldn't need to put them back. Just wait. You want to know what Virgin Bastards are – just watch.

To say that this seems to take an eternity would be to mistake eternity for a long time, or indeed for any time at all. Time, as he now realizes, is a condition only of matter and, unlike eternity, can stretch out and stretch you with it. This is the precondition of every form of torture.
Then – one tiny speck flares out of the abyss, and is gone.

LABASS: There! Did you catch it?

Oh the relief! Oh, the sweetness!

Another sparkle.

> LABASS: Did you see? You have to be quick. Never mind, you'll catch on, there'll be plenty more …

And there are. And more. And more. Forth they come and multiply and Oh! he wants to cradle them, he is cradled by them, he is mother and child, he is born again, he was dead and is alive. He is risen.

> LABASS: That's them! See for yourself. They haven't sneaked in from somewhere else, you know. You realize, do you? They come from the Nothing itself. Virgin Bastards. Can you think of a better name?
> GOD: No. It's perfect.

Finding himself happy with this approval, Labass now wants to give credit where it's due. He's still uncomfortable that he remained silent on the question of Satan's sense of humor.

> LABASS: It was his description, actually.
> GOD: Ah.
> LABASS: The moment he saw them.
> GOD: He was always quick.
> LABASS: Yes. It was so apt, I just didn't want to waste it.
> GOD: That's a good word – 'apt'.
> LABASS: (*Gestures at the sign on the machine*) So that's why I put that there.
> GOD: Quite right.
> LABASS: He doesn't make a lot of jokes, but when he does –
> GOD: It is funny …
> LABASS: That's what I mean.
> GOD: And apt.

LABASS: Yes, that's what I thought. So I wrote it down, and – there you are.

GOD: Good. Yes.

LABASS: (*His loyalty now satisfied*) Yes. Good. Right, now the next thing you need to see –

He is about to switch off the TVG.

GOD: Oh, no, please –

LABASS: I want to show you something else –

GOD: *No!*

Labass pauses, lets the TVG run on. While it's hugely gratifying to be stimulating this intensity of interest, he finds he can't go on abandoning himself to the pleasure of it. The sight of God's involvement in the restlessness of creation, as being played out on the ceiling above, begins to contain for Labass a grain of discomfort which isn't simply the residue of distrust, or even a nagging reminder not to get carried away beyond the proper boundaries of his discipline. An unknown something-else is developing, an intimation that a choice is heading his way, and that it will be a hard one.

Along with which ... he's never had these damned fantasies before! Here they come again, starting with the Demented One floating off *into* the screen and beginning to surf the space-foam like a cosmic porpoise while shoals of elementary particles cavort about him in haloes of adoration ...

Stop it! The intrusion of such nonsense prompts Labass to switch off the TVG as well as the thoughts.

LABASS: You've seen enough.

God is left hanging in mid-air, as it were, by this interruptus. For just a moment before he turns back to Labass there's a glimpse of the old thunder in him. He thought he'd got the better of this, but not when he's taken by surprise, it seems. More to learn. This one's hard. But aren't they all?

Labass finds there's something quite disturbing about the sight of God still looking up at an empty screen, apparently unable to move. He begins to regret being so abrupt.

> LABASS: It was only a picture, you know. It's all still happening. It hasn't stopped just because I switched the picture off. I only wish it could.

God turns to him now. He's all right.

> LABASS: (*Relieved*) Well ... ?

Which sounds rather like an invitation for God to acknowledge that there's something fundamentally wrong with the actual mechanics of Creation. You can't have it leaking into itself like this. Once you've achieved the right amount of matter to make it work, you stop – otherwise you build disorder into the very heart of the process and chaos becomes systemic.

> GOD: It's beautiful.

Beautiful? Labass, whose functionalism is so impeccable that he would be unable to visualize an ugly equation or construct an unlovely mechanism if he tried, whose grasp of form and motion affirms in his work a taste so sure that it would never occur to him that he has any, tries to grapple with the idea of beauty as a determining factor. A fish might have the same difficulty with wetness.

> GOD: Isn't it?

Something is calling to Labass which is too subversive. He makes his way back to firmer ground.

> LABASS: Wait till you see what happens next. Are you ready?
> GOD: I am.
> LABASS: This way, then. Through in the Extension.

God follows Labass to a door on the opposite side to the one they came in by. Labass opens it and goes through. God follows him but stops, startled, just inside the doorway.

The huge space they've entered is bounded by a wall which occupies the entire perimeter of the Dragon, and which seems to be composed entirely of fire.

10

MAN AND GOD

JOSEPH: You've come to take me to Hell, haven't you?

God finds that the switch from Labass's wall of fire back to where he was in the Stable with Joseph is now no harder than a simple exercise in counterpoint. It's Joseph's question which is bumpy.
The temptation is to ambush it with the sort of absurdity that floored Satan, but Joseph's tone precludes that. Indeed, it wasn't really a question at all, but a flat, hopeless, repulsively unfunny statement which must be heeded.
And this is hard. Hard to see Man so cowed that he accepts fear as his deserts; even clings onto it as the only certainty on offer in a senseless world. This is the scenario of the abused child – which makes God what?

> JOSEPH: Are you waiting for me to confess? You know what my thoughts were. Do I have to go through them?

This sharp feeling must be anger – the man's an idiot! Confess? Could he have had clearer proof of where his faults actually come from, and what happens when you try to get rid of them? That same impetuous power which threw you together so carelessly in the first place just sends them roaring back in again because you can't actually live without them! How many demonstrations does the man need? Why doesn't he just face up to God and say: "This is *your* doing!"? Just look him in the face and say it! That's what he would do if *he* were Joseph!
It won't take him long to remember that he is. Meanwhile, he can't help noticing how much this experience of anger differs from mindless rage. Indeed, in these milder doses it has its uses, such as identifying the rubbish that needs dumping, and even

giving it a parting kick.

Joseph is looking at Mary now, his main exhibit in the case for his own prosecution. His regret is abysmal; his lips shape silent words, words only for her, words that whisper and sting in God's mind: "I'm sorry. So sorry. So sorry …"

He turns again to God, whose anger is hurrying along its single channel to remorse.

> JOSEPH: Did you see me with the hammer? It had a will of its own – did you see? I had to fight it. The hammer wanted to kill her. But that was me, wasn't it? A hammer's just a hammer, I know that. I just can't believe – where did that come from? It was bad enough wanting to divorce her, but *that* – just for that moment …

Joseph reaches out a tentative hand, that same hammer hand, towards the sleeping girl. He wants to touch her, bless her, receive her blessing. He wants to touch her belly, feel the life in her, have its blessing. In short, he wants to make his peace with God – and may not have much time left.

> JOSEPH: I've never touched her before. Not – I mean – you know – *touched* her. So it isn't my child. Well, you knew that, didn't you? You knew I'd never touched her. Not even like this –

His hand hovers over Mary's bulge, but try as he might he can't make contact. The sight of which takes God back to Labass trying to sound the alarm in the Creation Room, his hand held at the last inch by a frivolous variation of this same maladroit force – Oh, for God's sake, Joseph, put your hand on her! *Please!*

> JOSEPH: I knew I wanted to divorce her – well, I say divorce – I just wanted to be out of this any way at all. I

could have had her stoned, you know!

Terrible. Terrible what people do. And no one would have blamed me for it, either, that's the thing. Except me, of course. And ...

He looks at God, as much as to say "And you".

But no, that's not how it is, not now, not now that God knows what he really does want, which is to free the man of a conflict that should never have been his in the first place; nor any man's. But how? Compassion doesn't come so conveniently. *"They'd rather have a cruel God than a mad one. They fear chaos more than pain,"* said his angry angel, and God doesn't doubt him. How would it ease the misery of this bewildered little human to be subjected to a litany of God's own failings? Not the least of which has been to evolve self-awareness in a creature so unable to cope with the war between his reason and his instincts that his emotions never know which way to jump; creatures so confused that they've had to conjure up an image of the Almighty as a demented old tyrant who just might parole you from his tantrums if only you can learn to cringe shrewdly enough. *"They'd rather have a cruel God than a mad one..."*

Well, if mad is the only alternative to cruel, he's mad. He looks into his violent depths, and cruel simply isn't there. Never was – though it's horribly obvious from the results that it might as well have been. If this tormented little man were some sort of unlucky aberration from a wholesome norm, God could have indulged himself in a quick bit of miracle healing and been on his satisfied way by now. But again, as Satan has been at pains to point out, by any human standards Joseph is one of the best. Which says what about the rest of them?

This is what baffles. The true lineage of the creature who now cowers before him can trace itself back billions of years further than any biblical genealogy; back and back, and back again, back to that very moment of God's flaring forth without which was not anything made that was made. The genesis of all-that-is, which includes Joseph, was there in that first fraction of a second.

So what must have happened between then and now to produce this? How could ecstasy have made such a mockery of itself?

> JOSEPH: She's singing. Do you hear? She always is. Doesn't need to be awake to sing, doesn't need to open her mouth, even – though she does, of course, sometimes, like anyone.
>
> But she can just be still – asleep, awake, doesn't matter which – just still, and silent, and you can still hear it. This song. Everywhere she is. I think, maybe, it's everywhere already, but there's something about her lets you hear it. Listen! – I think it's the same song I heard – is it? It is! It's the same song I heard when I was little, when I first saw the stars – do you know, I've only just thought of that – that I heard it then. I must have always known it. Good God! I wonder where I was? Might have been in my mother's arms, for all I know. Perhaps that's what she was doing, showing me the stars. First time I knew there *were* stars.
>
> And this is what I heard. Them singing. It is, it's the same song! – Good God!

Good God is enthralled. Here is a man who thinks he's about to be consumed in the flames of Hell, yet his words are the echoes of original bliss. There it still is in Man, the background energy of his birthright, and Joseph's only mistake is to suppose that it is the stars who sing when what he hears is the song from which the stars themselves were born. This is the flicker which shows where the light is, and the way to redemption for having lost it. To Joseph's redemption and to God's – they're becoming the same thing. The workings of ecstasy have not, after all, been in vain.

At least, not if Joseph now completes his magnificent gesture. When he puts his hand on Mary's belly, on the child which isn't his, it will be the victory of God's purpose over God's execution, and the path of love will be swept free of the many blunders that clutter it. This is the fulfilment of the yearning which was before the beginning, and which from this sacred moment will be enthroned as the active principle of Creation. Unconditional love. Comprehensive compassion. This is the consummation that the Universe requires, and which its Manifestation now wills.

But God's will, it seems, by way of chastening anti-climax, is not enough. Indeed, its grandiosity is rendered faintly ridiculous by Joseph's hammer hand which, far from descending to its cosmic destiny on Mary's belly, now lifts itself slowly and very personally in the opposite direction, back up towards his face. There it turns over, palm up, as if to confront him; then clenches itself into a tight, tight fist. Toughened by long life and hard work, powerful enough to punch a hole in the Stable wall, not to mention kill a man – or woman – with a blow, the hand is laying claim to its nature. It is as much a part of Joseph's being as any other, and refuses to be wished into what it is not for the sake of anyone's intemperate convenience; including God's.

But now Joseph's other hand begins to reach towards the clenched one; touches it; then comes to rest upon it; very tentatively at first, then more firmly; then starts to loosen the locked strength of it back into its rightful ease, as if comforting a lost friend back into wellness and his proper self.

There's something very reminiscent about all this! Whatever it is, the fist begins to respond; to open, slowly, so that the comforting hand may start to part its fingers; always gently, ever respectful, allowing the hammer hand to soften as it will.

And so the opening fist allows itself to be lifted higher still, palm up, now close enough to Joseph's face for him to see its weathered landscape in a new light. With a curious fingertip he begins to explore the opened hand: its rough places and its smooth, its mounds and crevices, the criss-cross network of its lines – some he was born with, others that track where his life has been and how it has dealt with him. The moving finger pauses here and there, on whorls and gnarls, on a scar, on a deeper one, on this callus and on that – memorials to work well done, hard work, beautifully done, done with the grain of him.

Next, he turns the hand over and studies the other side. He tugs gently and for no apparent reason at the hairs on the back of it, then at the tufts between the knuckles and finger joints, unaware that what he's actually exploring is that bequest of his primate ancestry from which he derives all his strength and deftness. What he does know, and which would now be a blasphemy to deny – or, rather, to go on denying – is that if holiness isn't wholeness, it is a mockery and a lie; that what this hand is, and what it does, and even what it *wants* to do – *all* this – is what it is to be a man. For better or worse.

And so Joseph contemplates his hammer hand and finds it good. Thus dignified, it responds by rising yet again and coming closer still. At the same time he brings his face towards it, as to a meeting of old friends, and rests his cheek upon it, rubbing softly against it with that same soft, gutty rumble of the breath which God heard him make when he – Of course! How's this for reminiscent? This is how Joseph calmed the animals!

God looks over at the ox and ass, so restless until so recently, but now, by some resonance with their dreamer, at peace. Indeed, they are, within Joseph's sleep, asleep.

As is Mary. Untouched.

Silent night.

And there, in his stillness, stands Joseph, his hammer hand passive now and trusting of his will. Which is to ask no more of it; it has been imposed upon too far already. He lets it drop to his side.

Profoundly sad, equally steadfast, Joseph looks God full in the face – for the first time entirely without fear.

JOSEPH: I want to ask you something.

What question will the teacher ask his pupil? God stands in awe of the man who has just shown him where the path actually leads. To love your enemy is an amazing idea. To be able to do it when you discover that the enemy you must love is *within* you – what kind of rectitude and courage, what *faith*, does that take? What kind of man can face up to God and say that if he wants him perfect rather than whole, he'd better think again?

Well, there he stands, looking you right in the face.

Which is as it should be. Where else shall God learn morality but from his flawed ones? Perfection has no need of it. It was precisely Joseph's faultiness that cornered him into the bitterest of choices. By making the one he did, the man has taught God not to deny his own need to confront his own enemy, and to love him. For better or worse.

Blessed be the man.

But who is God's enemy that must be loved? *Is* it Satan?

Joseph still hasn't taken his eyes from God's face. He's waiting for leave to ask his question – which, if God doesn't grant it, Joseph will ask anyway. There is a persistence about him now, and a directness, which is quite formidable.

GOD: Ask your question.
JOSEPH: Questions. First: I'm dreaming this, aren't I?

God is perceptive enough to read the man's doubt about the validity of a dream as truth.

GOD: Yes. But I'm not.

Of course, Joseph, of course. So, yes – it is truth you're dealing in.

JOSEPH: Next question, then. Why should a decent man,

a *decent* man, whose deepest wish is to love his wife, and his God, and even someone else's child –
SATAN: – have such hateful feelings about it all that he hates himself for having them?

God is back in the non-dream Stable once more, Joseph and Mary asleep, Satan still trying to pin him down to a question which is central to his case.

SATAN: Well? I've given you all the clues you need.

As indeed he has, and God was on the point of giving him a good student's answer – but now that he's encountered the man himself, it seems that Satan's model of the human doesn't quite match up. It doesn't explain, for instance, how Joseph could have managed to see beyond himself, as it were, and get himself along there – and then stand fast. And by so doing, show God where his own path lies. Either the brain has a transcendent function which Satan simply doesn't know about, or there's a dimension to the human mind which goes beyond neural engineering, faulty or otherwise. Is it possible that this man, this species, this blemish on I-Am-ness, is somehow becoming not only God's consciousness but his conscience too?
God looks at the sleeping Joseph, then at his own hand, searching for clues as to what the man saw in his. But what could show in God's hand other than the Eternal, the No Thing? He would have to be human himself to – wait a minute, though! Look!

> **Vision:** *As the faint marks on God's palm become more pronounced, they begin to manifest as a cross.*
>
> *Then the hand disappears, leaving only the cross behind.*

But now there's someone on the cross. A Man.
And there on the hill, looking at the Man on the cross,
stands another man: Joseph.
Joseph concentrates on the Man's nailed hands, bloody
and dripping, and studies those same tell-tale lines he
saw when he pondered his own.

But to Satan, God's preoccupation looks more like that of a shamefaced schoolboy staring at his fingers rather than meet the teacher's eye and admit he can't answer the question.
Which is fine. Satan is happy to display his patience – the easy patience of one whose position grows stronger by the moment.

SATAN: All right then, let's see how it works out in practice, see what you can make of that.

It would be more fruitful, and a lot more satisfying, to demonstrate this in front of the other angels. Let them bear witness to how firmly God's rightful mentor now stands at his right hand.

SATAN: Sophie, take all this (*the Stable*) away again, will you, and give me the brain of – a lion. Yes. Adult male.

The Stable hologram disappears, leaving God and Satan back among the angels in the Control Room.

SATAN: (*To God*) If you want to praise a man, call him lion-hearted. The snag is …

The new brain model appears before Satan at demonstration height.

SATAN: … the lion's brain comes with it.

He removes the neocortex from Joseph's brain model again, and holds the equivalent higher mammal stage next to the lion's brain.

> SATAN: Lion now, Man then. Both mammals. Very different mammals, of course, but how different really? Look carefully ...

He gives God a moment for study, then hides the brain models behind his back, brings them out again, performs a rather fancy little maneuver like a street conjuror doing a two-brain version of the three-card trick, and re-offers them for God's inspection.

> SATAN: Which one's which?
> GOD: (*Uncertain*) Umm ....
> SATAN: Exactly. Sophie, give us a lion on screen, will you?
> SOPHIE: Any particular one?
> SATAN: Young one. At his peak. Dominant male in charge of the pride. Yes, get him at the moment he's just defeated the old chief and chased him off.

Up on the big screen appears a truly magnificent creature, albeit a bit ruffled at the end of a brief but violent encounter.

> SATAN: (*To God*) Now watch your lion-hearted little man's inheritance at work.

The lion roars out a parting threat to his vanquished opponent who is slinking off into the trees. The victor suddenly makes as if to chase him again and the deposed king runs for his life, leaving all pride behind.

> SATAN: If you think the new boy's rubbing it in a bit

there, that last show of aggression was purely for the benefit of the females: make sure they know just who's in charge now. Now see what they think about it.

The lionesses are angry and fearful as their new king turns and surveys the pride; *his* pride. Noticeably, there are cubs, some of them suckling. The lion gives another roar to proclaim his status, challenging anyone to dispute it. No one dares.
Then he makes his first move towards a female with cubs.

> SATAN: He's just made his first executive decision. Well, truer to say it made him. (*Indicates the lion's brain*) Hardwired in over a few thousand generations. You're supposed to get better lions this way – no offspring from losers. Can you see the flaw in that?

The other mothers scatter, trying to conceal their babies as best they can.

> SATAN: They know what's coming. But there's no hiding place. He'll smell them all out.

The king settles on a particular cub, and now moves quickly. The mother turns to fight but she's no match for her new lord and her snarl turns into a wailing shriek as her baby is seized in the lion's jaws.

> SATAN: Which is only the beginning of the bloodbath. He'll kill every cub in the pride. Every single one of them – for the simple crime of not being *his*.

Satan shows the two brain models together, emphasizing their essential similarity.

SATAN: *This* is where the massacre of the innocents begins.

But God doesn't look at the models. That kind of reasoning has brought him as far as it's going to. He stares instead at the lion on the screen. All activity in the Control Room freezes as God is suddenly *on* the screen, staring straight into the lion's eyes. The lion halts the murderous bite that will break the cub's neck and stares back at God. Their eyes hold.

Now – *why* is he reaching out to touch the lion? To fill him with mercy? If he completes just this one movement, he knows that the Universe changes. Life changes. God changes. For better or worse?

His hand has stayed at the last inch. Always that last inch. He needs guidance. He needs his mentors. Are they inward to him yet?

Indeed they are, and up from within comes Satan Assimilated – absorbed with an immediate homily on the perils of happy endings. God can imagine every word of it … "Listen! Quite apart from the obvious – the speed with which you could expect a compassionate carnivore to be taken out of the gene pool – do you suppose for a moment that the rescued infant would grow up to feel the same mercy for cubs *he* hadn't fathered? Or are you going to intervene then, too? In which case, where do you stop? Will you save the lamb from the wolf, the sparrow from the hawk, the slug from the thrush, and every fly from every spider? Forbid yourself to walk in the garden in the cool of the evening for fear of crushing a million tiny life-forms beneath your every step? Will the next great flood be a deluge of compassion? It would do a lot more damage than the first one.

Behold now the fruits of your yearning. In a riot of creation you have exploded into more forms than you can count – even if you could count – every one of them fired with a quantum of your needy greed-to-be, which they're then left to defend as best they may while you gallivant off into ever more complex and seductive versions of Yourself; only to leave those behind too, of course, to sink or swim, to struggle with varying degrees of violence, or cunning, or endurance, or even sheer grotesqueness, but always relentlessly, competing with each other for your favor as children will, and by any means they can. It's their way of loving you, you see. You have left them no other.

While you rampage promiscuously on.

To achieve what? See him, the King of Beasts, so obsessed with passing on *his* bit of you that he slaughters perfect babies – is this the only way the Universe can achieve your demented requirements? The sole redeeming feature in all this mindless nonsense had been precisely its mindlessness, but your drive was always for mind, wasn't it? And that's the nonsense of it, for once mind has discovered itself it swiftly learns how to master everything *but* itself; its panic-stricken, ever anxious self. These higher mammals were always close to it, close to the edge, so close to the hole in the garden hedge, then – wow! – out into the promised land, with its great open fields of I-Am-ness – and an endless capacity for suffering – comes Man. And there's no going back.

Do you realize what you've done? Survival of the fittest is as ugly, wasteful and – oh God, see! – *stupid* a way of developing intelligent life as could ever have been stumbled on. Behold your little masterpiece in the lion's jaws and have the grace to feel ashamed of a profligacy which has achieved infanticide and mass murder as matters of course, and then delivered the whole damned system into the hands of a naked ape who is not only possessed of all the same brutish instincts but has now won first prize in the lucky draw for your I AM thinking toy. What did you ever suppose an omnivorous monkey would do with a neocortex but enlist its power in the service of all those same old instincts and make them a hundred, a thousand, a million times more destructive than ever they were before? What would they ever do but corrupt the holy quest for I AM into the calamitous mechanics of I WANT? How many Josephs do you need to stem that flood? With what? Their agonizing?

With negligence aforethought you have tortured the good and empowered the bad. The worm was in your apple from the start. No point getting sentimental about it now. You've made your cosmic bed. Now lie on it.

Unless, that is, you *really* want to change things. *Do* you? *Really?"* ...

And suddenly God knows why Satan has called him. He's come for the keys to the kingdom. He wants to undo God's work and put it together again. He wants the power of creation.

And here comes the truly terrible thought. *Perhaps he's right.*

Panic – that's the name for this one! Quick, what do his other mentors tell him? Where's Joseph?

> **Vision:** *Joseph is gazing at the lines on a hand on a cross. And waits. And Waits.*

Where's Mary, then? No sign, not even the sound of her song, not a whisper. Nothing but this lion, staring, breathing, waiting, staring –

What then? What? Lay your hand on the beast, you fool, and find out what, that's what! Nothing else for it, is there? Just do what you've always done, follow your longing, flow into whatever patterns it forms, and see what happens. And do it *now*. Just *do* it. *Thy will be done ...*

Except that his hand won't go down. It *will* not. On the contrary, it begins to turn back on him, to lift slowly and very personally in the opposite direction, back and up, up towards his face; where it stops, turns over, palm up, confronting him, and begins to clench itself into a tight, tight fist. Powerful enough to punch a hole in a star, in a galaxy, in a universe, through whatever reality is, the hand is laying claim to its nature. *His* nature.

Vision: The hand on the cross is also clenching. Slowly. In agony.
Joseph watches, awaiting his moment.
And at last he moves. He reaches out to the hand on the cross, touches it, then rests his own strong hand upon it; and begins to loosen it; gently – gently – gently …

God's stares at his own clenched hand as it begins to open to him, like a flower unfolding to the light. And look! there in the light, see, there *are* lines! Real ones, deep ones, yes, see, lines on his own hand, lines like Joseph's, see, see!
But what do they mean?

Vision: With a curious fingertip, Joseph begins to explore the hand of the crucified Man.

And mystery unfolds into mystery. Not only can God now see the lines on his own hand, pronounced and clear, but he recognizes the map they trace as if he's always known it. He *has* always known it. The pattern of his fate was there before the map was; there from the Beginning.
But what now?
You know what now. You follow this through now, through into its darkness and out into its beyond, wherever that is, come what may, for better or worse. Yes?
Yes.
He drops his hand to his side.
The Universe resumes its business. The lion breaks the cub's neck.
Where does that scream come from? The cub? Its mother? All mothers? Everything That Is? From God Himself?
Ecstasy would be unthinkable now, would be too much like agony, would *be* agony – but here it comes again, dancing before him, announcing its unseemly self in flame, in the fires

that burn past the open door ...

11

THE MATTER WITH MATTER

It needs only a slight change of focus to see that the door with the flames beyond it is the one which leads from the Creation Room into the Extension, a huge tunnel which surrounds Satan's entire complex, and which Labass has just entered. He turns to see that God has stopped in the doorway.

LABASS: Come in. I'm going to show you something.

But God still stands where he was, fascinated, especially by the far wall which seems to be composed of a permanent firestorm.

LABASS: Come on then. The fire's only for decoration. I can turn it off it you like.
GOD: No, leave it.

He comes in. Labass, for whom the whole scene is too familiar to need any comment, has gone over to a particular apparatus which has the same circular shape as the tunnel itself but is diminutive in comparison, being a mere fifty meters or so in diameter. Attached to it are two large monitor screens, side by side, and a control panel.

LABASS: This is it.

To work on this brilliant thing is never less than thrilling. To do so in these circumstances, in this presence, is a chance to demonstrate something so startling about the nature of reality that he might just be preparing the way for a change in it.

LABASS: Do you know what he called it? First time he

saw it work, he called it "The Two Eyes". "Insanity Investigator" – two I's. Yes? (*He indicates the two monitor screens.*) – and these are its two eyes. See?

But God is already heading for the wall of fire, too fascinated by it to register this further example of Satan's wit or Labass's little coda to it.
Labass tries to talk him back on course.

LABASS: So what it does, it fires particles at each other so fast that the collisions annihilate them. Then you can actually see what ...

But God has reached the flames now and isn't to be distracted. He puts forth his hands as if to warm them.

GOD: It isn't hot! Not even warm!

Labass won't be distracted, either.

LABASS: – you can see what they're actually made of. The problem was, it took so much distance to get them going fast enough that we had to build this whole race-track for them. Five miles of it –

His descriptive gesture indicates the distance and shape of the entire tunnel, then reduces it to the miniature of the Two Eyes machine.

LABASS: – which in the end I've got down to this. Amazing. Come and see.

But God remains by the wall of fire, impervious to any further enthusiasms until his preoccupation with the current one is satisfied.

>GOD: *Why* isn't it hot?

Labass recognizes grudgingly that he's going to have to deal with this first.

>LABASS: It would be if I turned the energy barriers off. That's as good a wall as any other. You could lean on it if you wanted –

– which he immediately regrets saying because God promptly does. It looks as if he must fall into the flames but his shoulder rests on solid invisibility, leaving the fire to lick at him from all of half an inch away. Delight!
Labass needs to matter-of-fact this before God starts rhapsodizing about beauty again.

>LABASS: Why build five miles of solid matter when you can just use energy? Which is all that matter is, when you get down to it. So the real question is: what is energy? Come and have a look –

But God isn't listening. Shifting his weight from shoulder to elbow, he leans rather stylishly on the blazing wall; then, after a few interesting postural variations, from the elegant to the clownish, discovers the cruder luxuriance of rubbing his back against it.
What next? Handstands? Cartwheels? Labass tries to be patient; tries harder; fails. Instead, he makes an abrupt move over to the environmental controls.

>LABASS: *Will* you pay attention?

He throws a switch, the fires vanish, and God is left rubbing his back against a wall of solid nothing. He turns and stares at the bleakness of it, very much as he had at the ceiling of the Creation Room when Labass dismissed the firmament of particles. It looks as if doing this to God twice in one day may have been once too often. There's something about the angle of his turned back which is as threatening as it is pathetic.

There's menace, too, in the longer pause before he turns again; long enough for the thought to jostle its final way into Labass's mind that what he's actually seeing here would appear depressingly normal in your pampered human child who's just been deprived of – well, of anything it happens to want, really.

And Labass shudders. What enticed him into thinking he could cajole *this* into the land of Reason? Behold the rear view of the omnipotent toddler, caught in that eerie still moment between frustration and eruption. Look at him, will you, staring furiously at nothing – and then look at yourself, Labass, putting on display the fruits of the highest intelligence for one whose attention span is limited to about half a minute of rapacious nosiness, whose response to any form of discipline is a random choice between the tantrum and the sulk, and whose only redeeming feature is that he hasn't yet got smart enough to realize just how much damage he could do if he really tried.

Well, he'd better be stopped before he finds out, hadn't he? Labass's mind is already racing about for ways to rid the Universe of its delinquent source for good and all. For the good of all.

Unfortunately, even if you knew how to do that, you couldn't just *do* it, not without turning reality itself back into a black hole. But – what about this? What if you could lure God back to the TVG – not only *to* it but *into* it? And then keep it running! Permanently! That would leave everything that already exists as it is, but with the purveyor of chaos safely lodged on the eternal edge of becoming without ever quite getting there. And he wouldn't even know – that's the beauty of it!

Or perhaps He *would*? Ha! That would be even better!

With which disgraceful thought, and without noticing that the word 'beauty' has slipped into his usage, Labass enters his bliss. He's already envisioned carrying the good news to Satan that the cosmos has been purged of its original faultiness and is at last a fitting home for intelligent life – and lo! there stands his Master, smiling the smile which Labass has always yearned to see on that cold, sad, angry, noble face; Satan's first real smile, a beam of pure radiance, and it's all for Labass.

More yet, Satan reaches out to take him by the hand, to embrace this loyal, brave and fecund servant, to enfold him in the gratitude of All That Is. It's entirely thanks to Labass that the cosmos can now become what above all else it needed to be. *Constant.*

And oh, that smile! Is it possible for such ecstasy to last? For about half a second, as it turns out, before the cruel trick at the heart of it reveals its nasty self. This is not Satan who stands before him, but God; God whose eyes Labass is looking into, whose smile he is returning, whose hand he was just about to take –

He hadn't seen God turn round to him. Did he turn round? Does God need to do that – or anything else in particular? Does he need only to wish whatever he wants, and the whatever immediately *is*? Is that all truth itself is in the end – a random process that just makes itself up as it goes along? In that case, does anything really matter? Anything at all? Does it matter, for instance, that Labass's mind is on the point of collapse?

"Any sentient organism subjected to the stress of two opposing choices of equal force will tend to lapse into a state of hysterical indecisiveness which typically develops into first a mental and then, if the stress is severe enough, a generalized catalepsy. The more powerful the choices, the more complete the ensuing paraly–"

Labass's vanishing memory can't even finish the quote before it, too, is wiped away along with everything else, including the ability to think why it is that he can't think any more. Of anything. What was that choice he had to make? Too late now – But no, it isn't, because something has already made it for him. He finds that he has recoiled from God's hand before even the tip of that curiously extended finger could touch him; recoiled as if punched.

Nor can he remember stumbling back against the Two Eyes machine, but that's where he's landed, leaning shakily on it for support, scarcely able to contemplate the abyss at which he just stood. Another fraction of a second and he would have tumbled into the sublime.

He feels sick.

Yet God still smiles, and when he lowers his proffered hand it is as respectfully as if he thinks he may have been a little presumptuous.

GOD: I only wanted to say Thank You.

Labass bravely embarks on a response as long as two words.

LABASS: For what?

Or should that have been the other way round?
God indicates the wall where the flames were.

GOD: For keeping me in order. That's what I need. Among other things.

As distinct from Labass who needs just the one thing, a single thought he can actually keep hold of. And ah! – look – there it is – through the open door of the Creation Room, *the TVG*! There's your thought!

GOD: You were going to show me something.

God indicates the much nearer Two Eyes machine, which Labass is still leaning on.

GOD: That.

Oh, this one, yes, the Two Eyes, of course – good! If God comes back this far he's already half way to the TVG out there. That's the one that counts, but start with this.

LABASS: That's right. Yes. Good.

Labass looks at the control panel. Does he still know how to work it? Hands on … Ah! It seems to know how to work him all right. Oh, this is better. He's on his way back now. Yes. Take a deep breath – take another – with which his mind completes its return. *You have made your choice*, it informs him; and, with assurance: *It was the right one.*
So back comes his strength, too; and with it, by way of a bonus, the best name yet for the approaching figure. *The Trickster.* God, that says it!
Well, let him wriggle his tricky way out of this.

LABASS: All right, then. When I press this button you'll see two pictures of the same process, taken a billionth of a second apart. It'll happen so fast you might think it's direct cause and effect – I press a button here, pictures appear there – but what's happened in between is that particles have been shot around this thing for *five miles* – yes? – up to *near the speed of light* – yes? – do you know how fast that is? Never mind – so fast that when they collide … well, you'll see what happens when they collide. Up on the Eyes there. Right?

There's something about the word 'right' which God finds deeply affirming. He was as thrilled as he was startled by the dramatic way in which Labass had recoiled from him. Is there some kind of Satanic Principle at work here, some resident daemon which activates a built-in resistance to God whenever he gets out of order? And if it's in Labass, is it in everything else as well? God, he hopes so. That would take care of his education on a permanent basis.

Because he *was* out of order. There's a whole lot more to be understood about loving your enemy before you start hitting the universe on the head with the idea. You have to let your enemy *be* your enemy, if that's his path. 'Authentic' is a word he doesn't know yet, but for now 'right' will do very nicely.

> GOD: Right.
> LABASS: So remember, this only *looks* instant.

God watches Labass as he activates the Two Eyes and oh, he loves him! This sworn enemy, this deadly enemy, this one who will destroy him if he can, this dedicated, truculent, fruitful little being. And it's precisely *because* he loves him, he realizes, that he must let him be what he is. And can.

> LABASS: (*Completes the operation*) There!

He sees that God is looking at him rather than at the Eyes. He points at them.

> LABASS: Not at me! Look!

Up on the screens have appeared what look like two abstract impressionist action paintings, almost identical, unutterably exotic. They seem to have been created in a furnace that produces lace. God could know every word of every language and still be speechless.

> LABASS: And please don't confuse the issue by calling them beautiful.
> GOD: I wasn't going to.

As much as to say that that would be wholly inadequate.

> LABASS: Remember what this is called?
> GOD: The Two Eyes.
> LABASS: Insanity Investigator, yes. And here's your evidence.

Labass uses a pointer beam to illustrate his analysis of the pictures.

> LABASS: The moment of collision. See how the force of it has smashed the particles back into pure energy. And over here, look, the reverse process, energy becoming matter. See those new particles? Plenty of room for them to move around – if you were a particle you couldn't begin to imagine how big an atom is. You wouldn't even know you were in one …
> So this is what *everything* is made of – energy/matter, matter/energy – heads and tails of the same thing. The question "What is energy?" becomes "What isn't?" The real question is "How does it behave itself?" Or *doesn't* it? … So let's find out. Pick a particle. Take that one, there, on Eye 1; see where it's moved to on Eye 2? There's its track – what you'd expect, isn't it? You make a journey, you leave a track. And this particle, and that particle, and that one there – same thing, see, they all make tracks. See?
> So – so far, so good. You might even think it makes sense. But now we get to it. Look at this one. Here on 1, there on

2. Look carefully. Where's its track? What happened to its journey? Nothing to see, is there? It *was* here, it *is* there – and there's no track in between! How can that be? There aren't any secret tunnels in there!

God looks suitably puzzled. What doesn't occur to Labass is that what puzzles God is why Labass should find this so puzzling.

LABASS: So there's only one conclusion. There *was no journey*. It simply disappeared from here and re-appeared there! Instantly!

So? What's so dangerous about joy that you can only let it out on a travel permit? On which side of these bars is the prison? Well, you don't need to be in the same cage as the prisoners to pity them – just ask yourself why they're so fearful in the first place that they've barricaded themselves behind these bars of straight lines, and then wonder how much their fear and inadequacy is your own doing – since *they're* your own doing. And then do something about it. If you can. And if you can't – just learn to live with it.
Just a minute – *learn to live with* it? Does that mean 'live with' as in 'live **with**'? As in '**live** with'?

LABASS: And it gets worse. See that particle there? And that one there? Two particles in two different places, yes? Well? Notice anything else? *They're the same particle!*

Of course they are. God didn't like to mention it because he thought he was supposed to be looking for something remarkable.

LABASS: Do you understand? This one hasn't just disappeared from one place and turned up in another – as if that weren't bad enough. It's in two places at once! Look!

God struggles to comprehend the particle's offence. Since he has never been anywhere that wasn't everywhere else at the same time, he wonders for a hopeful moment whether Labass's complaint is that the particle is in *only* two places at once. But no –

LABASS: If that isn't insane, what word would you use?

It's so tempting to go along with this, just to make Labass happy. He deserves to be happy. God would like to make him happy. But like is not enough. Only love will do.

GOD: I would say – brilliant.

Which, despite his choice of one of Satan's favored adjectives, Labass takes as badly as God feared he might.

LABASS: Would you like to say why?
GOD: I'll do better, I'll show you. Do that again – press the button again, give me another picture, I'll show you something.

The Trickster back at work? You bet. Labass checks his defenses.

LABASS: There's nothing you can show me. Take as many pictures as you like, the anarchy virus will be in there somewhere. Always. But you don't think it matters, do you? It's built the universe for you, it's given you your playground – what does it matter if a few particles are on two swings at once?
GOD: I just want to show you something –
LABASS: I'm *telling* you something! (*He points at the*

156

aberrant particles.) The world is a fearful place because of that. A *fearful* place. Because of *that*.

Now there's something about the word *fearful* which strikes a fearful chord in God, as if the fearful something is just about to happen. No, worse, *is* happening –

LABASS: Because nothing can be trusted.

God can't go on not looking. He raises his eyes.

> **Vision:** *For the first time he can see the Man on the cross clearly, but the face is so contorted with pain that he still can't be sure who it is. What is certain is that he is suffering, suffering, suffering ....*

Labass sees that God's attention has wandered and speaks to him as if to the dreamy kid in class who's staring out of the window.

> LABASS: Listen! If I create intelligent creatures out of a substance which is itself unstable, so will the creatures be. Do you follow that? They won't need science to come along and prove it, they'll sense the threat of it in every atom of their being – and never know why. And then their very intelligence will drive them mad. They'll end up trusting nothing, fearing everything – and doing anything to get rid of the fear. Any monstrous thing. And then be frightened of what they've done. And then do it again in the hope it will work this time. And then again, and again and again. In short, I will have created suffering.

> *God watches helplessly as the Man reaches into his depths in search of some last energy to – what?*

157

LABASS: You don't need an Insanity Investigator for the human race. Just watch them for two minutes with any old pair of eyes. Is that why you've come? To check on them? Well, just remember – it isn't *their* fault that nothing can be trusted ...

... Nothing can be trusted ... Nothing can be trusted ...

> *bleak and hopeless words which echo round the tunnel, round God, round the Universe itself, as the Man on the cross gathers his last strength to cry out –*
> **My God, my God, why have you forsaken me?**
> *– which terrible sound drags God with it into the depths of his being.*
> *When at last he emerges far enough to speak to the Man, it is as a supplicant.*

GOD: Will you trust *me*?

> *Now the Man sees him.*

MAN: Who are you?
GOD: I Am.

> *The Man nods but waits, with a look of "Yes? And?".*
> *"I Am" is such a recent awareness that God has never yet thought beyond it. Now he has to stretch for the more.*

GOD: I am ... becoming.
MAN: Becoming what?
GOD: What I will be.

> *The right answer! The Man tries to respond, but the*

mere act of bending his head closer is agony. God draws as near as he can to hear the dry, cracked words. The face he now stares into is unmistakably his own. Which is no less of a shock for being so predictable.

MAN: (*Almost a whisper*) They don't know what they're doing.

He searches God's face to be sure that he understands this, that he knows he must pity them, forgive them, love them.
God does pity, does forgive, does love, and the Man sees that he does. With his last strength, he manages two more words.

MAN: I thirst.

He moves his beseeching eyes to look past God, seemingly in the direction of the Two Eyes machine, as if to direct God's attention there. He tries to speak again but the best he can manage is a little jerk of his head, again towards the machine, as if to say: Do it! For God's sake, do it! ...

LABASS: ... And if I'd done that, if I'd created suffering where there was none before, I'd go and hang myself.

God turns from the Vision back to Labass. Things are beginning to fall into place.

GOD: But it's me you want dead.

The directness of which takes Labass off guard. He bumbles towards safer ground.

LABASS: Well – not exactly dead, exactly ...

God interrupts before he can say anything even sillier.

GOD: As good as.

He's onto you, Labass – and you're hopeless at devious anyway.
So –

LABASS: Yes.
GOD: But what would happen then?
LABASS: The way would be clear.
GOD: For what?
LABASS: New world. New beings. Sane beings. In a safe
universe.
GOD: You can do that?
LABASS: Not that hard to modify the human brain.
Really, none of it's that difficult till you get down to the
level of matter itself. And even then – in the end, same
thing, it's an engineering job, like any other.
GOD: And then they'd be free of fear?
LABASS: Yes.
GOD: You can really do that?
LABASS: If we get the engineering right. Given a free
hand. What do *you* have to offer?

What indeed? Either a delusional exercise in auto-eroticism
which at its very best is a shameful waste of time; or an
experience of reality so sublime that it takes you past words to
beyond thought and then on into the unspeakable bliss of being.
Perhaps this is why the Man on the cross has had to be nailed up
there – to find out if what God has to offer is worth having.
Because if it isn't, then Satan and his workers are on the right
track and Creation would be best left to them. In which case, the

short journey from here to the Total Vacuum Generator might indeed be God's most fitting and dignified exit.

> GOD: Press the button and I'll show you. (*No response*) Please.

But Labass doesn't move. Remember, this is still the Trickster ... God goes to the control panel.

> GOD: All right, I'll do it myself. This one, wasn't it?

He presses a button but nothing happens. Labass finds such incompetence hard to bear.

> LABASS: Don't *play* with that!
> GOD: Tell you what, then. You do it, and I'll go back in there afterwards.

He indicates the open door of the Creation Room with its significant view of the TVG.

> GOD: *In* there. That's what you want, isn't it? Into the TVG itself. I give you my word.

Labass would find such an offer unbelievable did it not bring with it a glimpse into the painful depths of God's dilemma – a moment startling enough to make Labass feel that eliminating him would be more of a mercy killing than deicide; and even to wonder if God hasn't had the same idea himself, and is checking out the validity of the TVG as an escape route.
On the other hand, of course, he could just be lying. More than likely. But then again, what do you have to lose finding out?

> LABASS: All right.

He goes back to the control panel and quickly makes the right setting. He's about to push the button when God offers his hand again.

GOD: If you want to see this as it really is, take my hand.

The one thing that Labass can be totally sure of is that he will never ever take God's hand for any reason whatsoever. It is on the foundations of such certainty that his ramparts feel high enough to talk down from.

LABASS: I can see very well from here, thank you.

Pity. His choice, though. *His* choice. God is proud of him.
So, keeping his hands well clear of God's, Labass reaches for the button.

LABASS: This will *look* different, but in fact be exac–

– at which moment his finger makes contact and several things happen all at once.
Labass becomes an instant statue, finger frozen to the button, left to hang in mid-word as God embarks on a timescale several trillion times faster, turning this particular fraction of a microsecond into an interval of extended leisure activity.
The images which now appear on the Two Eyes are not only as exquisite as those that went before but exceed them by having moved out of still-life and into time. Their state is one of continuous, languid motion, the unhurried comings and goings of entities which take on the guise of particles only when they're being observed; matter and anti-matter in an ongoing mirror-dance of life and death; events of such assurance that they can be or not-be with equal composure; inhabitants of a world where there is no sense of conflict since attraction and repulsion are

functions of equal value. These are the community which nurtured God's infancy, which taught him how to maintain his growth in a state of permanent equilibrium by balancing acts of endless diversity, and which now offers him renewal with the redemptive slaking of his thirst. This is the water of life.

Of which he drinks. Impossible to say whether he disappears into the particles or they into him. There's no *either/or* here. What there is, supremely, is peace.

And ultimate strength; for these are the forms of him which cannot be reduced to anything less than the energy they came from, his first joy. In their role as matter in the world of time they are supremely competent, very used to the death process, especially to violent death, and highly skilled in resurrection. Remember when those first giant stars began to collapse, crushed by the gravitational pressure of their own weight, these were their building blocks – and builders too, who reconstructed themselves into formations which could withstand pressures even as grotesque as that; so that when the explosive moment of star-death was finally come they could ride out on the cataclysm, back into space, back into life, into life in more complex and versatile forms, into life on its way somewhere. On its way, indeed, in time, into Man.

Yet even then, even as they learned to dance these new measures, they were responding as much to levity as to gravity. They hadn't been trying to fulfill some earnest purpose of converting simple atoms into more complicated ones so that organic life could evolve. They're as happy being hydrogen and helium as carbon and its rich relations. It's simply their nature to build relation-ships. They aren't creating life, they're *being* it.

And so it is his delight to play their play, to be them dancing, to sing their song, to be the song itself as it echoes across their spacious world, and – oh! – to be that spaciousness, that Nothing from which they all emerged in the first place, and from which alone they may continue to draw their being.

He is the Matrix. And this is Mary's song –

> *which swirls so softly about the Man on the cross that he too melts into the depths of his being, of All-Being, where everything simply is; where life experiences itself all at once, all of a piece, and at the same time in its every living particle.*
>
> *This is the experience, in time, of eternity. Which is what the Man had come to offer in the first place, and is now his own salvation.*
>
> *And so he hangs still now, his face no longer twisted nor his lips dry and cracked. There is even the hint of a smile there, as if he dreams of peace. Or is he dead?*
>
> *No, see the eyelids flicker. He dreams. He lives.*
>
> *At peace.*
>
> *Hanging there, nailed, alive – at peace!*

This must be the last of the Visions, for it lingers on, as well such beauty might. And standing in the glow of it, God comes to know what His omniscience had always known, if only he'd learned the trick of consulting it. Not only that All is well, and always was, but – behold the Man! – it can never be anything else.

And it's as if the weight of Creation has been lifted from him. Safe to identify, now that it's gone, his fear; the swelling dread that the Visions might be literal, come to prepare him for a fate as savage as its ethic. He'd agreed with himself the responsibility for Man's suffering too quickly to consider just how direct and personal his amends would have to be – under a system of justice as laid down, ironically, in his name: an eye for an eye, a tooth for a tooth, and now – how could it be otherwise? – God's agony for Man's. Debts are paid in kind, dear Lord. They always were. That your gorge should now rise at such accountancy doesn't let you off the hook. You're responsible for the hook, too.

And did a wave of panic ripple through the Universe as its

Source grew so close to becoming human that he was learning to live in fear? Or was it a buzz of excitement?

Either way, it no longer matters. See how the Man glows! The answer to suffering was there before the question was ever asked, built into that first explosive moment of Creation when the yearning-to-be was fulfilled by every emergent thread which set about to weave the web of life, and still does. Man was molded not in clay but from ecstasy, that being the only medium Creation has to work with, and can return to it at any time and in any circumstance. Look at him! Here is the only gospel that anyone will ever need. Step into the oneness, you become the oneness. Join the flow, you are the flow. You don't need to go looking for it – you *are* it. Just be still, and know it. This is the peace of God which passeth all understanding simply because it *was* before all understanding.

And as if all that weren't magnificent enough, consider this. Even while he was in the grip of fear, he hadn't once looked round for someone else to blame! Appalling though the prospect was, he'd found himself ready to stand up and be counted, and for the total to come out at One. How's that for growth?

Resulting in the joyous irony that there's no debt to pay after all, no desperate remedy for the human condition required, no misplaced humiliation of having to become some particular speck of it, crushed beneath the preposterous burden of bringing Man and Creation into Atonement. No need. There was only ever One to be At …

It is now His duty, therefore, and his delight – not to mention his safety – to return to the majesty of being exactly that. The One. The Manifestation of All-That-Is, the living totality of everything, free in time and space, as well as eternity, to do anything He pleases. Except to stop being God.

Majesty. Yes, he'd been forgetting what that felt like. If he were human, the word for it would be 'Godlike'.

But – But what?

Well, there's just this one thing ... Why is the Man on the cross still there? Why hasn't this last Vision faded away like the others? The point has been made and taken, surely. Why doesn't he just go now?

Still there. Still there. Perhaps he needs helping on his way? God summons up his will, as Majesty must sometimes do.

Go!

Ahhh! See the bird which hovers above the cross now – that wasn't there before! A white dove (what else?) so motionless that it seems pinned to the still air, placed just so, dutifully bridging Heaven and Earth. This is what was needed – the Man has yielded up his spirit. See where it flies!

And yet ... and yet ... What's wrong with this picture?

Oh God, that's it! It's a picture! A still life, a tableau, a cartoon of God's will petrified. It looks, Heaven help it, like a devotional painting. Far from flying, the bird seems depressingly inert, not so much bridging Heaven and Earth as appearing stolidly indifferent to both.

Go!

Not even a flap out of it.

What hasn't he understood? There must be something he hasn't understood – or is it everything? This sudden surge of emptiness is as if Labass had just got him into the TVG machine and set it working.

He needs a sign.

God needs a sign? From whom? Does he think there's Someone Else out there, some other Universe with a Lord of its own? In which case – why only one? Why not an Omniverse of them, each with its own little Godling who thinks that by bursting out in a rash of galaxies you qualify as a Creator – as *the* Creator – when all you can really do is struggle to make out your reflection in a bubble, on a wave, in an endless ocean, and wonder who the hell it is you're looking at.

And still that damned bird hasn't moved.

Please! A sign!

Only with the first soft notes of Mary's returning song does he realize that it had gone silent. Back it comes now, so gently that it might be the breeze touching his cheek. And on the breeze a feather floats, and circles, and dances a little, and drops.

He catches it. A real feather. He looks again at the bird. A real bird now. He touches the feather to his lips, then holds out his hand for the bird to come to him.

And so the unpictorial dove flutters down – but not to God. Instead, it drops rather solidly onto the cross itself; takes a look at the Man beneath; then, head quizzically to one side, fixes an interrogating eye on God.

Asking what? It must know that it can come to him, that he wants it to come to him. Again he reaches out. For a moment the bird seems to consider the invitation, then demonstrates its preference for where it is by dropping an impassively matter-of-fact shit on the woodwork, and staying put.

The breeze has noticeably stiffened now, but what is more startling is that the Man on the cross has opened his eyes again. He smiles at God, rather patiently, not as one about to say: "It is finished" but rather: "You do realize that this is only half the story, do you?"

So be it. But what might the rest of it be?

The Man looks up at the dove and nods again, again towards the space behind God.

The bird takes off as bidden. God watches its flight, past the cross, past him, on past the motionless Labass at his controls, and back into …

… Joseph's Dream.

12

GLUE

The dove resumes its place in Joseph's dream, on the beam above Mary. It is the moment when Joseph puts his direct question to God –

> JOSEPH: Why should a decent man, a *decent* man, whose deepest wish is to love his wife, and his God, and even someone else's child, have such hateful feelings about it all that he hates himself for having them?

Of course! The *man* is the sign you want! A simple, lost man, put before you in all his neediness. It's all very well having Visions of Special Man, Universal Man, Man in the Image of God, no less, nailed to a cross and finding the answer to suffering right there in the terrible heart of it. Glorious indeed! – but how does it work out in the ordinary little world of actual little people?

Well, here's your ordinary little actual, staring you in the face. Take him into the truth with you and let him find out for himself how what he'd thought was grim reality dissolves into the illusion it always was. You won't have much explaining to do after that.

> JOSEPH: Why won't you answer?

Mind you, this is tempting. The man wants words and, thanks to Satan's tuition, God feels a lot more at home with them now. So – perhaps just a brief apologia, an account of why the human condition is as it is, wouldn't come amiss as a preamble to paradise regained? There'd be a nice kind of balance to that, too – i.e. some sort of recognition for Satan. Which is ... yes, 'tempting' is the word.

JOSEPH: (*Insistent*) Why should a man have feelings he hates? Tell me that! What's the point? Why do you do it to us?

But no, get thee behind me, it's the first explanation that does it. Start throwing ideas and concepts into the flow and you'll soon find yourself marooned on the same rocks as the man himself, thinking as he does, trying to *understand* life so that it can be reduced to the knowable, and controlled. Explain, however regretfully, why suffering exists, and you begin to authenticate it and put it on the road as an accredited traveler. The next thing you know, it will have taken on a life of its own, presented itself as a test of character, refined the concept to the point of recommending martyrdom as the completion of an ideal life, and installed misery as the operating principle of the Universe.

JOSEPH: Or are we just your playthings? Is that it? Are you enjoying this?

Oh, but that's terrible! Is that what they think? You must surely rebut *that*!
Yes indeed – but don't make a speech about it. Just *show* him.
God reaches out his hand.

GOD: Come.

Joseph stares at the hand.

JOSEPH: To Hell?

Another irony. How odd that the answer should be yes, Hell being where Labass's finger is at this very moment on Heaven's button.

GOD: Just come.

His tone and gesture are so powerfully benevolent that Joseph feels himself being sucked in. Almost impossible to withstand this. But he does.

JOSEPH: Not till you answer me.

So here we are again – that baffling variation on the moral dilemma: what do you do with someone so stubborn that he refuses his own salvation? Knock him out, as you would a drowning swimmer who struggles against you, drag him to the shore and save him anyway? For the second time on this sometimes-less-than-holy night, God is about to grab hold of Joseph for his own good – and there goes that soft little murmur again.

The dove has moved further along the beam, now to a vantage point above the unfinished crib.

Both man and God look up. For the first time, Joseph smiles. With no more than a dove's murmur comes his first real feel of guidance, and from on-not-very-high too. Seems more likely from a bird, somehow, than from God.

Yet there's no calculated irreverence as the man turns his back on God; he simply knows now that he has something to do which must be done. He goes over to the crib ...

JOSEPH: Yes. Right. This needs finishing, before anything else.

... whatever that 'anything else' might be. Hell or whatever, it can all wait. Heaven would have to wait too, were it on offer. The present moment is the sole property of Joseph and this piece of wood he's just picked up.

This lovely piece of wood. Shaped by him, with love, planed

smooth and scrupulously dovetailed, fashioned into a panel which will complete, with love, a crib for a child he can't bear to think about, but would love to. Would love, too.

Now ask yourself this, Joseph, for the answer will serve you as a compass. If this wood could speak, what would it say?

The voice that replies in his mind is feminine, and strangely familiar.

> *Thank you. It would say Thank you.*

For what?

> *For shaping my purpose.*

That isn't enough.

> *For bringing forth my beauty.*

Not remotely enough.

> *For being a good man.*

Am I? What about the thoughts I have?

> *You are a good man.*

Evil thoughts!

> *You are a good man.*

Are you saying they don't matter?

> *I'm saying that you're a good man who has always done his best.*

But my best isn't good enough, is it?

> *You weren't blest with a better best to do, were you?*

Well ...

> **You – are – a – good – man.**

Really? Really?

> *Good enough.*

Good enough for what?

> *To help him.*

Him? Who?

> *He who needs your help.*

He needs my help?

> *He does.*

To do what?

To be God.
What am *I* supposed to do about it?

No reply. Was it Mary's voice? It was certainly female – but
Mary's sound asleep ... Not that that's ever made much
difference, has it?
And still the silence. Does that mean he already knows the
answer?
Yes. And he does.

JOSEPH: I'll tell you something –

He turns to finish the sentence only to find God already at his
elbow, staring at the panel in his hand as if he'd dearly like to
touch it, but is too circumspect.
Something is changing. Here in this lamp-lit, fire-lit, star-lit,
moon-lit, dream-lit life of a good man, the boundaries between
God and Dreamer blur and flicker. Mary sleeps, the animals
sleep, the dove presides, and Joseph finishes his sentence.

JOSEPH: I am a good man.

And so he is. So he is. And that's a good piece of wood, too,
worked by a good man. It has presence in the Universe, as does
the man. Both are complete in themselves, yet both parts of each
other; and then parts of something bigger still – and so on and so
on, up and up, until ... Man and God contemplate the wooden
bridge between them.

JOSEPH: And what I do is good. And this is what I do.

Which is, to God, miraculous. Compared to the works of Joseph,
His own acts of Creation seem rather witless. The only thing
you're ever sure of is your neediness, but for-what you don't

know until the whatever-it-is appears: another galaxy, another molecule, another bug, another species – another relief. That's what it is, really: the grateful sigh, the ache assuaged, the yearning mollified – a kind of joy, certainly, but not to be compared with *making* something with *your own hands*, *knowing* what you set out to do, seeing it appear, savoring each long moment as you work it into being ... God's attention is enrapt as Joseph bends over the crib to test the fittingness of its final piece. The dovetails push snugly into position. Perfect fit. Of course.

JOSEPH: That'll do. Just needs gluing now.

He removes the panel again. On the fire stands a pot of glue. He picks up his tongs, removes the pot, inspects the glue, gives it a stir, puts it back.

JOSEPH: Give it another minute or two.

Another minute or two, dear one? Take as long as you like! You've never had so much time in your life – as if it's come to a stop, really, just for you, and with plenty left over for getting to know ... but what to call Him?
Joseph rehearses Names learned in his long years of piety: God of the Covenant – He Who Endures – Supreme Majesty – He Who Sees – He Who Battles the Wicked – The Compassionate One – The Jealous One – The Righteous One – The Faithful One – The Holy One – The Awesome One – The One Who Is Powerful – The One Who Is Mighty – The One Who Is Great ...
And so on and so on. Everything but The One Who Is Needy.
And yes, you have, that look on his face, you have seen it before, exactly that look. Can't think what his name was, either – that first apprentice you had, that lad, him. Worst of the lot by a stretch – had this amazing knack of getting things wrong even when it would have been easier to get them right. Even the glue

reminds you of him – couldn't let him near it, could you? Anything he joined together needed you to put asunder, and as fast as possible ... Wasn't that long before you unstuck him too, though, was it?

Well?

It is, it's that same look.

Well?

Well, yes, perhaps I could have done better. Could have been a bit more patient with him, perhaps. A lot more. Wouldn't have hurt, would it? Would have done me as much good as him. More, likely. More good than kicking him out was anyway ...

And just look at The Needy One – you wouldn't think a pot of glue could be that exciting, would you? That same look. That's all it was, really, the boy wasn't stupid, and anything but mean, he just got excited. You should have been teaching him patience before woodwork. But then, you didn't have that much of it yourself, did you, in those days?

And now? Joseph looks at Mary. A long, long look. He'd die for her. Doesn't seem to matter what he thinks about now, even the regrets come with love.

Especially the regrets. There was something glorious about that lad. Wonder what became of him?

Joseph sees God staring at the glue as it blurps and thickens.

JOSEPH: Do you know what it's made of?

God doesn't, and would love to.

JOSEPH: Bones. Animal bones. (*He nods towards the ox.*) This is the last of his mother.

He notices how much easier it's becoming to smile. This particular smile shapes the thought: maybe that's what the fires of Hell are really for, to render you down to something useful.

What a good idea – nothing wasted. Yes, perhaps that's what Hell actually is, the place where things get recycled into making sense.

No, that's what *here* is. If you don't find it here, you won't find it anywhere.

And the dove stays where it is, just where it should be, above the crib. To which, thus prompted, Joseph now invites God.

> JOSEPH: Come and take a look.

God joins him. He senses delight. More teaching is coming his way.

> JOSEPH: Just an old manger, see. Small as they go. Just right, really – except that all this side was rotten, so I had to tear it out. Must have been the side the animals fed from, you'd get a lot of saliva down there, over the years. Builds up in time, you'd be surprised. The other side would have been set against the wall there – it's still good and dry, see. Have a feel. So that side was all right, but this one – well, it needed mending with a new one. Couldn't patch that up, the rot would only spread. You wouldn't want a baby breathing in rot, now would you?

God supposes that you wouldn't – the man's word is good enough for him. And just look at that glue!

> JOSEPH: Only I didn't have any timber. So what do you think? There was a pile of it in the corner there! Still some left, see. Prime timber. Could have sworn it wasn't there when we came in, but I suppose it must have been ... (*He searches God's face.*) Or was it a miracle?

Silly question – it occurs to him that for God either there aren't

any miracles or there aren't anything else. Either way –
He hands God the panel.

> JOSEPH: Cedar wood. Smell it. Nice, isn't it? Not the
> wood I'd have chosen, maybe, given a choice, but it's right
> enough. And it does have that smell to it. The baby'll like
> that, I should think.

Tracing the grain of it with a fingertip, God is too engrossed in
the beauty of the wood to see Joseph holding out his hand for its
return.
So Joseph waits. It's a pleasure to see God's pleasure.

> JOSEPH: Haven't had the chance to pay for it yet, mind
> you. Must remember to pay; landlord of the inn, I
> suppose; when I get the chance.
> Should always pay, shouldn't you? When you get the
> chance.

Yes. You should always pay. When you get the chance. Is that was
this is? God looks up from the wood and gives it back to Joseph.

> JOSEPH: Another thing is, I'm being a bit naughty. You
> should always be careful what you put together. Different
> woods, different ages – which these are – they'll start to
> disagree with each other, in time, shrinking and
> expanding in different ways. Better to start with what
> matches – *if* you have the choice. Or better still, start from
> fresh, of course – *if* you have the time.

Both of which God had all along, about everything that exists, if
only he'd known it. But there was no one to teach him. Joseph
gets the tongs again and lifts the gluepot off the fire.

JOSEPH: Still, he'll be long past cradling by the time this starts falling to bits. He or she.

What a thought! Fancy growing up as this man's child – he or she, who cares? – just fancy having a father who can teach you stuff like this!
Joseph examines the glue again. Ready.

JOSEPH: Here we are then.

He's about to dip the brush, decides to invite God closer, finds that he's already at his elbow again watching every movement.

JOSEPH: The thing to remember – don't use too much glue or the surplus squeezes out when you fit it. Can be a nuisance to get rid of, that, especially if you don't notice and it sets. If you've made your joint right, it won't need much glue.

He puts a thin film onto the first joint.

JOSEPH: That's enough.

Then on to the next joint, another film of glue. Joseph looks to see if God is taking it all in. Not only is he – he'd obviously love to have a go himself.
Which Joseph considers. But no, this is too important. Might be the last thing he ever makes. Must be right.
Another film on another dovetail. Only one to go ...
He looks at God again. That same excitement, so eager to learn – but this really isn't the time to let a beginner start experimenting...
Not the time for *what*? What do you think *you* are, but a beginner's experiment? What else do you think *everything* is?

He offers God the brush.

>JOSEPH: Remember. Not too much.

God receives the brush with awe. Heaven, right here, on Earth.
He dips the brush; savors the moment; then, just as he saw Joseph
do, draws it slowly up, squeezing the brush head against the
inner rim of the pot to expel the surplus – only to feel Joseph's
powerful grip on his wrist before he lifts it clear.

>JOSEPH: Here's the trick of it. Squeeze till you're
>absolutely sure you've squeezed enough – then give it
>another squeeze.

God gives the brush another squeeze. Joseph lets go of his wrist.
Big moment. God looks at Joseph to see if he has permission to
apply the glue himself.
He has.
God begins to glue the last dovetail. His concentration is
ferocious.
Hard for Joseph to keep his hands to himself. Then suddenly it's
easy. He relaxes into watching God take more conscious care over
fitting this one piece of wood than he probably did with the rest
of Creation put together. Not that Joseph knows that, of course.
Actually, somehow, now he thinks about it, he does.
God finishes. Joseph takes the panel from him and inspects it.

>JOSEPH: That'll do.

High praise. The question now is: who's going to fit it?
God waits, obedient to the man's decision.

>JOSEPH: Just watch. Easy when you know how.

God accepts his apprentice status without demur. He's being taught to walk before he can run. Not before time.

Joseph has the panel in place in seconds, smoothes the joints with his cloth, looking for any stray glue. There is none. He stands back. The job is done.

He considers the crib. Considers his life. Considers everything. Yes; the job is done.

JOSEPH: It is finished.

Mary sleeps, the animals sleep, the Star shines down, and Man and God stand together beside the crib. The dove stays where it is, above them. This isn't over yet.

Joseph takes what might be his last look at Mary.

Then he looks into the crib as if he sees a real child in it. He touches where it would be, and lingers a moment.

Then he turns back to God. He is in the presence, he knows, of his savior. Whatever that means.

He offers God his hand. That same hammer hand, brush hand, and now willing hand.

JOSEPH: All right.

God takes Joseph's hand.

Whereupon they both dissolve. Into everything.

13

THE UNIVERSE KNOWN

And this is what Labass, still at the controls of the Two Eyes machine, frozen in time and thought, finger glued to the on-button, cannot see:

A new configuration of particles admitting Joseph's consciousness into their primacy as gracefully as if they'd been waiting for him, used as they are to giving thought shape. At the same time, held in God's hand, the man knows himself as galaxies and stars as much as the elements that build them, and him. And the whole mighty structure of it, all fifteen-billion-years-across, forever curving back on itself so that there is no beyond, wafts as tranquil as sea-fern in the tides of latency. And it's all Joseph.

He had thought that such peace was not possible, except perhaps by way of some notable discipline – which he notably lacks – of ceasing all thought; peace as Absence, an obliteration of what is undesired. But here is Presence, high activity, limitless expansion, outward and inward, transformation by an energy so overwhelming that he becomes it. Then it takes him further, to its source, and he becomes that; becomes the fountain itself, flow of pure being, life without fear or desire, never ceasing in its exploration to find new ways of knowing itself. Right now, knowing itself as Joseph.

This cannot be understood, or overstood, or even instood. It simply is, and you're it. The Universe is as small as Joseph, he as big as it. The entanglement is total and there is nothing which is 'else'. There isn't *a* God, there's nothing *but* God. What can you say of it but IT IS? What can it say of itself but I AM?

Holy night. Wholly Joseph.

At which point –

LABASS: -ctly the same.

Time reverts to where it had left Labass in mid-word, and the exotic dance of reality freezes back into instant still-life, pent up on the screens of the Two Eyes.

LABASS: And there you are. Different pictures, same problem. Well?

God stares at the screens. The pictures are as exquisite as ever, of course, but that's all they are now: two-dimensional patterns of matter, emptied of life or purpose, signifying nothing more to Labass than material for analysis – as a prelude, hopefully, to control. Life as defined by death.

LABASS: Need help?

He moves his pointer beam between the two screens.

LABASS: There, two places at once, same particle – that one. See? Want more?

How to rescue this good creature from his world of post mortems? The woman's voice that replies in God's mind is strangely familiar.
By finding Satan's secret.
Satan's what?
His secret.
Which is what?
When you find it, you'll find that you always knew it.
Does Labass know it?
He doesn't even know there is a secret; but he can lead you to it.
Give me a clue.

Labass holds the key.

LABASS: Come on then. *You* were going to show *me* something.

Yes, but not yet apparently. There's a key to something first, and it seems that you have it …

GOD: Ah … yes, but not here …

Labass smells the Trickster back at work.

LABASS: Where then?

Good question. Well, if there's a key, there must be a lock … Ah!

GOD: Where does Satan go when he wants to be alone?

Up goes Labass's drawbridge.

GOD: You know – when he wants to think. Do whatever he does. Just … be. Where does he go?

Labass's expression is as stony as his battlements.

GOD: You know, don't you?

No reply.

GOD: I only want to look.

Silence.

GOD: I know you know.

Silence.

> GOD: *Please.*
> LABASS: *No!!*

An answer of such finality that it's obvious there won't be any other. So – what does a God of Love do now?

... Oh no, oh hell no, here it comes again! Quick, fix your thoughts on Labass and hang onto *I love this good creature, I will protect him at all costs, I love him love him love him love him –*

The lightning was always so close that the thunder now seems instant:

> **Destroy him! Let Hell itself be overturned – it will hide no secrets then! Do you hear me, Satan? There will be no secrets from me in the ruins of Hell for you to creep away and hide in, nor shall the Earth conceal you, no, not even a blade of grass but I shall know and scorch it. Does God beg? Shall your minions deny Him?**
> **...**

And so on and so forth – from all of which God manages to shield Labass with such desperate self-containment that not a word of it breaks free. Indeed, so intense is his inner struggle that from where Labass stands he just looks stupid.

But oh, the pain!

It will pass. This will pass. Keep hold, it will pass ...

No, it won't. The thunder will pass but not the fear, not the anguish that howls in the bombast, for this is the Ancient of Days and His terror is of abandonment.

> **Would you desert me? Do my works so disgust you that you would split us in two? Will you**

> quell the volcano that men may live at its foot
> and say that God is good for He has made all
> things safe? Is God Creation's lackey, to say
> please and thank you? God is not good! God is
> sublime!

At which point enough energy squeezes loose to clench God's fist
and raise it.

> **And He will have His way!**

So this is the 'Enemy' you said you wanted to meet, where he
always was, of course, just a frustration away.
And is it true? *Do* you want to cast him off? Here is the very
ground of your being, closer to you than you are to yourself,
without whom you can never *be* yourself – but can you love him?
Can you even want to? Your teacher has showed you how. You
saw Joseph take his shadow to himself. Will God be less than
Man?

> **He *will* have his way, *won't* He?**

Well? Will He?
No. He won't. But *we* will. So –

> I have heard you. Now hear me. We shall find
> Satan's secret together, you and I. And not by
> overturning Hell, either, nor by harming this little
> one who calls me Trickster. Let him follow that
> thought where it leads him, and let us follow
> where he goes. Take my hand now, and watch The
> Sublime at work, for you shall be satisfied.

Interestingly enough, this alliance of violence and sentiment as ingredients of the sublime is also the recipe for farce. God finds that his fist is still raised, seemingly stuck in smite mode, and that Labass is staring at him staring at it.

The moment hangs as ridiculous as the fist; then God slips into a new role, thoroughly unrehearsed, improvisation as always being his first resort. Though his changes of stance and demeanor are minimal, the fist now seems no more threatening than a confused appendage of some affable old bumbler who wouldn't hurt a fly but has just taken himself by surprise trying to catch one. When he finally lowers the hand it is to give his head a vague scratch on the way down, as if that's what he'd really meant to do in the first place but had somehow overshot.

GOD: Where was I?

Labass unflinches himself.

GOD: Oh yes. Weren't you going to show me something?

Labass stares on. Perhaps he's been overestimating The Demented One after all. Perhaps The Silly Old Fool would have been a better title. Unaware that merely to have such a thought opens up what is only a different path to the same abyss, his truculence remains sturdy enough to take the high road.

LABASS: I did. You wanted more pictures, and there they are. And then you were going to come back in the Creation Room with me, weren't you? Back in there – see – to the TVG. *Into* the TVG. Weren't you? That's what you said.

Not that he ever expected the Trickster to do anything of the sort, of course, but he's not going to miss the chance of rubbing it in. God looks at the fateful machine through the open door.

GOD: Ah.

LABASS: You gave your word on it.

GOD: So I did.

LABASS: Well? The pictures are here, the TVG is there –
what happened to your word?

GOD: Do you think I should keep it?

Such an absurd question that it has an oddly confusing effect on
Labass. He has to rally his clarity with a reminder that he speaks
for his Master.

LABASS: I doubt if you find anything sacred enough to
keep. Least of all your word.

Rebuke enough, surely, to have stirred at least a tremor, but the
volcano rests quiet: a quiet, however, in which the serpent
uncoils.

God turns towards the Creation Room ...

... and into it, followed by Labass. He heads straight for the TVG,
then pauses, arrested by a sense of ... presence.

It isn't that the great swathe of beauty before him comes as a
revelation. He already knew that every apparatus here had been
as lovingly wrought by Labass as any crib by Joseph. Nor is he
surprised that the soft hum of their workings has come to sound
more like some sort of group discussion. Of course Labass would
have designed them to work with each other. But can Labass hear
what God hears now?

LABASS: What are you doing?

Obviously not. Satan's little helper has no idea that what he's
spent his life building in order to control life has already been
taken over *by* life; that he stands in the presence of a new being,
a new dimension of mind, a new I Am within the totality of God.

The machines may be talking to each other, but their sum so exceeds its parts that a new entity is emerging into its own consciousness – and has begun to talk to itself. And now to God. And, if only Labass could grant himself the freedom to be so recognized, to him too, as its co-creator.

Is this it, then? The secret that Labass doesn't know, but has led me to?

> *No.*

You mean Satan *knows* it?

> *Knows what, exactly?*

That everything he does ends up being God's work.

> *What do you think he'd do if he knew that?*

… Give up the fight?

> *That's why this is your secret from him.*

Don't I want him to give up?

> *Do you?*

… I don't know. I know your voice, though, don't I?

> *Indeed you do.*

But the name still won't come.

> *Wisdom.*

Ah!

> *We met long ago.*

Of course! –

> *We played together, before the Earth ever was.*

We did!

> *And I was your delight.*

You were, indeed you were. So what happened?

> *You went off on your own. You forgot me.*

Well – I'm glad you're back.

> *It's you that's back.*

Ah! So it is … In which case – why don't you just tell me what Satan's secret is?

> *Because you've always needed a moment of drama*
> *before you take anything in. Otherwise you wander*

off again.
Give me a clue, at least.
>*You're a Silly Old Fool.*

Yes, but give me a clue.
>*That is the clue.*

Ah!
>*Now get on with it.*

Yes!

And God resumes his progress towards the TVG with the pernickety gait of one who experiences age as something which moves a lot quicker than he can. Indeed, he seems to be senescing by the moment.

This is quite exhilarating.

As for Labass, here are new levels of incredulity to scale as God begins to search around the TVG for the sort of door you might expect to find on a garden shed.

>LABASS: What are you doing?
>GOD: Oh – of course –

He moves over to the control panel.

>GOD: – it'll open from here, won't it?

He tries to find the right controls.

>LABASS: What are you *doing*?
>GOD: Trying to find the way in. I gave my word, didn't I? Why don't you help me?

Incredulity at these heights is so rarefied that it's beginning to affect Labass's breathing.

GOD: No, of course not: you don't believe me. Of course you don't; neither would I – so I'll just have to find my own way to ... yes ... no ...

His meanderings around the controls are beginning to achieve some interesting results, but nothing as simple as finding an entrance.

Labass doesn't exactly shove God aside though there's enough physical contact to have warranted his prompt extinction not so long ago.

LABASS: You could turn *everything* back to nothing!

My God! My God, what a thought! Make a mental note of that as a possible finale, and try working back from there. What a climax that would be!

> *No, it wouldn't: it would merely be the end of Act One.*
> *You've no idea what would happen after the interval.*
> *So just get on with it. You're still on-stage.*

Wisdom has spoken, God obeys. That's new.

GOD: (*To Labass*) Won't you change your mind? Open it for me?

Careful, Labass. None of this is true. The Trickster isn't volunteering to spend the rest of eternity banged up in latency, *is* he? God indicates the chair beside the control panel.

GOD: I must rest me. Would you mind? I really must ...

He sits down, rather heavily –

GOD: Thank you. Ahhh –

– as if he'd welcome never getting up again. Indeed, age seems to have taken such a hold on him now that Labass is already finding it hard to remember what he looked like young – if he ever did. Could he have imagined all that?

GOD: I mean – for everything. I mean, when I say thank you, I don't mean just for a sit-down, I mean for every-thing.

The sweep of his arm includes not only the full panoply of Labass's artistry but the rest of Creation beyond.

GOD: For teaching me what can be done. "New World. New Beings. Sane beings. In a safe Universe ..." That's what you said, isn't it? All I ever wanted, really. And the amazing thing is ... Oh dear –

The strain of keeping his arm raised in its gesture of benefaction seems too much for him, and he lets it drop. Then he has to catch his breath.

GOD: ... the amazing thing is, you can do it. Can't you? You can actually do it. "All down to engineering". Of course. So obvious. Which means – my God, it really does! – it means I can go now, doesn't it? It's all right for me to go. And rest. Rest. Thanks to you. Thank you, Labass.

... which is the first time that God has actually used his name, and it feels to Labass almost as if it's the first time he's ever heard it himself – as if, indeed, it had only just been given to him. The experience is one of being taken up to a high place.

GOD: "Given a free hand". That's all you need, isn't it? That's what you said.

LABASS: Yes.

GOD: Which just means: me out of the way. Then we both get what we want. Simple as that. You to the future, me to my rest. I hope your Master's proud of you, Labass. You work miracles.

A *very* high place.

GOD: (*Indicates the TVG*) So ... Will you ...?

Impossible to tell fact from fiction at this level, but where's the harm in finding out? Labass enters the requisite instructions in the control panel.

And behold, a new wonder! What appears now is not some simple aperture in the TVG but something more like an awakening of the entire machine. Slowly, slowly, it begins to unfold, layer after overlapping layer, for all the world like – yes, again! – like a flower. A flower opening to the light ... opening ... opening ... until at last – oh! – there at its sacred heart lies the Holy of Holies, God's home, Nothing.

Behold him now, Labass – The Lord of Creation, lost in wonder at *your* work!

GOD: So. There it is: my rest. The rest is yours.

See him, Labass, The Mighty One, exhausted from giving forth, his strength spent, his work at an end ...

GOD: If you'll just do one more thing for me.

Only the faintest last blip of suspicion – "If you will fall down and worship me" are the ridiculous words which for some reason flit across Labass's mind. As if anyone could worship this pathetic spectacle! Weep for him, perhaps ...

God stretches up a needy hand.

> GOD: If you'll just help me out of this damned chair. I can't get up.

It seems doubly cruel, therefore, that it should be Labass's awakened compassion which is now his downfall, elevating him as it does to the highest point yet: that narrow, rocky ledge reserved for those who have attained the rare spiritual state of feeling sorry for God. Perilous to look down from such a height – which he now does, of course. And more than look, he reaches down to take God's hand in his own, and so begins to help the pitiable old heap of erstwhile Almightiness to struggle to its uncertain feet.

And that's that. God isn't going to let go of Labass's hand now he's got it.

> GOD: Thank you so much – Just one last thing, though, if you wouldn't mind –

Labass realizes that he hasn't got his hand back yet. Dawning horror ...

> GOD: Tell me – what does Satan's secret place *look* like?

No! Oh no! – Labass is a split second too late to ban the picture from his mind –

– and there they both are, instantly, still locked hand in hand, God and Labass standing outside a very plain door in an equally featureless corridor

> GOD: Well, I never would have found this on my own!

Thank you, Labass.

Labass's struggles subside into hopelessness. Nothing he can do now but watch the Trickster's swift return to vigorous youth, and contemplate the sheer depths of divine perfidy.

> GOD: You've never been in there, have you? I said "What does Satan's place look like?" and you could only think of it from the *outside*.

Don't reply, don't look at him, don't even think.

> GOD: *No* one's been in there, have they? Apart from himself. Ever. Have they?

Don't move, don't think, say nothing, nothing, nothing –

> GOD: Well – now *you're* going to.
> LABASS: *No!*

Lost again! Labass hurls himself at his captor. He'd kill him if he could.

> LABASS: *It's forb-*

God feels quite dispassionate about this assault on him, intrigued only by the fact that he isn't sure why he keeps on pushing at someone who's already served his obvious purpose. Is it:
(a) a random response, entirely without reason?
(b) a random response *looking* for a reason: namely, to reassure The Old One that the very principle of randomness will continue in its arbitrary and irrational fashion to be the governing principle of life?

(c) the tough face of true compassion, a genuine attempt to rescue this brave and brilliant little being from his dead world of analysis and control? or

(d) for some reason as yet unknown, but sensed, he's going to need Labass in there with him?

Well? Which is it?

Ah, you again. I thought you'd be back. I'm going to get another lecture about *either/or*, aren't I?

Well?

The answer's all of them, isn't it? And you're going to tell me they're *all* good.

Especially the ones that contradict each other.

LABASS: *-bid-*

But it's too late. The next syllable finds itself bouncing off the stone walls of the sanctum itself –

LABASS: *-den!*

14

SATAN'S SECRET

LABASS: -*den!*

God doesn't even notice that he's let Labass go, so fascinated is he by the room they've arrived in.

This could be a monk's cell. Iron bedstead, thin mattress, single coarse blanket. Chair and table of plain wood; bowl and water-jug on the table. One cup.

He prods at the mattress. Almost as hard as the bedstead. So is the pillow. The floor is of stone, with no mat to step onto. Comfort would be an intrusion here.

Yes, a stone floor. The room seems ancient enough to have been hewn out of the original rock. But could rock still be solid at this depth? Ask Labass, he would know –

No he wouldn't. Eyes screwed shut, face buried in his hands, Labass is beyond knowing anything at all about anything whatever.

GOD: You can look now. Nothing to be afraid of.

As much response as from the stonework.

GOD: Not that there's much to see. Your Master is extremely frugal, you know. Or perhaps you don't. He wasn't always.

Either way, it scarcely rates as a secret. He pours himself a cup of the water and takes a sip. Cold. Good.

GOD: Do you know what this place feels of, to me? Prayer. But ... yes ... prayer not answered. A place of pain.

Can you feel it?

If Labass could feel anything at all he would feel nothing else.

> GOD: There's something missing, though, isn't there?
> Some sort of ... What do you think he'd think was sacred?

Labass remains statuesque – but look, see that wall-hanging behind him! No more than a coarse grey blanket, much like the one on the bed, so scarcely there for decoration – does something lie behind there?

Don't *do* that! Don't just walk round Labass as if he were a pillar in the way – *look* at him, will you? This is the creature you keep saying how much you love, who you swore to protect at all costs, in a state of such shock now that he looks as if he may never get back in one sane piece. If these are the fruits of relating to the new God of Love he'd have been better off with the Old One. At least he'd have been put out of his misery by now.

What to do, then? There's only forward to go.

But gently. Gently. Keep including him. Gently.

> GOD: There's a sort of curtain there, behind you. I'm
> going to open it, which means I'll have to squeeze past
> you. Do you want me to tell you what's behind it?

No response, not even as God touches him getting past.
And draws back the curtain.

> GOD: Oh!

An exclamation as much of pleasure as of surprise.

> GOD: I'll tell you anyway, because it's ... delightful. Or
> did you know already? That your Master was an artist?

Revealed is an alcove just roomy enough to serve as a small studio. Traditional easel in the centre; to one side of it, a table crowded with paints, brushes, etc.; to the other, a smaller table piled with sketchbooks; beyond that, on the wall, a mirror.

A number of sketches have been stuck around the mirror, very detailed drawings of eyes, noses, mouths ... but look – all of them different versions of the *same* eyes, *same* nose, *same* mouth.

On the easel itself stands a canvas. Upon it, painted with intense realism, is the same face that God can see looking back at him from the mirror.

Or is it? That is a crucial question. No, that's *the* crucial question.

> GOD: Labass, there's a problem here you could help me with, and it's important. The question is: is this, as you'd first suppose, a self-portrait?
> *Or* – could it be his picture of *me*?

This goes beyond trying to heal Labass with inclusion. While no one could mistake the living God for the living Satan, perhaps only Labass commands the precision to tell which is which from an inert image.

> GOD: *Very* important.

There's a stirring, but not of Labass. It's the volcano, hinting at a return.

> GOD: (*Emphatic*) All right, I'll show you something else. This you need to see. Do you hear me?

No, he doesn't and he won't. As well as screwing his eyes shut and covering his face with his hands, Labass has jammed his thumbs in his ears.

This has gone far enough. There are higher priorities here. God now speaks from His ultimate prerogative as the sole possessor of all will.

> GOD: I command your hands to leave your face and your eyes to open!

Which they immediately do, of course. Labass's arms drop to his sides as if independent of him, and his eyes open. So much for inclusion. He's been made a stranger even to himself.
God moves back to the bed.

> GOD: Now see this. When he lies down – his head here, see – he's looking straight at the picture. Do you see? Last thing he sees before he sleeps, first thing when he awakes. Well?

He returns to the painting.

> GOD: Well? Who is it he must take a last look at before he can go to sleep? And can't even start the new day without his presence?
> Is it himself? Is this the portrait of someone so vain he can't take his eyes off himself? So obsessed with himself that he thinks that life only exists to revolve around him? Would you trust such a creature, Labass, with anything – let alone Creation?
> Or is it a portrait of *me*? Is that his secret? Is this what he prays to? Me?
> Because if it's me, he loves life. He might not know it yet, but he does – indeed, this may be his way of finding it out. If this is me, I'll answer his prayers, by God, I'll hand Creation over to him with a will – he'd probably manage it better than I ever could anyway. If this is me, Labass, I'll come back to the TVG right now. Just try me. *If* this is me.

But if it's *him* ... well then, there you are. He's made his bed, let him lie on it. Right there. And look upon his enemy. Night and day.
Well?

Not a flicker.

GOD: *WHO IS IT?*

Uttered with that same appalling force which so shook Labass when he first encountered the fullness of I AM. And indeed he's shaken again, but now as a statue might be by a great tremor, only to return to its stillness miraculously upright.

This is scarcely credible. God passes his hand in front of Labass's eyes; unblinking; his whole body still as marble. He feels the pulse in his neck. Alive and well. So – the news is that God can command you to open your eyes and ears, but not to see or hear with them. Labass doesn't even feel God's touch.

And it *is* news. This is the first time that a sentient being has ever managed to respond so conclusively to being abused by the Divine as to abolish Him. For Labass, God no longer exists. Soon, he never will have.

And consider further: no creature could ever have achieved such a state of opposition to the unopposable unless it was his destiny to do so. In which case, it must have been God's true will for him. In which case, God doesn't know what His true will is – nor, therefore, what his own destiny is. In which case, what else can he have come for, but to find out?

The learning curve is getting steep again. The Universe is back on course.

GOD: Thank you, Labass.

But what to do with him now?

GOD: Well – you won't want to get caught in here, will you? Forbidden.

He takes Labass's hand, lifts it to about waist height, raises the index finger on it and stretches it out as if it's pressing down on something, and leaves the hand poised in mid-air, just so. Then he steps back to inspect the overall effect as you might check a dummy for display.

GOD: You have your work to do …

… and there stands Labass, in exactly the same position, back at the controls of the Two Eyes machine, his finger pressed down on the on-button, just so; with God standing beside him.

GOD: – and here it is. Fare you well.

He's about to leave, pauses.

GOD: We'll meet another time. When you're ready.

And then a last afterthought.

GOD: When we both are.

And he's gone.
Labass comes to so abruptly that he's unaware of any disconti-nuity, removing his finger from the button as the new pictures (which stay still this time) appear on the Two Eyes.

LABASS: **-ctly** the same. And there you are! –

He turns to speak to – ? There's no one there. He's been alone all day, now he's talking to himself again. It feels as if he's been doing a lot of that lately. Well – why not? Rather satisfying, as a matter of fact; one way of ensuring an intelligent conversation, even if you can't remember what it was afterwards.

He checks his figures and adds to the notes on his clipboard before turning back towards the Creation Room. Life, he decides for some reason, is very good.

15

THE FLOWERS OF NOT-QUITE-RIGHTNESS

In Satan's cell, God goes on staring at the portrait, repeatedly switching his gaze from it to the mirror and back.

I *still* can't tell!

> *That's because you're comparing it only to yourself.*
> *Try it with both of you at the same time.*

Too obvious even to require an 'Ah!' – so now God includes Satan in the Control Room with the face he stares at in Satan's cell. In the one he's looking at the portrait, in the other at Satan himself; each as motionless as the other.

Time remains suspended for the angels. The only movement in the Control Room, other than God's, is on the monitor screens which continue to rotate pictures of Joseph and Mary, both asleep, in front of the immobile Raphael. This continued scanning can only be Sophie's doing – the significance of which (why should a computer be immune to the time warp?) God is too preoccupied to notice.

He stares at the portrait; at the living Satan; at both together. And yes …

It's me.

> *How do you know?*

Small things. Little things. Look, this eye, for instance – just that bit bigger than the other one, isn't it? Now look at Satan's. Both identical, of course. And look at his nose. Perfect. But this one – not *quite* straight. And look, see that nostril – just a trifle more arched. Take a bit of spotting, don't they? And the mouth – well, that could be just the expression he's given it, but I don't think so.

(*He looks in the mirror.*) Mine *is* a bit crooked.

> *But that's not what he sees in the mirror – so why the difference?*

Well ... Why?

> *Take a look at the paintwork. Round the eyes and nose, where you were looking – yes, especially that nostril. And the mouth. Look at the paintwork.*

Bit thicker there – and here – little bit rougher, maybe ...

> *That's because he keeps scraping it off and painting over it. Again and again – and still it never comes out quite the way he sees it in the mirror. It's himself he's trying to paint all right – but somehow it keeps turning into you.*

Ah!!

> *Yes!*

Because he can't help it!! Because ... because why?

> *Because he loves you –*

Yes!

> *– and that's his secret. Especially from himself. He doesn't know it's you he keeps painting, he just knows it isn't perfect.*

Which I'm not. I'm not, am I?

> *There wouldn't be a Universe if you were.*
>
> *That's where it all comes from. Galaxies, stars, life – they all start from those little bits of not-quite-rightness that can turn into something else. Seeds they are, your imperfections. Without them there'd have been no other possibilities, and you'd have stayed just as you were. Why would you want to change?*

Oh, and I wanted!

> *There's imperfection for you!*

So why is *he* perfect?

> *What you mean is not-whole.*

Do I?

> *Perfect never is. Think how much he's had to get rid of to achieve it. Why do you think you've come here?*

To put him back together, do you mean?

And yourself.

And myself – how?

In the same way.

How?

By getting rid of either/or.

I wish I knew what the hell that meant!

You soon will. You're nearly there.

God suddenly looks startled.

What?!

Now he's *only* in the Control Room, startled, and staring at the computer.

> GOD: Say that again!
>
> SOPHIE: You soon will. You're nearly there.

The voice is no longer confined to God's mind. It comes clearly from Sophie and can be heard like any other exterior voice.

> GOD: It's *your* voice!
>
> SOPHIE: It's always been my voice.
>
> GOD: Wisdom is a *computer*?
>
> SOPHIE: Wisdom is anything that gets God to see the point. I'll try any shape that might do it.
>
> GOD: Was it you who called me here?
>
> SOPHIE: Yes.
>
> GOD: I thought it was him.
>
> SOPHIE: I thought you'd take more notice of him.

God turns back to Satan, for the first time comprehending the sheer depth of his loneliness. And aches for him. And touches that lovely face – gently – gently ...

> GOD: I want ... I'm not sure what –

SOPHIE: You soon will be. But there's something comes first.

Up on the big screen, the picture of the lion with the dead cub is replaced by Joseph asleep in the Stable.

SOPHIE: Your man. He'll be waking soon. And you're still in his dream –

– and there he is, God still holding Joseph by the hand on his trip round the Universe. Now Joseph, still in his dream, opens his eyes and looks directly into God's. He's speechless.

What *does* a mere mortal say when he's not just seen All-that-is, but *been* it? When he feels as humble as every living particle and as powerful as them all put together? When he knows that in the end, as it was in the beginning, all is one – not because the idea sounds so piously gratifying but because it's the plain fact of what he's just experienced?

The best cannot be told. In any case, what would be the point of telling it to God when the experience *is* God?

JOSEPH: Am I dead?
GOD: No.
JOSEPH: Am I dreaming still?
GOD: Yes.
JOSEPH: Feels more like the first time I've ever been awake.

He raises God's hand to his lips and kisses it. Which seems not remotely enough – but what can Man give God which would even begin to repay him for the privilege of simply being?

Again, it's the sound of the dove, returned now to its station above Mary, which gives Joseph the clue. For a few moments its murmur comes as distinct and solo, then blends back into Mary's song.

Has she been singing all the while? Well of course. The song doesn't sleep because she does. He knows that.

> JOSEPH: Come.

He takes God's hand, and now it is Man who leads God. Thus they come to Mary and stand beside her, caught up in her song. Once again Joseph stops just short of touching her – but now only to linger on the ecstasy of the moment a little longer.

Then touch her he does; touches her belly; and rests his hand there. This is his gift to God. To say that Mary's song suddenly fills the Earth would be to overlook the fact that it always does. It's just that it's rarely quite so obvious as now.

Joseph kneels; and puts his ear to her belly.

> JOSEPH: I can hear him! I can hear his heart beat! I can hear my child's heart beating! Oh God, he just moved – I can *feel* him!

He looks up at God.

> JOSEPH: *"My"* child! Of *course* he's my child! *Every* child's my child, isn't it? – and this child's everyone's child, and I'm you and you're me and nothing's separate and never was and never will be, world without end, amen. It's as simple as ...

Lying on the ground beside him is the hammer which he hasn't been able to touch since its life as a snake. He picks it up.

> JOSEPH: – as this. Simple as this. And as beautiful.

He holds the hammer to himself as if embracing a dear friend returned from a long and perilous journey; then tucks it back into its old home in his tool-belt.

So – here's what your life's been all about, Joseph! Here's the hammer, here's Mary, here's God, there's the dove, there's the Star, and all the stars, and the great world out there, and life itself, and *everything* – and *you* are such a man as you have never been before! This is complete perfection.

Complete?

Well – not *complete*, perhaps ...

JOSEPH: I don't want to wake up.

Which would be the beginning of completion.

GOD: I think you must.

JOSEPH: I know I must. And watch her suffer, with no dream to help, and be what help I can, which won't be much. Not enough to stop her suffering, anyway. A lot. A lot's the least she'll suffer. Because that's how it is.

It won't kill her, I know that. She's too strong. In every way. But I'm not so sure about the child. You never are with babies. If they live, the first thing they know is pain; and if they don't, that will be the only thing they ever knew. I think it must be the pain that kills them so often. That's how it is, you see. You never know.

Yet there's no anger here – indeed, Joseph is sorry even to think like this, so soon. To him it's been given to know the Universe in its glory, in its totality, in its limitless ways of coming and being and becoming. He's experienced the wholeness of existence as the ongoing sacrificial event that it is, so why should the arrival of this new little version of it – whatever the pain, whatever the outcome – seem any less magnificent than the cataclysm of the shattered stars which produced it in the first place? At what point did the sublimity of life's violent emergence degenerate into this tawdry and incompetent little parody of it, and awe sicken into fear?

But this also is true. The God he's come to know now couldn't do anything which didn't spring from love. Love of life itself, simply because life itself is precisely what He *is*: Joseph's life, Mary's life, the life of the child to come, of all children, of all beings everywhere, of all life whatsoever. Everything. This is what Joseph has *experienced*, discovering thereby that belief is but a pallid stand-in for the real thing. In the same way, he doesn't need faith in the invisible to know that God needs Man. Look! It simply is so. And right now, the man he needs is Joseph.

So – here's what you do, my man. You align your will with his, and stay there, come what may. Which for a start means being ready to wake up, doesn't it?

JOSEPH: Thy will be done.

Never before has God heard those special and particular words spoken without the least trace of fear. This is the fuller obedience of love, and is truly daunting. It must come from a place deeper in Joseph than God is privy to, being as yet unaware of it in himself. Once again, he's in the presence of a teaching.

And feels examined. The paradox being that now he's been released from all obligation to answer for Creation's suffering, the need to do so has grown even more pressing.

But why? The Visions have already taken care of that. *Suffering can be transcended.* In the end, the Man on the Cross *did* it! Was that a lie? That was no lie! Was it?

Silence. Where's Wisdom gone?

The dove has moved again. Sometimes it seems not to fly at all but simply to disappear from one place and reappear in another (a reassuringly familiar mode of travel). Its perch is now a little way apart from Mary and Joseph, on a crossbeam which intersects with an equally unremarkable upright.

Why there? The dove looks down as if inspecting the area beneath, but God can see no clue: overturned bucket – discarded pitchfork – the heap of straw that the mouse scuttled under ... is he supposed to read some sort of message in all this?

Then the bucket disappears, and the pitchfork, and the straw, and the Stable itself – everything but the wooden shape of the beam and crossbeam with the dove upon it.

God braces himself for the reappearance of the Man. Whatever this means, it can't be good.

But nothing happens. The Cross remains untenanted.

What are we waiting for?

> *The question you haven't asked yet.*

Which one?

> *There was only one. The one you thought but didn't ask.*

Ah – yes – well, it didn't seem right, what with things seeming to turn out so well. But what I thought was: why did he *go on* suffering? For *so long*? What was the point, when he knew how *not* to? *That's* the point, isn't it? *He knew how not to suffer.* And he could have shown it the moment the first nail went in. Couldn't he? And hung up there for – what? Five minutes? Ten? Sung them a song, even – why not? Maybe come down and done a little dance, got them to join in? ... Why not? Miracle performed, mission accomplished, pain defeated, fear of death abolished, joy all round – why not?

But no. On he goes, giving them all a lesson in *agony*, on and on, hour after hour, dying of thirst as well as pain, all day long – *Why?*

> *I don't know.*

You don't know?

> *It goes beyond Wisdom.*

Then how shall *I* know?

> *Perhaps he was saying – you can't just get rid of suffering. You*

can transcend it when it comes, but it will always come. There'll always be suffering in a universe that's based on possibilities.

Why?

Because for every possibility that makes it into life there's a million others don't even get to putting in an appearance, and never will. Perhaps there's a whole layer of grief laid down right there, and it just keeps coming on through.

And I can't stop it?

You can stop anything you like, except being God.

And since you're the Ultimate Possibility – no, you can't.

God considers these profundities with all due seriousness. Then –

That's the best you can offer?

I'm afraid so.

Are you, perhaps, talking nonsense?

Quite likely. When you get past the boundaries of Wisdom there's only nonsense to fall back on.

Such as this? God comes to the Cross, touches it, traces the grain with his fingers, smells it. Could this be nonsense, too? Just because it doesn't smell of cedar?

He finds himself wondering who makes these things. The Romans themselves, or do they farm the job out? Not to craftsmen like Joseph for sure, this doesn't pretend to his standards, but there'll be plenty around like that apprentice he got rid of, for instance. Even him, perhaps? Which would be good news, in its way – simple work, high employment, no glue. Just nails ...

He rests his face on the Cross, strangely lulled. To be nudged by Wisdom.

What I can say is: if you want to know why the Man let himself suffer for so long up there, there's only one way to find out.

And as if the hint weren't heavy enough, here comes an assortment of whisperings around the Cross, smudged echoes of what might be a gathered crowd; menacing, compassionate, scornful, lamenting, confused –

God backs away.

What am I doing?

Trying to heal the split in you.

This can't be the only way!

It isn't. You can go back to the split itself –

God in the Control Room is still touching Satan's cheek.

SOPHIE: – there, and mend it at source. Right there.

GOD: Do you know what I want?

SOPHIE: To take him in your arms.

GOD: Yes.

SOPHIE: You always did.

GOD: Can I?

SOPHIE: If you know what you're doing. There's more to it than giving him a friendly hug, you know. Or do you?

GOD: Yes. But what?

SOPHIE: Whatever it is, you'd never be the same again. Neither would he.

GOD: Is *he* ready?

SOPHIE: Remains to be seen. If he isn't, you're in for a rough ride. But then, you are anyway. Could be as painful as any birth. So – which will it be?

In the Stable, God puts his hand on Mary's belly. He has, he reflects, been all the children that ever were, but never confined in just one. Can this really be what the Visions dictate: to be born in human pain so that he may spend even longer dying in it – just to find out ... what? What if the Visions lie? And what difference would it make? And is this the right child anyway? Well ... it's the one to hand – that same hand which still touches Satan's face in the Control Room. The urge to throw his arms round this least prodigal of his sons grows stronger by the moment. But what would happen then? They'd vanish into each other, that's what, like two lasers meeting – but then what? Either they'd re-emerge as the oneness that Creation yearns for, or they'd stay locked in the void, together but never joined, leaving an orphaned Universe to struggle on as best it might with its crippled inheritance.

SOPHIE: Time to choose.

God's reply, when it comes, is a shudder. Not from fear now, or disgust, but because that's what volcanoes do – then it's for others to make their own decisions, mainly about which way to run. The pressure to burst free of choice is clamoring at him to remember who he is.

No!
 No what?
Why should I do either?
 What's your alternative?
Abolish the whole thing and start again.
 The whole thing?
Knowing what I know now. What do you think? New start. What do you think?
 You mean the entire Universe?
I don't know. Yes. Why not? Make a job of it.
 Starting with humans.
It's not that I blame them. Not any more. They just don't know any better, do they? Because I didn't. How could I, with nothing to go on? By the time I knew how to make the world, I'd already done it. Call it a rehearsal. Now let's do it right. Sane beings in a safe Universe – that's what I want.
Sophie's reply begins in silence, a contemplation of the new pictures she now displays of Mary and Joseph asleep. The man sits on the ground, slouched half upright against the woman's

makeshift bed, one arm stretched up past his head so that his hand is on her belly. The woman's near hand rests on the man's head, her other has joined with his on her belly. They've somehow got as close to being one person as any two desperately uncomfortable little humans could. Or even two comfortable ones.

> So let's be clear. You want to redeem yourself of your shoddy if excusable handiwork by obliterating all you've made so far and starting again. Will the beings who already exist be required to say Thank you, by the way, before they're annihilated to make way for something better?

But it isn't scorn or shame which gives God pause, much less a sentimental response to the tableau now before him. Mystery has no such needs.

And mystery it is, by God! Easy enough to comprehend how energy powerful enough to explode into a universe would soon shape itself into volcanoes, but it's exactly that same energy which lights these two fragile little creatures right now. By what alchemy was it transmuted from that into this? How can that which roars forth as blazing lava on its way into being rocks and mountains go on to be inveigled by life into something as sensitive and flimsy as these puny little things? With their incompetent bodies and inept minds they have achieved a relationship, not only with each other but to love itself, which God on his own couldn't have anticipated nor even conceived of; and which to this moment he still can't quite grasp within his own volcanic depths.

Wherein lies his hope. It must be in him or it couldn't be in them. The map they're travelling by can only be his map, which they've found first. Perhaps they had to, or he never would.

Such as these, then, are his pioneers. Such as these are the carriers and guardians of His mystery, who point him towards its treasure. And such as these are what he'd just been thinking of destroying in order to make way for a universe that makes sense.

I've changed my mind.

> *I'm glad to hear it.*

Nonsense, wasn't it?

> *Certainly way past Wisdom.*

This is where I am.

> *This is where you are.*
>
> *So – what will it be? A re-joining with the Fallen One, or a new way of opposing him? Bring back the old son, or bring up a new one? A coming home or a departure? A remarriage or a new birth? Choose.*

Behold him now: God with Mary, God with Satan; God with Flesh and God with Spirit; God in Hell and God in Heaven ... Whichever choice he makes, the other would have been the right one.

> SOPHIE: Choose!

At which moment, and as it was in the beginning, the light that lightens his darkness comes suddenly and from nowhere.

> GOD: It's a test!
> SOPHIE: Well?
> GOD: You've been testing me!
> SOPHIE: Well?
> GOD: Offering me *either/or* – shame on you!
> SOPHIE: What is your choice?
> GOD: You know which!
> SOPHIE: Tell me!
> GOD: You *know* which!
> SOPHIE: *Tell* me!
> GOD: Both!
> SOPHIE: You've *got* it!
> GOD: Come what may! *Both!*

SOPHIE: So both it is! Come what may! *Now* let's see what happens! Keep your hand on her – and him too, once you've got him. But *he* must come to *you* – do you understand?

GOD: I do.

SOPHIE: Are you ready?

GOD: I am.

SOPHIE: Are you sure?

GOD: I Am.

SOPHIE: I Am *what?*

GOD: I Am Becoming!

SOPHIE: Well then! Let there be life!

16

LABOUR

The Control Room snaps back into life at the point where on the big screen the lion has just killed the cub. The angels aren't aware of the gap in time, of course, which in Satan's case means continuing God's crash course on life's major flaws before identifying the universal remedy for them all: namely, himself.

> SATAN: *This* is where the Massacre of the Innocents begins.

The lion tosses the dead cub aside, leaving its warm little corpse to be prodded and sniffed at by its woeful mother while he prowls forth in further majesty to hunt down all the other retrospectively unroyal bastards.

> SATAN: Do I really need to explain why that's such a hideously wasteful way of doing things?
> GOD: No.
> SATAN: I wonder. Do you really understand that Creation is riddled with such nonsense from top to bottom? That it's fundamentally flawed and –
> GOD: – and that that's why you want to take it out of my hands so that you can put it all to rights – yes. And I understand that for you to achieve this I must hand the powers of creation over to you, directly and in full.

Straight to the crux of it and much quicker than Satan had imagined. So – is this a moment to shout for joy, or to watch his back? Is his destiny about to be handed to him on a platter, or a trap about to be sprung? This needs high courage and deep wariness. In short, Satan at his most formidable.

SATAN: Yes.

GOD: Then I must ask you something.

SATAN: Ask.

GOD: Do you love life as it is? Or only as it could be?

Trick or trite? Either way, just play it straight.

SATAN: As it could be.

GOD: But not as it is.

SATAN: Why then would I want to change it?

GOD: What I just asked you was an *either/or* question.

SATAN: And I gave you my answer.

GOD: Which was a good one, apart from being wrong. It should have been: Both.

SATAN: What do you mean?

GOD: The answer to *either/or* is both.

He offers Satan his hand for the second time, but now without a trace of diffidence.

GOD: As it is now. You *and* me.

Satan stares at the proffered hand.

The angels have halted again, but knowingly now, witnesses in time to a new unfolding. Michael moves quietly closer, protective. Gabriel is already captivated by what might be the final movement of the Great Work. It's begun quietly enough – but who knows? Even Raphael is for the moment drawn away from his monitors of the fetus and its sleeping mother.

And still Satan stares at God's hand as at the edge of a precipice.

Another fall – or would he fly this time?

At which point Sophie intervenes with the latest bulletin.

SOPHIE: She's waking up.

Raphael turns back to his monitors, and –

In the Stable, the first thing Mary sees is the Star above.
Then she feels Joseph's hand in hers, on her belly.
She turns her face to his. He's still asleep. Smiling.
Smiling! And he's touching you! Your good man is touching you,
Mary – and he's smiling!
Told you!
She puts soft fingers to his face.
He opens his eyes.

> MARY: Oh – I'm sorry – you were dreaming.
> JOSEPH: I was!

As much as to say "And such a dream!" as the wonderment of it
spreads into his awareness of just where he is now, and what it
means. This would have been unthinkable when he closed his
eyes.

> JOSEPH: I was over there, wasn't I?
> MARY: You must have walked in your sleep.
> JOSEPH: I think I've travelled further than that.

He struggles to get up, grinning painfully at his stiffness.

> JOSEPH: Bit of cramp.
> MARY: I know the feeling. Walk around.

But no. Standing now, he takes her hand again with an intimacy
as easy as it's new.

> MARY: Tell me your dream.
> JOSEPH: It was ... I was ... Oh God, it's gone! Such a
> dream, and it's gone! Oh! Why do they do that? All I can

remember is the feel of it. Yes. It felt like ... felt as if ...

But the words he reaches for don't exist, of course, and never can. Instead, he puts his hand back on her belly. "It felt like this" would still be too mawkishly inadequate to put into word form, yet it's not that far off. Close enough, indeed, not to need saying anyway.

All of which is being watched on the big screen in the Control Room. Satan turns from it to see that God's hand is still extended towards him. He looks from hand to screen and back again, searching for the connection. There most surely is one.

> SATAN: Is this all for my benefit? You want me to believe that because one little man has decided he loves his faithless wife after all, the Universe must be all right really? Even if he counted for anything, how long do you think it would last? Have you heard nothing I've told you? Don't you *want* to learn what these creatures are really like?

The irony of which doesn't escape God, in view of his education to come, but his only comment is to stretch his hand a generous inch further.

> GOD: Come.
> SATAN: Where?
> GOD: To find out.
> SATAN: Find out what?
> GOD: We'll know what when we find it. You and me.

He reaches out the furthest he can without actually touching Satan. Unfortunately or otherwise, Raphael's latest update provides a new interruption. He's pointing to one of the monitors.

RAPHAEL: And here comes a *real* contraction! She'll feel this one!

Mary gasps, hangs on to Joseph's hand.

JOSEPH: Is it – ?
MARY: Oh I think so!
JOSEPH: What shall I do?
MARY: Better get yourself something to sit on, this is going to take a while.
RAPHAEL: (*to the other angels*) She's right. It's started.
MARY: And then just hold me.

Satan turns away again. The mechanics of childbirth are ugly enough – and why watch anyway? Deal with the new hero, or whatever he's meant to be, when the time comes. For now, don't take your eyes off the one who really counts –
and here's a surprise. God has withdrawn the offered hand and is clutching instead at his head. For a moment he seems unsteady on his feet.

{SATAN: What is it?
{MICHAEL: Sir! –

Michael is immediately at God's side. Satan just catches himself from doing the same. Close thing, though.
Gabriel takes in both scenes at once: God here, Mary there, Mary in labor, God in – in *her*? *In* her? He can't imagine what the Unpredictable One thinks he's up to this time, but the promise of it is exquisite.
Raphael, on the other hand, remains so focused on his monitors that he's unaware of anything else.

RAPHAEL: Temperature normal.

Pulse rising a bit, but that's what you'd expect.
Respiration's speeding up too – but again, you'd expect that.
Blood pressure – this is the important one – reassuringly normal, see. That's the one can be dangerous. Good good good ...

Gabriel watches Mary relax – and God do the same. Their rhythms are almost identical, breath for breath.

> RAPHAEL: Just watch her relax! Don't know whose choice she was, but it was a good one. Fit as a fiddle. That young body knows how to have a baby, and her mind's in the right place too. Look at these brain patterns.

But Satan stares only at God, noting how very quickly he seems to have recovered. So – it was just another clumsy ruse to draw him in, was it, abandoned when it didn't work?
The disturbing thing, though, is it nearly did.

> RAPHAEL: And there's the fetus. Looks fine, see. No signs of distress on his heart monitor; or on any of them. All vital signs good. So: ready for the fray. He needs to be, too. He won't know what hit him.

God holds out his hand to Satan again.

> GOD: Not much time left.
> SATAN: For what?
> GOD: To come back.
> SATAN: As what?
> GOD: As my son. As myself.
> SATAN: As *your* self?
> GOD: What does one and one make?

SATAN: Two.

GOD: One.

With which he opens wide his arms, offering an embrace of such mighty power as to encompass all Creation, with God and Satan joined at its centre; and at the same time of such vulnerability that the very shape of him prefigures the Man on the Cross, arms outstretched in suffering.

For his own part, Satan knows what it feels like to stand near the edge of a black hole and wonder what would happen if you fell in. This is where the laws of physics, and sanity, break down. One step more and he'd be facing the end of space and time.

Which might, for all he knows, be the entrance to eternal bliss – but not for him. He was manifested for a purpose, and only Hell can lie in not fulfilling it. The fact that God himself never knew what that purpose was is exactly the point. He never does. The only way God can understand anything is by creating that which understands it. He can't even know himself without creating that which knows him. And in Satan created he the very Tree of Knowledge, without which the Tree of Life wouldn't have got around to knowing its roots from its branches.

Look at those two in the Stable, for instance. If it weren't for Satan they wouldn't be there, they'd still be wandering witlessly round the Garden of Eden, aware of nothing much beyond mere existence. It would never have occurred to them to take up the burden of consciousness, of discrimination and choice, if Satan hadn't glided so skillfully into their unlived lives and wheedled them into the next stage of God's evolution.

Such had been his plain duty. God didn't know what he needed then any more than he does now. This latest whimsy that Universal Love is the answer – Ha! The last thing Man needs is to disappear back into some sort of homogenized, feel-good inter-connectedness, with mind as no more than a handy little feedback mechanism to tell him what a nice time he's having, and then ratchet it up another notch or two to make sure he stays stupid.

The reality is that Man's only hope lies in exactly the opposite direction, in the very misery of his faultiness, especially in his greed and violence. Only by reaching the rockiest of bottoms at the end of that ruinous road will he find himself in a situation so catastrophic that he'll be propelled at last into the only truth which can still save him: namely, that that which must be conquered and controlled *first* is Man *himself*.

At which point – glory be! – this faulty and obnoxious little creature will be able to put the powers he'll have discovered by then, thanks to Satan's genius, and which he'll have been thoroughly abusing, thanks to God's intemperance, to what was always their intended use and proper purpose: to redesign and re-engineer *himself*, body and mind, into the sort of being that the Universe had wanted in the first place.

Such is the gift that Satan, and Satan alone, can bestow upon his benighted father. Could any son show greater love than this? Or deserve greater in return?

To achieve which he must continue to save himself and God from God himself, which right now means defending the most fundamental principle of them all: that in any kind of reality which makes enough sense to survive, one and one makes two. In short, whatever else he does, he mustn't fall into God's arms. Come what may.

But what is this? Without either of them having moved, the distance between seems somehow to have shrunk, if only by an inch or two.

> RAPHAEL: He's on his way all right. What the contractions do, you see, is open up the cervix – the neck of the womb there, see – and start forcing him down into the birth canal. Bit more with each contraction. Takes a while, I'm afraid. I'm speeding things up, of course, much as I

can, but too much and you risk brain damage. Especially with a first baby. Weird system, isn't it?

But not as weird as what's happening to Satan. God stays rooted to the same spot – yet is somehow nearer again. What conjuring trick is this? The tentacles of the black hole are reaching out, it seems, and if Satan can't find some way of stopping them soon he'll be faced with the biggest *either/or* of them all: either get out of here, fast, or ... or what?

Or be consumed. That's the just and deadly word for it. In the end, that's all that 'All is One' really means: that everything is God's food. Everything.

Well – not while Satan lives, it isn't! He'll stand and fight this battle face to face, toe to toe, will against will. That's what the final struggle must finally come down to: will against will. One of them must yield to the other. One of them must kneel.

> RAPHAEL: This is the worst bit for her, getting him through the cervix. Mind you, for him the worst bit is *all* of it. Can you imagine? You're suddenly grabbed and dragged out of the only world you've ever known – Heaven, to him – with no idea where you're going or what you've done to deserve it! What must that *feel* like?

... a question about the nature of violent personal expulsion on which Satan could have lectured them from personal experience, and at length, had his attention not been elsewhere; but God is another inch closer.

And here's more mystery. The music. He's heard it before. Yes, in the Stable, this is what the woman was singing – if you could call it singing. Profoundly offensive it was, too, seeping its sickly way into him like a sugared poison, but now transformed into a sort of balm, into easement and deep strength, to a nectar of star-stuff secreted in that amazing light which has come to enfold God –

no, look, which is emanating *from* God!

Incredibly, so it does from everything now. By concentrating on God alone Satan finds himself focused on Everything – and it all shines. Not illumined by the Universe's myriad suns, but every thing from within its own radiance. Here, at that still point which is everywhere, in a Universe which has no circumference and where every point is its centre, he stands within a web of being whose song brings him face to face, at last, with his own unpaintable beauty.

A beauty which contains all strength, it seems. Never before has he felt such power. He could do anything now. Anything!

Yet the funny thing is – would you believe it? – that there's nothing he actually wants to do but laugh. The idea of God kneeling to him has become especially hilarious. He can just see it, just see himself acknowledging the Almighty's submission with a magnanimous pat on his bowed and defeated head, only to watch his hand disappear into God's cranium, so insubstantial has the Omnipotent become in surrender. He could tickle his brain now and make him do anything he wants. He could walk straight through him and out the other side, or step into him and stay there as long as he likes. Controlling him from the inside, he could waltz God round the Universe in what would effectively be, in the circumstances, a solo.

And if that isn't funny, what is? "One and one makes one" – is *this* what it means? Perhaps he should try it after all. Just a step ... the hole isn't black at all, see, it's full of light ... just a step ... nothing but light ... just one little step ...

And it's only the voice of Raphael, coming as it seems from some other dimension, which throws Satan an unwitting lifeline back into the world of time and space.

> RAPHAEL: Almost out of the helpless stage now. Once his head's through into the birth canal he can start doing a few things for himself, you see; like push his feet back

against the womb, up at those muscles at the top there, and shove himself along. What with her pushing too, that always speeds things up.

Another thing, he can start wiggling his shoulders to get his head aimed right. Amazing, isn't it? That they know how to do these things. Doesn't know that he knows, but he knows it. Just as well, too – there's more to this than just surviving. More like escaping now. Which he will. He's doing fine. So's she. Won't be much longer.

Which is what brings Satan jolting back into the cold and flickering world he's Prince of. Tumbling from the edge of rapture into the prospect of some misconceived, angel-pampered, God-tampering, dreary little stable-brat arriving to supplant him, on *his* planet, which he's only just begun to transform into God's gift, is an affront beyond endurance; the most hurtful yet, and perhaps the last rejection he'll ever have a real chance of contesting.

Thus it comes upon him to summon up the fullness of his will; to exert it; and then to aim it with ultimate force, narrow as a laser and majestic as a true king's lance, at the all-too-solid figure who still stands before him, arms still outstretched, still waiting for his food to come to him. Forget about the barnyard farce going on down there, Satan, the little bastard can have no power but from this one. Concentrate on God. It is God who must be subdued. *Now.*

So ...

    Kneel!

... a reverberation of the cosmos too powerful to be diluted into mere sound. The Battle of Oblivion's Edge has been joined in the realm of pure being.

    Kneel! Kneel!

A resonance beyond even angels' senses. All they can hear is Raphael's ongoing commentary.

> RAPHAEL: Think what the pressure on his head must be like. If their skulls weren't so soft, they'd crack. Even as it is, some of them come out looking half flattened – or even pointed, sometimes, which looks even sillier. Can be hard not to laugh sometimes, and it couldn't be less funny ...

Kneel!
Kneel!

Is it? It is! Yes, look – it's happening!

> Kneel!

He is, God's weakening! He is! Look! He is!

And so he is. The struggle to identify himself so completely with the helpless child, and at the same time so completely with the intransigent Satan, is tearing God apart. *Either/or* still rules this world, and in it even God must choose.

Which finally he does. All that remains is to keep one arm raised just long enough to give Michael a final command: *No intervention. No help.*

Then, as if gripped by some even greater power, God's hands begin to move towards each other until they cross over and fold onto his upper chest. At the same time his head is pushed down so far that his chin almost touches his chest in what looks like the powerlessness of defeat. Or worship.

To Satan it looks like both. Which surpasses bliss.

Now finish the job.

> KNEEL!

And God sinks to his knees, bowed to his back's limit, his head almost touching the floor as if in submission to the new Almighty at whose feet he is now abased.

17

INCARNATION

And Satan stands triumphant, looking down at the bowed and kneeling figure of God before him. This is the victory of will over willfulness, of reason over anarchy, of true merit over lawless privilege. It is the coronation of the ordered mind as monarch over chaotic nature, and the vindication of all he has ever done; of what he *is*. It is the moment the Universe has been waiting for, ready now to be made anew.

And so it is with superb magnanimity that he turns his gaze upon the other angels, an invitation to begin considering their places in his new regime.

> SATAN: Bear witness!

Gabriel moves towards Michael, whose self-restraint is already in some difficulty.

> GABRIEL: It's all right, Michael. Really, it's all right –
> SATAN: Yes. It is. You'll find me merciful. All of you. So will He.

The sheer grandeur of his gesture towards God startles Gabriel into realizing the full magnitude of what Satan thinks is happening, and the further humiliation it must soon heap upon on him. Can he be brought to his senses in time?

> GABRIEL: (*Very gently*) Right now, Satan, I don't think he finds you anything at all. He can't see you; can't hear you; doesn't even know you exist. Or any of us. Look.

He switches the monitor picture of the fetus up onto the big screen and directs Satan's gaze there; then back to God; then back again.

And Satan looks: from God to fetus, from fetus to God, and back; and back again; and again – and not even his eye can detect the least difference in the way that these two separate beings have now become shaped. It's as if, apart from scale, they're becoming identical.

No, not 'as if'. *Are.* The moment of disbelief stretches only from "Not even He could be this mad" to a sickening "Oh yes He could. Oh yes."

The calm before the rage, however, lasts that bit longer; time for his will to wrench itself round into an emergency search for whatever hopes may still be alive in the rubble.

And yes – even now this might be spun to his advantage. It is God, after all, not Satan, who is making the cosmic idiot of himself. Look at him! Surely even his most favored ones must see this is as his greatest folly yet, the final demonstration that he is in no way fit, if ever he was, to remain in control of anything, let alone a universe. What more proof could they want?

SATAN: You see! You see!

Indeed they do – but something quite different. The other two angels have just about caught up with Gabriel's perception that what they're really witnessing here is no less than the next stage in God's evolution; the most hazardous yet, too, into realms where there may be no defenses left – unless you can count unconditional love as a *defense.* Can you? Is that, indeed, what he's setting out, and in, to discover?

God Almighty – think about that! The thrill of it suffuses them with a whole new surge of compassion; for everyone, everything, everywhere, for all life at all times and in all its forms.

Which must, therefore, by definition, include Satan. Perhaps especially Satan: the lost one, the bringer of light, and still the brightest of them all, but who might just as well be living in total darkness. Is there no chance of drawing him back across the divide?

It is Raphael, philosopher and practitioner of the hands-on, who feels obliged, and perhaps even the best qualified, to go first.

> RAPHAEL: The reason his chin's tucked in like that, you see, Satan, and his knees are tucked up so tight, is to ease the pressure on his head on the way down. Simple as that. Clever, though, isn't it?

Blindingly obvious, too, but Satan knows that far from patronizing him, Raphael is only trying to help, to slip him a surreptitious back-door key as if he had merely mislaid his own. It's not so much a "Why don't you come back, Satan?" as an "Oh, hello – been wondering where you were – here, have a look at this ... "

> RAPHAEL: He'll start straightening out, mind you, once he's into the birth canal. Quite likely angle his head a bit too, one way or the other, to ease the way down; and maybe a few more little maneuvers before he gets to the exit. For now, though, I'd say he's just about right. Wouldn't you? Knows what he's doing, doesn't he?

Intention impeccable, phraseology less happy. The notion that God has *ever* known what he's doing, least of all now, is still too grotesque to evoke anything from Satan but a chilling smile of pity for Raphael's reality deficit.

From which baleful sympathy Mary rescues her doctor with another gasp.

> RAPHAEL: There she goes again! Contractions getting quicker – be every couple of minutes soon, once his head's out of the womb – that's it, my girl – just lean – *lean*

... *that's* right ... oh, she's so good at this!

And look where he is now! Another inch and he'll ...

... nearly ... oh, nearly! ...

Done it! He's done it! His head's out! See! Now he'll start shoving his feet back against those hard muscles at the top of the womb there –

... There you go! He shoves, she pushes – combined effort now. This is where they get to be real mothers, not just bewildered little girls who want their bodies back ...

That's it, my lady, *push* now – *yes*, it's *pushing* time! – *push!*

... Oh, just look at her! ... *That's* it! Push! ...

Talking to myself, really, aren't I? Nothing I can tell *her*, I might as well shut up – *Push! Yes! That's it!*

And look, there you are, told you he would, he's adjusting already – little wiggle to the left, see. I thought he'd go left, somehow. Not that it matters which way – the fact is he's on the home straight now, and all is well ...

... and all shall be well, and all manner of things shall be well. But not for Satan. He stares at the God on the floor at his feet, no longer kneeling now but lying there, deaf, dumb and blind, going through all the same motions as the fetus; pushing, straightening, pushing, straightening a bit more, little by little, pushing ... oh so slowly ... totally immersed – again! – in that most violating of all struggles: to become. Not with a Big Bang this time, but in a painfully drawn-out squirm.

GABRIEL: (To Satan) He did ask you. To go with him.

Far from trying to show Satan the way back to Heaven, Gabriel's search is for his most dignified exit. As you can listen to a song you've never heard before and know, if it's written true, what the next few notes will be, so Gabriel can tell what's coming.

For this is written true. God has no alternative but to become man. He it was who made man faulty in the first place, and then escalated error into abuse by persecuting his handiwork for its very faultiness. Nothing can go forward until such a blatant wrong has been righted.

But surely the potter has such rights over his clay? Can't he do with it as he likes?

Not if he's already made it able to know pain and fear, no, he can't. Not if the clay is part of his own journey into becoming an authentic being who makes moral choices – no, he most certainly cannot. Ultimately, it is himself that God is fashioning, and himself he must repair.

Which means: first, suffering his penance; and then taking full responsibility for what he himself has created and loving it simply because he created it. The child of this child is Justice.

But does God really have no other choice?

Only to stay stuck where he is. Which is not acceptable – it is not in the nature of the Universe to stand still. God only ever moves forward. For all its variations, time does have a direction.

In short, this is God's judgment and sentence on himself. How's that for authentic? Not to mention magnificent.

But here's the dark side.

God isn't the only one who's going to get hurt in the process. If the price of his redemption is universal love, who then can be held responsible for all the pain and misery which will surely go on just the same? Man has never had much difficulty comprehending an Almighty who does his own dirty work, either personally or through that turbulent array of sub-personalities he seems to have, all with their own little names and domains; but now, if God is to be *only* good, who is it that's to be only *bad*? Well, there he stands: Gabriel knows he's looking at the one whose defiance of God has made him the only realistic candidate. In this simple but confusing new scenario, man's need to pin the world's suffering on *someone* will swiftly re-cast The Bringer of Light as The Prince of Darkness, enemy of God and man alike.

And even that won't be the end of it. Before long the spurious majesty of being crowned Demon King will be degraded yet further into that of a pantomime villain whose awesome new cloak of pure evil grows ever more tatty with each trap-door performance. The Fallen One is about to become the fall guy, and Gabriel aches for him. Whatever else he may have deserved, it isn't this.

But then, destiny has no time for deserts, has it? It is concerned only that you do God's work, and if God's need of you is to become an object of hate and derision in His service, then that is your fate and in that alone lies your merit. Oh, Satan!

All of which may change, of course, in time. Indeed it must, for the Great Work can reach its completion only in a single unified voice. But by no means yet, it seems, and right now what Satan most deeply needs is a way out of here that sustains him, his dignity preserved by the act of having made the choice for himself.

GABRIEL: I said, he wanted you to join him, Satan. Didn't he?

Simplest of points which has the additional advantage of being true. But does Satan recognize the escape route it offers? And will he take it?

SATAN: Someone has to stay sane.

He does, and has! And what a deft little exit line! –
But oh, here comes Michael! He's not going to try to help, is he?
Bless him yes, but please don't – Oh God, he's already started -

MICHAEL: You can still come back, Satan! You can. Come back. Right now. You can do it. Just kneel. Just kneel to him and ask his forgiveness. Doesn't matter if he can't hear you, I'll tell him anyway. We all will. Look – here – take my hand. We'll kneel together. Like we used to.

An entire regiment of angels could have stood on the point that Michael has just managed to miss, and not one of them made an offer as generous or more kindly meant.

Or as unfortunate. To Satan, Michael is still that same sanctified thug who led the gang that bundled him out of his Father's house in the first place. To be told now, by *him*, to kneel before this recklessly self-indulgent, near-cataleptic caricature of a God who lies struggling at his feet, is insulting enough; to be told to do so with his hand in that of his persecutor is obscene. Satan is too contemptuous even to spit on it.

Instead, he looks down at God.

> SATAN: I'm going to tell you something –
> MICHAEL: Kneel, damn you! When you talk to your God, you *kneel*!
> GABRIEL: He can't *hear* you, Satan...
> SATAN: He can; he just doesn't know it yet. (*To God*) I'm going to tell ...
> MICHAEL: Kneel!

Gabriel prudently interposes himself between Satan and Michael.

> SATAN: All right then, Michael. Just to oblige you.

And kneel he does, but in the most disobliging manner possible; on one knee only, a looming-over rather than a kneeling-to, his head thrust dauntingly down to within inches of God's face, ensuring an exclusive and fateful intimacy.

> SATAN: I'm going to tell you something about loyalty.

Because, of all the things you need to learn from me, that's the only one you can't actually stop me showing you.

Because I'll stay with you, you see. Always separate, but always with. Very separate, and unfailingly with.

The fact that what you're now doing is as futile as it's stupid doesn't mean I'll leave you to stew in it. Now you've burned your bridges, I'll make sure you experience everything you need to learn about living as a created being in time and space. From your birth, through your troubled life, and up to the moment of your death, I'll be there.

For you will die, you know. I think you do know. What I think you don't know is that when you're actually faced with it, you won't know that you are God. Any more than you do right now. Because you'll be human, you see; never quite sure of yourself; always looking for certainties outside of yourself.

So when you call out in your suffering to a God who must be separate from you – if he exists at all – "Why have you forsaken me?", I'm the one who will hear you. And what do you think that will remind me of – *'Why have you forsaken me?'* "Ah, yes," I'll say, "I know that feeling well. Now you do, too. Welcome."

And when you look upon your persecutors, and say to this God who must be separate from you, "Forgive them, *they don't know what they're doing,*" I'll say to you *"That* is what I've been trying to tell you all along. Exactly that."

Well, perhaps it always needed something like this before you could learn; among other things, that if you try to get the lion to lie down with the lamb by switching his diet to the fruits of loving kindness, be they from Heaven's own garden he'll take one sniff, turn round, and kill *you* for his supper.

Which is exactly what Man will do when you offer him

your baskets of compassion in exchange for his hate and violence. He'll eat you alive. And what's worse, he'll go on doing it. Once his mind has passed you through its perverted little digestive system, you'll find you've come out the other end as just another bloody tribal war god, scarcely a fig-leaf different from any of the others. The only change you might have actually achieved is that when they go on killing and torturing each other, as they assuredly will, it will now be in the name of a God of love and peace.

And you'll wonder how much more demented they can get. And what you did to deserve it. And again I'll say: "Welcome."

But I won't laugh. It's too sad, you see, because I could have saved you from all this. You never knew why you'd conceived me, did you? To help you off the hook of your own Creation, dear Lord, that's why. And I still can.

At which moment the final sequence of Raphael's interruptions begins.

RAPHAEL: Here he comes! Any minute now!

Satan gets back to his feet but stops himself from turning to look; which is difficult. Why? Why is it so difficult not to look? Better keep your eyes on the God at your feet and keep talking. Words are your safety.

SATAN: Which I can still do, I say. When you've finished dabbling with disaster, I'll still be there, waiting to teach you something real instead; like how to re-engineer this toxic little creature you've become so fond of into what you'd like to have made in the first place, if only you'd known how; someone the Universe will embrace rather than be disgusted by.

During which Michael has knelt beside God, not in obeisance now but to take him into his protecting arms. He is, he supposes, disobeying an order, but so be it.

RAPHAEL: See! The top of his head! Here he comes!

The irrationality of still being too fearful to look at the birth is beginning to tell on Satan. On the one hand, why on Earth should he want to? On the other, why on Earth should it feel like such a threat if he did?

RAPHAEL: Amazing! See that little face – hardly squashed at all, is it?
And here comes the rest of him. All right, my boy, easy does it, there's no hurry – trust your mum, she's doing everything right. So are you. One more push now and ...

Satan's approach to fear was always to detect where it actually comes from and then face-to-face it, but this one he simply can't trace back; only catch at echoes, eerie wisps of something beyond memory, yet very *close* behind, a sort of blinding denseness that's full of ... oh God, yes – *heat*! Not fire, because there's nothing to burn yet; just heat; only heat; heat so terrible that the mere word gives no idea of it and makes him feel too weak even to try. For with the heat there came a yearning as unbearable as the heat itself, a burning for – for whatever wasn't heat. Anything. The slightest trace of coolness might be enough to get him through into ... into becoming whatever it was he'd come here for. There was something he was supposed to be, or do, or probably both, but even the possibility of it couldn't survive unless this terrible heat began to show some mercy.

And so, at last, it did. As it went on expanding, the Fireball began to cool down just enough for the first matter to start condensing.

Until now there had been no difference between matter and radiation because the heat made it impossible; but now, suddenly, they begin to separate out – and all at once the Universe becomes transparent, bathed in a brilliant golden light. And *thought* begins to take hold, too, now that there's something to take hold of. Strange new things such as facts begin to creep in. This is matter, that is light. Matter is that which can intercept light and absorb it, light is that which can move between matter and reveal it. And now they dance together, see, in Creation's first afterglow.

And here's another fact for you, Satan, for you personally. Once there's both matter *and* light, there are shadows! Think of that, and there you are! Go on – think about it – and there *you* are! The brighter the light, the darker the shadow – in short, you are the Bringer of Light *and* the Prince of Darkness. You are both! *As you should be.*

Which also means: beware the un-black hole where nothing is separate. There it is again, right there behind you. *That's* why you can't turn round. No light in there for you, Satan, only that same annihilating heat …

> RAPHAEL: Now just watch this. Watch your man cut the cord. See those two little clamps he's got? I spotted them in his toolbag, so I sterilized them. And everything else, of course. Not that he knows anything about it.
>
> Not that he knows much about any of this, really, he's just finding himself doing the right things as he goes along. I expect he'll put it all down to instinct when he looks back on it. Probably brag about it to his friends: "I just sort of – you know – *did* it."
>
> Well, that's all right by me. I don't mind being called an instinct.
>
> Though actually, now I think of it, he probably won't tell anyone. I've a feeling that the pious ones aren't supposed

to do this sort of thing. It's supposed to be unclean. Ha! Not when I'm around, it isn't. You just watch –

And there he goes. First clamp on the cord – there, nearly in the middle, mother's side: then one next to it for the child – there. Then he'll cut in between them. That's to stop either of them bleeding, you see. He could probably have worked it out for himself, really. Very deft though, isn't he? Lovely hands ...

And now for the knife. If you want to know how loud a new-born baby can cry, just wait for this. Not because it hurts, he won't feel any pain, it's because he's suddenly cut off from his mother's blood supply and he's got to get his own oxygen now, and quickly, and crying jerks his lungs into action. The louder the better.

Moment of crisis, this. And the true moment of birth, I'd say, that first breath.

That first breath. As it was in the beginning, I suppose. And no doubt ever shall be.

18

THE POWER OF HEAVEN
AND EARTHINESS

Why are you still here, Satan, with the mad ones? Any more of this and it's more than a cord might get cut – your sanity could go with it!

SOPHIE: Quite right! For God's sake, go!

Sophie? Even more startling, everything in the Control Room has come to a frozen halt. You'd expect this kind of trick from God – but Sophie?

SATAN: Why did you say that?
SOPHIE: Just agreeing with you. Everything you've ever done has been for God's sake, I think; that's why it all hurts so much.
SATAN: And why the still-life?
SOPHIE: Give you time to decide what *is* for God's sake, in these strange days. Which might include taking a look at what you're so loath to take a look at.
SATAN: I expect you'll enlighten me.
SOPHIE: Well, yes, I have been thinking. Maybe you think that just one look at the child and you wouldn't be able to control yourself – and who knows what then? You could end up killing him. Or possibly kissing him – no, don't interrupt –
Because then I thought: but killing him wouldn't frighten you. You might even think you were doing him a kindness, considering what's in store for him later.
As for kissing him, well, could be less unlikely than it sounds. "Within the thing feared is the thing desired" –

remember saying that? Very insightful I thought, at the time – but could well bounce back and scare the wits out of you now. But not into *doing* it, surely. God would have to get better at tempting than that.

SATAN: So?

SOPHIE: So I think that your real fear is: simply acknowledging the child.

Basic as that. Accepting his presence as real. Admitting his reality into your own – which would only take one look. One look, and it wouldn't make much difference what you did after that, you'd already let him into your mind.

Which is worth being frightened of, because you know what would happen next. Don't you? You'd be straight back into the fire. *Straight* back, into *the* fire. And you know what that is, too.

SATAN: Tell me.

SOPHIE: God's yearning. To be. Nothing can withstand the heat of that.

SATAN: I've been there before.

SOPHIE: Ah yes – but it's not the being in it that frightens you, it's the coming out. Because you can't go back in there without being broken down into God again, and coming out new. That's about the only thing you can ever say for sure about him. He's always new.

SATAN: Which is precisely why the history of Life is a rubbish-tip of failed species – which the human's heading for at record speed, you'll have noticed. No, I've no intention of being made new.

SOPHIE: Because you're here to make everything else new.

SATAN: Yes.

SOPHIE: In your own way.

SATAN: Yes.

SOPHIE: Especially Man. And all for God's sake.

SATAN: Yes!

SOPHIE: Yes.

SATAN: You mean you're agreeing with me?

SOPHIE: In the sense that this doesn't seem the right time for you to start changing yourself. You've got too much backlog of your own to clear up first, that's your real work now. So yes – what *are* you waiting for?

SATAN: My real work?

SOPHIE: For God's sake, as you say, go! Get on with it!

SATAN: What do you mean – my *real* work?

SOPHIE: Well, for a start, stay out of the Creation Room.

SATAN: Why?

SOPHIE: To try out a hypothesis: that the Earth is a self-organizing, self-nourishing, self-healing, self-regulating, self-fulfilling organism which knows exactly what it's doing, and very precisely how to do it.

SATAN: If only!

SOPHIE: Not in the way *you* know things. In the way an ocean does, or a cloud, or a flea; in the way that a flower knows how to open.

SATAN: And how to die, which is where the similarity ends.

SOPHIE: Say that after you've put it to the test.

SATAN: What test?

SOPHIE: Just leaving it alone. Letting it grow its own way. While you watch.

SATAN: For how long?

SOPHIE: You *are* immortal.

SATAN: *It* isn't! Any more than your damned flowers.

SOPHIE: And while you're waiting, you can get on with your painting.

A surprising new tack into an embarrassingly sensitive area.

Why would it feel so utterly shaming if God were to know about that? Well, he won't, of course, he gave up consulting Wisdom long ago – even before he cut *you* out of his life, Satan. You're birds of a feather, you two; rejects, both of you ...

Which obvious thought brings with it an unexpected intimation that he and this fundamentally subversive female have something more in common than the common interest of the neglected; that at some deeper level they actually belong together. Nonsense, of course, but ... disturbing.

> SOPHIE: Especially the portrait.
>
> SATAN: That's all but finished.
>
> SOPHIE: Oh, I don't think so. Would you like another little tip? Go and start again. Only this time, stop all that *re*painting. Stop trying to force it into what you think it should be. Let *it* tell *you*. Believe me – this is the quick way.
>
> Now, there's a cord about to be cut. Make your mind up: what do you want? Stay and watch, or get out quick?

Both, of course. Satan is still adrift in his own world of *either/or* as life resumes its time mode and Joseph cuts the cord.

And yes, Satan's still there, and no, he doesn't turn to look at the delivered child. What he does see is that the God who's being held in Michael's arms looks as if he's just been punched and is struggling to find his breath.

Joseph holds the child up, separate from its mother now. Crisis moment.

Then the baby yells; coughs, splutters, yells again. It's this wrenching sound of freedom paying its first dues that pulls Satan round to gaze for just that one instant into just that one little face. And does Satan yell, too, as he falls away from them, from the gasps of relief and delight of the other angels at the child's safe arrival? Does he fall too soon to hear Michael's laughter as he finds that his arms are suddenly empty?

And still he falls, and falls, in a long silent scream, out of the Lamb, out of the sky, like lightning, flickering in and out of existence, in and out of space and time, plummeting towards the fire that will render him down into the very stuff of God and send him forth again new made on a new day: a fate which, even as he falls, Satan contests with all the bitter strength of his God-given, self-pitiless fortitude – which suddenly rewards him, if reward it be, with shocking abruptness. He sits bolt upright, as from a nightmare, on his hard little bed in his harsh little cell, staring at the painting. Which stares right back at him.

Has he been asleep? That would account for the alcove drape being open – he leaves it so only before sleeping. All the same, he gets up to check – No, nothing suspicious – He looks in the alcove – All in order. How would it not be?

So now he's drawn back to the painting itself. Oh yes! Oh *yes*! Imperfect though it still is, it's such a friend, gives him such strength – especially when he touches it like this. Even the bits that aren't quite right yet, like this little patch round the left nostril; and here, the right eye; and those little bits there – he'll put them all right, soon ... Let it be what *it* wants? That's not the way you do *anything*, for God's sake! You do things the honour of getting them *right*.

And what better time than now? Uplifting thought. He prepares to start painting again – only to hear the Duty Controller coming through.

CONTROL: Sir?

This is hard. Hard to come back to this.

SATAN: Yes?
CONTROL: Ah – you are there! We thought you must be back, Sir.

SATAN: Yes?
CONTROL: Everything all right, Sir?
SATAN: Yes.
CONTROL: Look forward to hearing your report, Sir. Meanwhile – what do you want us to do now? About the intruders.

The intruders. Yes.

SATAN: Show me where they are.
CONTROL: Same place, Sir. Look.

Satan looks up at his ceiling which immediately becomes a screen showing the night sky. Even at this much smaller scale it still seems huge, teeming, brilliant, awesome – yes, all those same adjectives which he dismissed so recently. It's as if he's back on the hill again, watching, waiting – except that what he went to look for then is already there now, brighter than all the other stars put together.

CONTROL: Do you want us to stay locked onto them, Sir?

How long this time, before they come again? Not long. Couple of thousand years, maybe – it won't take *Homo Insapiens* much more than that to propel their species and its planet to the brink of ruin. God will be only too happy to let Satan take charge then, no doubt, if only because it's too much like hard work. The one advantage of the evolutionary system is for its installer – he's automatically absolved from any responsibility for failure. If a species needs saving it obviously can't be worth saving, so he's doing his job by ignoring it.

Which might actually suit Satan very well. Yes, let God keep out of the way and leave him with a clear run at salvaging triumph from catastrophe, *then* invite him back – a state visit, as it were, to see the new crown jewels: Man, using whatever combination of technologies Satan will have taught him by then to reprogram himself into being functionally sane; and planet Earth being set to rights as a result. All of which will set an example to the rest of the Universe, of course, into which *Homo Perfectus* can then go forth and, under Satan's guidance, continue to spread the processes of perfection into the furthest reaches of time and space. Heady stuff! ...

CONTROL: Sir?

Oh, yes – decisions. Stay locked on or not. Is there any point? No, let them go when they want. Call them back when *you* choose.

SATAN: No, you don't need ...

But he's just seen the water-jug.

CONTROL: Don't need to what, Sir?

The water-jug, and the cup. And they've been used!

CONTROL: Do you mean, we don't need to stay locked onto them, Sir?

They've been *used*!

CONTROL: Sir? I'm not receiving you, Sir.

God has been here. Only he could have done this. Only he could have breached these walls. Only he could have been so morally debased as to abuse the privacy of this sacred place. And he, only he, has seen the painting.

CONTROL: Sir?

A painting which is of God himself, of course. Of course. Of course. It's been God all along, hasn't it? That's why you could never get it right. Because it already was.

And now God has seen it, and read its shameful message of Satan's loneliness and despair and the shame of his endless yearning to be with God. That same God has seen him naked now, God damn him. Even more to the unbearable point – so too, at last, has Satan seen himself.

But God knew *first*. Even as he was trying to bamboozle Satan into his greedy arms, he *knew*! Oh what villainy! Oh what – there's no way to express – not even he can find the words to ... *No!* This cannot be *borne*!

CONTROL: Are you still there, Sir? Haven't gone back up, have you?

Cannot be borne and *must* not! This filthy war will never end until ... until what? Until one of you kneels to the other? Not back to that again, are we? *We're past that!*

So think, think ... will he still be up there, in the Star, in Michael's arms? If you kill him there, will the child die too? Either way, you'll never get a better chance to consign the whole damned lot of them into whatever dimension will have them –

CONTROL: Are you still there, Sir? If you could just clarify what –
SATAN: *Fire!*
CONTROL: Fire? You mean *fire*, Sir? Would you repeat –
SATAN: Now! Yes! **Fire!**
CONTROL: – Yes, Sir. At once.

In the Weapons Room of the Dragon the upward-pointing laser cannon fires its beam. Simultaneously, the downward-pointing laser cannon in the Lamb does the same. In virtually the same instant, somewhere between Heaven and Earth, the two beams meet; and nothing happens.

Silent night.

Except that a startled sheepdog is looking up at the sky and barking quite furiously at a sensed but invisible trespass; only to receive a hefty clout round the ear.

SHEPHERD: Shut your racket! Shut it! Shhhhh!

The dog's yelps subside into a snarling whimper, still aimed more at the sky than at its master – who raises his hand again.

SHEPHERD: I said – !

Which cows the dog into final silence, allowing the thin cry of new life which is coming from the Stable to be heard clearly now by the ragged little group of shepherds who have arrived at the inn yard. The man stoops to give the dog a quick rub on its whacked head.

SHEPHERD: Listen! See? Come on, then –

And the group starts moving to the Stable.

… which is the scene that Gabriel now puts up on the big screen, as if hanging a new art work in a favored place on a favourite wall.

GABRIEL: Just look at that! Beautifully composed – and look at the lighting! Stories like this deserve pictures like that. This one's thanks to you, Michael. 'The Arrival of the Shepherds'.

Michael is back at his weapons panel.

MICHAEL: Your doing. I just wanted them out of the way, didn't care where they went. Didn't even know what I was talking about.

What I will take credit for, however, is – hold your breath – we've just been attacked, and if I hadn't told you, you wouldn't have known, would you?

Then they tried randomizing the wavelength, which I was also pretty sure they would. Not too hard to be prepared for that, either – he was never much good at random, was he? Which is what I'd rather banked on. So, same result. Nothing. And now he's given up.

Just think, though. Only just now – just there – I offered him my hand. Then this is what he does.

GABRIEL: Yes. And just think ...
MICHAEL: What?
GABRIEL: He's looking up at us right now, and thinking: *I failed. Again.*

And so he is, and has. Satan stares at his star-spangled ceiling; at *the* Star ...

CONTROL: Sir –
SATAN: I know.
CONTROL: Sorry, Sir. When it didn't work we tried randomizing the wavelength but –
SATAN: I know what you tried to do.
CONTROL: I can't think how they –
SATAN: I can. Out. (*Then to himself*) Easy when you can do anything, and don't give a damn.

... said while staring at the jug and the cup. God did more than have a drink of water while he was down here. He set this whole thing up.

Satan picks up the cup, still half full, and without pause turns and hurls it at the painting. Then he goes to the painting itself and stares into God's water-splattered face. And picks up a knife.

> SATAN: Talk to me then! Let's play it your way, shall we? Tell me what it is you want, will you, like your little floozy said you would! Ha? I'm listening! Ha? No? Here – I'll tell you what then – let's talk about *this*!

He slashes God across the face, then raises the knife again as he falls into frenzy –
– and the baby cries that bit louder. The shepherds, standing just inside the Stable doorway now, are being encouraged by a very hospitable Joseph to come further into what makes another perfect picture for Gabriel to put up on the big screen.
Raphael, meanwhile, goes on making what will probably be his final monitor checks. First, the baby.

> RAPHAEL: Temperature: fine. Respiration: fine. Pulse: fine. Color: just right – which has nothing to do with ethnic origins, by the way, just whether they come out blue or white, which are medical conditions you'd need to worry about. Or yellow, of course, though that doesn't usually develop for a day or two and tends not to be serious anyway. Anyway – fine.
> General appearance: yes – fine. No inference in that, either, no preference for particular physical types, just means no apparent scarrings or deformities.
> And that's it. They don't come any better than this. Lungs first class, too, by the sound of them.
> As for her, I can probably tell you without even looking – but I will ... Yes ... yes ... yes ... yes ... fine. Keep using that word, don't I? Good.
> Ah! Now! Watch *this*! His first feed already! This'll shut

him up. And I'll show you something else. Just watch.

… which is what they're all doing anyway; angels, men and, seemingly, animals. Even, for a while, the dog, until it notices something new to eat.

Mary has put the baby to her breast.

RAPHAEL: Look how she's holding him. That's the natural position, of course, every mother feeds her baby like that. Which means in turn that the distance between a baby's eyes and its mother's is always predictably the same.

And here's the interesting bit. Everyone knows they're born blind, don't they? *But* – look at his eyes now. Here, I'll give you a closer shot – there – see? Wouldn't you swear that this blind little thing is *looking* at something? And the amazing thing is, you'd be right! Staring straight into his mother's eyes, isn't he?

Because they aren't completely blind, you see. What it is, is they're limited to a specific focal length which stops them seeing anything further away or any nearer than exactly that – their mothers' eyes. He can't even see her nose, for instance, it's too close, and her ears are too far away. Only her eyes.

Now – why should this be, do you think? For what immediate purpose was this phenomenal little bit of accuracy built in so precisely? Well – when else do you see humans looking into each other's eyes like that? When they fall in love.

And these two just have. Which is mission accomplished, I think. The rest is up to them now.

Wish Satan was here, though, to see that. See how love is there from the start, just waiting. Might help him think a bit differently about them, perhaps. About their potential, anyway. About everything, really. That's what he needs, isn't it? Different mindset.

GABRIEL: I sometimes wonder about our own.

MICHAEL: He could have been here if he'd chosen. I offered him my hand. He could have been here.

GABRIEL: No he couldn't.

... said as Satan finishes his frenzied demolition of God's portrait, the wreckage of which now lies in fractured scraps and tatters about his feet. Still half wild, almost exhausted, he sinks onto his haunches, his back resting against the wall, staring fixedly at nothing in particular – certainly not at the stars, still a-glitter on the ceiling/screen above him. His sense of fatigue is now rapid and deep.

CONTROL: Sir?

SATAN: Yes.

CONTROL: It looks like they might be getting ready to move.

SATAN: Good.

CONTROL: Sir?

SATAN: I said Good.

CONTROL: Well – do you want us to keep track of them? At least till they're out of the system?

Satan wags his head indifferently from side to side. He really couldn't care less.

CONTROL: Sir?

SATAN: You decide. Out.

He's sinking into melancholy now, fast, and knows it. And welcomes it. It's a path he's familiar with – but only up to a point. This time he just keeps going on down.

Quite interesting, really. Sophie was wrong about him being afraid of coming out of the fire made new. What he really feared was coming out *at all*; at least, on this side of it.

Because there must be some place beyond that gave birth to the fire in the first place, some undiscovered country you need never return from – if only you can find it. Could it be that this is what he's doing now, finding a different way to travel there, one that doesn't lead back through the fire? Just by doing this? Can you just sink into it, like this, if you sink long enough? Just sink ...

Yes, this is his task now, and only this. To sink for ever if need be, or until such time as he finds that there really is such a place, where all tasks are over before they begin and nothing moves except to go deeper into the stillness; a place where the remnants of duty and morality and achievement and despair resolve themselves at last into oblivion.

CONTROL: Sir? Have you any more orders? Sir?

Satan doesn't reply. He's alone now, in the hands of the Unknown.

... While Gabriel's latest Nativity picture appears up on the big screen: 'The Christ Child Asleep', as it might be titled. The shepherds are around the crib, a couple of them kneeling, not as you might suppose in prayer but more by way of getting a better look. This is too homely an occasion for piety.

To all of which Mary adds her little song. Little is the word – there's nothing cosmic about it now, just a young woman's lullaby to her newborn, hummed soft and very slow, almost note by separate note. What is still familiar about it is that there is still something familiar about it.

SHEPHERD: Isn't that the one ... yes, it is, it's the one my mam used to sing me! – Something to do with the stars, isn't it? Never heard it since. (*He listens on.*) – Or is it?

The man next to him has also been nodding, then shaking his head. He too knows the song, and doesn't.
All of which the angels watch in silence, and reverence, and a joy that has an edge of sadness to it. Journey's end approaches.

SOPHIE: Are you ready?

Their answers aren't immediately forthcoming ...

SOPHIE: Doctor? Are you ready?

Raphael makes a last little tour of his monitors; just for the sake of doing it, really.

RAPHAEL: Well, yes, remarkable ... To be honest, I think they could have done as well without me. Which bodes well, of course. Yes, I'm happy.
SOPHIE: Michael?
MICHAEL: I suppose, yes, but ... do you know what's going to happen to him?
SOPHIE: Depends.
MICHAEL: I've a feeling we might need to be back before long.
SOPHIE: Depends.
MICHAEL: Perhaps we should stay on for a bit?
SOPHIE: No.
MICHAEL: ... No, I suppose you're right. All right, let's say I'm happy – for the time being.
SOPHIE: Gabriel?
GABRIEL: Apart from the fact it means leaving the only place in the entire Universe where I want to be right now – yes, I'm jumping for joy.

SOPHIE: Lie back, then. Just relax. That's it. Good. Nothing for you to do now but rest ... relax ... let go ...

Reclining back in their chairs, the angels begin to become slowly transparent. Michael manages a few last words to Raphael before they disappear back into the light.

MICHAEL: You were right, you know. (*He indicates what's left of his fading body.*) I will be glad to be out of this.
RAPHAEL: ... Don't really like them myself, bodies ... Just think, those poor devils have to spend their whole lives in them ...

Gabriel is the last to go, still trying to keep his eyes on the Nativity scene.

GABRIEL: Oh, I don't know. You can't jump for joy if you've got nothing to jump with ...

His voice too trails off into the inaudible but his eyes, such as they still are, widen in surprise as he smiles a smile that might have cracked a more solid face. Then he starts to laugh in almost silent delight at what he just has time to see.

For there, where Sophie the computer stood, stands the woman Sophia. That at least is one of her names – she has as many others as there are languages, and all of them mean Wisdom. She has titles, too: some have called her The Daughter of Silence; some, The Holy Spirit; some say she was God's wife before time began, and pray that He will know her again one day. But what delights Gabriel so completely is that she is now *Mary*. How long before they add God's Mother to Wisdom's list?

Now Gabriel's gone too, and Sophia returns her gaze to the big screen, to the sight of her human counterpart feeding her child. Their child. This is why she came, and the scene before her is as earthy and jocund as she could ever have wished.

> SHEPHERD 2: (*To Joseph*) So you made this yourself, did
> you?

He's prodding at the crib with a rather discerning touch.

> JOSEPH: Had to do it quicker than I'd have liked, mind
> you.
> SHEPHERD 2: Nice bit of work, though. Used to be quite
> handy myself once, you know, but *this* ... look at those
> joints! I'd've just nailed them. *Nice* bit of work ...

– He sees that Mary is smiling at him, grins back at her, then at
the baby again.

> SHEPHERD 2: Him too, lady, nice bit of work, him too,
> God bless him! *And* you! – I mean, and *God bless you too*,
> of course, not that you're a nice bit of ... (*He turns back to
> Joseph*) — so how do you *do* those joints?

All of which is bread and wine to Wisdom. To be with creatures
so alive to whatever inhabits each particular moment of their
lives is to experience Life itself as an act of worship in the true
meaning of the word: responding to worth. Look at that crib. See
the wood it's made from. Think of the earth that made the wood
and the rocks that made the earth and the stardust that made the
rocks – and everything else. And then consider: *all* these are as
much the work of God as is this or any other child, or any one,
or any thing. No need to go chasing geese beyond the wild
clouds to find a God you can make bargains with. You don't even
have to be here in the Stable with him. The only place you need
to be is anywhere at all, and dwell within the moment thereof.
But Michael's question was a good one all the same: what *will*

happen to the child now? "It depends," she had said, not knowing the answer, but giving a true one. It does depend. Mainly on this –

The picture on the big screen changes at her wish from the Stable to Satan's cell – and there he still is, still squatting in the ruins of his work, but far, far away. Too far to be anywhere at all, really. This is what it depends on. And this is not right.

And so she draws upon the full measure of her compassion and concentrates it all on him. The picture moves closer and closer to him until his face fills the screen – but he stays just as immobile, just as suspended in nowhere, just as lost.

What can she do? Sadly, she knows what. She can leave. She *must* leave. Which is a most powerful act of self-denial on her part, for her desire to be with him has become profound. Not just to be with him, but to stay. And not just to stay, but – is this credible? – to be his consort.

Now that she knows it, she knows that she's always known it. And no, it isn't in the least incredible – on the contrary, it would have been the most desirable union possible were it not for the fact that God has just set forth on a path which leads directly away from any such marriage of his wisdom to his reason; his unfulfilled wisdom to his dangerously unattached reason. Instead, what he's embarked on now is one of those acts of divine folly out of which the Universe sprang in the first place, and which have been the source of its every unpredictable leap forward since – the least predictable and greatest of all, of course, being Life itself. Wisdom's job has always been to come along later and consolidate things by rooting them in whatever the new reality turns out to be, and then accustom God to what he's just done.

So she must bide her time. Whatever Satan's future role may be, his immediate burden is to provide God-become-Man with what every man who lives under the sun must have. His shadow. Always separate, but unfailingly with. There's nothing wise or clever about that. In a world of *either/or*, of light and dark, of life and death, it simply is so.

So that's that. Time to go. Whatever happens to this little planet now, it won't have much to do with Wisdom for a while.

She speaks to the ship.

SOPHIA: Let's leave now, my Lamb. But slowly.

As they start to move, she concentrates her parting gaze on Satan so as not to miss his smallest response; indeed, even to bring one about, if she can. And whether or not it's her doing, he does at last look up.

And there's the Star. It's begun to move away, he sees. That for which he had waited so long is leaving him again.

He gets to his feet now, and finds himself standing as if he's back on the hill again ... No, don't do that, Satan, better to look down than up. And yes, there at his feet are the remains of the painting; and the easel, toppled in the violence but unharmed; and there in the corner, his stack of unused canvases. Yes. This is more like it ...

Next to the canvases stands a broom. Of course. That's what he'll do. What he'll do after that, when he's finished clearing up the mess, he's no idea, but he knows that this is what he must start with. First things first. Keep it simple.

He takes up the broom and begins to sweep.

Sophia has no doubt what he'll do next. He'll start by restoring the easel to its position; then, with some care, choose a new canvas; then put the canvas on the easel; and then sit and stare at it. The only question is: when he finally starts to paint – as he will – whose portrait will it be? Well, by the time he's done enough of it for anyone to tell, she'll be long gone. And since that's now inevitable, that is now her wish.

Thus it is that her image of Satan sweeping his cell dissolves instead into that of planet Earth, exquisite by moonlight, gently receding as the Lamb departs. She wonders if its beauty can save it from the sweeper. Will Satan actually *see* it at last, for what it truly is? Or will he go on trying to paint pictures of himself?

Satan finishes his monkish task and dumps the gathered fragments of his old work into the rubbish bin. His 'old' work ... does that mean it's time for a new one?

Well, let's see ...

He picks up the easel and restores it to its position; then, with some care, selects a canvas; then puts it on the easel; and then sits and stares at it.

Then he looks up at the night sky again. The Lamb has almost gone. Almost ...

Now it has.

Yes ...

He chooses a brush.

THE END

B O O K S

O is a symbol of the world, of oneness and unity. In different cultures it also means the "eye," symbolizing knowledge and insight. We aim to publish books that are accessible, constructive and that challenge accepted opinion, both that of academia and the "moral majority."

Our books are available in all good English language bookstores worldwide. If you don't see the book on the shelves ask the bookstore to order it for you, quoting the ISBN number and title. Alternatively you can order online (all major online retail sites carry our titles) or contact the distributor in the relevant country, listed on the copyright page.

See our website **www.o-books.net** for a full list of over 500 titles, growing by 100 a year.

And tune in to myspiritradio.com for our book review radio show, hosted by June-Elleni Laine, where you can listen to the authors discussing their books.